mr. X
GET OUTTA TOWN!
EPISODE 1

W.L. Liberman

McArthur & Company
Toronto

First published in Canada in 2005 by
McArthur & Company
322 King St., West, Suite 402
Toronto, ON M5V 1J2
www.mcarthur-co.com

Library and Archives Canada Cataloguing in Publication

    Liberman, Wili
    Mr. X / Wili Liberman.

    (Get outta town ; episode 1)
    ISBN 1-55278-548-3

    I. Title. II. Title: Mister X. III. Series: Liberman, Wili Get outta town ;
    episode 1.

    PS8623.I34M48 2005   jC813'.6   C2005-905409-3

Cover: *Katarzyna Kozbiel*
Composition: *Mad Dog Design Connection*
Research: *Krista Glen and Laurel Rhind*
Printed in Canada by *Webcom*

The publisher would like to acknowledge the financial support of the
Government of Canada through the Book Publishing Industry
Development Program, the Canada Council for the Arts, and the Ontario
Arts Council for our publishing activities. We also acknowledge the
Government of Ontario through the Ontario Media Development
Corporation Ontario Book Initiative.

10 9 8 7 6 5 4 3 2 1

EPISODE 1

1

The computer chirped. The cell phone bleeped, the iPod raged, the PDA chimed and Xerxes Frankel laughed, just loving it all. Email. He pulled up the message and listened to the hum of the printer as the page slid out. He scooped it out of the tray.

"Hot," he said to himself, scanning the message. Then he nodded and smiled. "All right," he said again. "The race is on."

No time, he was thinking. No time to lose. He grabbed his helmet out of the closet and jammed it on his head while steadying the handlebars of his ultra-light yet uber-strong mountain bike.

"Time to head out to the Boulevard of Broken Dreams," he said, aware that no one else was listening. At least, he hoped not. After all, it was 5:40 a.m. That's right, in the early light and he had school that day.

The sun filtered over the horizon casting long shadows. The morning air was damp but Xerxes felt warmth seeping into his arms and legs as he pumped the pedals streaking up Paris Avenue. Funny, he thought. That's where he'd be heading very, very soon.

The Boulevard of Broken Dreams was his name for the most treacherous ride in his neighborhood. Cutting across Paris, hanging a left at Detroit Street, burning it up Rotterdam, then taking the vertical hill straight up Mecca, Xerxes powered up, working the gears like a musician. Oh man, could he feel it, lactic acid searing his legs and coming off the saddle, he grunted and groaned as he inched to the crest. You needed to balance perfectly or you'd just topple over at the arc of this monster hill. Xerxes sensed the strain in the bike, thought he heard the gears quiver and crack. Man, he thought, what I do to keep myself going and he laughed, well, snorted to himself.

Climbing the hill up Mecca wasn't the hard part, oh no, that was easy. No, it was the other side that was the hard part. Xerxes hit the summit and stepped down, letting himself breathe for a minute or two. He surveyed the world. The light mist was beginning to burn off. It was going to be a perfect May day. May was his favorite time of year, that transition period between spring and summer. The days warming up, the world greening, nature shrieking in his ears, it was all very cool, he loved it. But it was time to get serious. He walked the bike across the plateau, a distance of 30 meters, maybe less. On the other side, the view expanded but disappeared at the same time. In front of him, was space. Far out into the distance, he saw the expanse of houses, neighborhoods cut into the hillside, roads snaking through the subdivisions and farther out, steel towers marking the edge of the downtown core.

Xerxes glanced down at his feet. Are you ready? he asked them, and tapped his toes in response. Affirmative, Captain. One deep breath. Exhale. Another deep breath. Exhale again but slowly, sending out a constant stream of air, storing energy in those red corpuscles.

Xerxes set his feet into the traps and balanced, hanging in air for a long moment, then applied pressure to the pedals but not too much. Momentum would not be his problem on this side as he stared down the path to seven, not six, not eight but seven hairpin turns before hitting a straight-away where he'd have the bike up to 70 kilometers and then the drop-off where the road ended.

The Boulevard of Broken Dreams was a road to nowhere. Some developer had this big idea. Build all these houses and these roads and people will come. Problem was that he bought up used railway lands and this chump discovered after he sunk all his money in, that the land was polluted, lead and contaminants and toxins permeated the soil, making it uninhabitable. The guy went bust but not before leaving this section of road in the middle of it all, starting and going and ending without connecting to any-thing else. Where the BBD ended, he'd put in a wooden stairway, 647 steps to the bottom.

Xerxes flew through hairpin number six. The bike wobbled but he brought it under control. The wind whipped at his face and he shivered. Centrifugal forces pulled at the bike but he kept his position tight and streamlined, adjusting the handlebars when feeling the curve of the road. Rushing air howled in his ears and he converted it into the roar of the crowd as he flashed into the velodrome carried by the energy of the multitudes yelling his name in unison. Okay, cut that, he thought and focus. Checking the speedometer, he banked hard to the left and climbed the wall practically horizontal for a split-second. If he reached out with his right hand, he'd touch the road surface and burn holes in his riding gloves, so that wasn't going to happen. The view straightened out as Xerxes prepared to enter the last hairpin. Sixty kilometers now, keep it steady, keep it steady, he hunched forward slightly and leaned right, waiting for the drop, feeling for it, counting off when the front tire would start to slide. He pumped more power into the pedals and tore into the straightaway. I want a record, beat my P.B. I want 70 plus. In all the times, he'd ridden this route, he'd only managed 70 kilometers and today he wanted at least 71, if not more. The trick was to ease up before the end. You didn't want to fly over the stairs, no way, you had to take each one. Well, maybe hop the first few, that was okay.

He was thinking about that power bar now flattened in his back pocket. Should have had one before heading out. Too late now. Piston legs, keep on pumping, he prayed. Streaks of pain lit him up from his ankles, up his calves, seized the kneecaps and smoked his thighs. Must keep going. Xerxes couldn't see or feel his feet, it was all a blur and the burning in his chest? Heart's going to explode, flame out but through the pain and through gritted teeth and watering eyes, he smiled. The speedometer had hit 71 and the needle was wavering spasmodically, jumping like a hyped up tic touching on 72, yeah, 72, yeah, it hit the magic number. Immediately, Xerxes eased off. Wooden fence and platform 100 meters ahead, time to decelerate and take control because this part now, it was all about finesse, riding the bumps and the grinds. And guess what? The staircase curved too, winding its way down to the bottom. By the time you hit the last one, the world was spinning. It was like being on the fastest Ferris wheel in human existence.

Xerxes squeezed on the brakes and heard the whine of the pads. So high-pitched, it drilled into your skull. He shifted off the seat, kept his knees flexed and his arms loose and then took the first step, felt the bump of the tires and the jiggling of his insides as the bike bucked and jumped, first the front, then the back. Xerxes maneuvered the handle bars, skimming the scarred banister where so many people had carved their names. The staircase was narrow, barely wide enough for two people to pass without bumping shoulders and for him it was an elongated pen, the boundaries clearly marked. If he made a mistake, he'd hit the rail and sail 40 to 50 meters into space and make a hard landing. No way was that going to happen, even as he jostled the side and took some splinters in his elbow. Man, that bites and he gritted his teeth.

A man out walking his Beagle stopped and stared. He watched in awe and horror staring at the jerking, bobbing figure on the vibrating bike as the rider bounced between the rails and in any given second thought he'd hurtle out into space crashing on to the tarmac, and wind up a broken, crumpled thing. Even the dog remained still, growling deep in its throat. Time had stopped as the man held his breath. He thought about closing his eyes or turning away but couldn't. He had to see how this turned out. The bike shot out from the last step hurtling toward him. The rider reared up and pulled back on the handlebars sending the bike into a sideways skid. The man heard the scraping of rubber on cement. Still, he didn't move as the figure slid closer and closer. With a gut-wrenching tug, Xerxes braced his right leg and dug his heel into the cement surface wrestling the bike to a stop not less than a meter from where the mute man stood transfixed with his dog. Xerxes pulled up and bent over the handlebars panting heavily but after a few quick breaths looked up and smiled in triumph. Sweat rained on his shoulders and chest. Dust clogged his throat and he coughed.

"Sweet," he croaked.

"What the hell did you do that for?" cried the man with the dog, spittle forming at the corners of his mouth.

Xerxes laughed. Why would he do such a crazy thing?

Good question. And Xerxes Frankel, the seventeen-year-old star of his own teen travel show, had the answer. It couldn't be simpler. He was off to Paris, France. And guess what? He had accepted the challenge. Xerxes was riding his bike down the Eiffel Tower. All 1671 steps. The race was on.

If Xerxes had a fault, he was an unapologetic romantic. Here, as the host of a travel show, he had the opportunity to see the world. He hooked up with local teens in the cities he visited and they'd show him their city from their point of view. It was brilliant, magic. But there was always a challenge, some kind of quest built in. Like the challenge ride down the Eiffel Tower. Now that was cool, maybe dangerous but still, he was up for it. And they'd get it all on videotape. No, his fault was falling for his female co-hosts. Xerxes was a romantic, gave his all in every situation but wore his heart in a vulnerable place. That's one of the things that the producers of the show liked about him, his enthusiasm, energy and honesty. Xerxes was upfront about who he was and what you saw was pretty much what you got. And that was a tall, gangly kid with tightly coiled hair and a smooth, coffee-colored complexion. He laughed a lot—big, open, gut-filling laughs that made everyone else around him want to laugh too. He was infectious, with his sheer, pent-up energy…and that's why he was hired. To throw that energy back at the audience and get them excited about travel and adventure and new experiences.

After leaving the Boulevard of Broken Dreams and the spitting man and his Beagle in his dust, Xerxes sped home, leapt off his bike, hefted it on his shoulder and carried it down the concrete steps to his basement room. He glanced at his watch, just 7 a.m., about the time his parents were just starting to get up, perfect. He opened and closed the screen door carefully, trying not to bang too much but the door caught the bike's back wheel and rattled. Meanwhile, he fumbled with the lock, and the door to his room, swung open, well, screeched open actually. Hmm, need to get some oil on those hinges, he thought, then cringed a little as he heard a heavy foot come down hard on the ceiling. Whoops, sounded like his dad, Darius, he'd know that iron tread anywhere.

Hastily, he hung the bike up on its rack on the side wall, pulled open his drawers grabbing for some clean clothes, and then leapt into the bathroom slamming the door. In a second, he'd stripped out of his bike gear, dumped it in the hamper and had the shower going by the time his dad thumped his way down the stairs and hammered on the bathroom door.

"Xerxes." Pause. No answer. "Xerxes." Darius thumped the wood with the palm of his hand rattling the door in his hinges.

"What is it?"

"How many times..."

"What?"

"How many times have I..."

"What?"

"I said...how many times have I..."

"Can't hear you, the water's running..."

Darius swallowed his anger and opened the door. Clouds of steam engulfed him. "My God." The wrinkles went out of his pajamas instantly. Now that was heavy duty steam.

Xerxes popped his head around the shower curtain. "Hi, Dad. What's up?"

Darius took in the dripping face, the goofy grin and his anger dissipated with the steam. "What do you want for breakfast," he sighed.

"Oh, you know...the usual."

"Right. Ten minutes," Darius said and backed out of the room, appreciating the instant coolness after he'd closed the bathroom door behind him. The usual consisted of Eggs Benedict and crêpes with syrup. Ever since Xerxes had told them he was off to Paris, he wanted only French food and that didn't mean fries or poutine, for that matter.

Fifteen minutes later, Xerxes had demolished his breakfast in two minutes flat, brushed his teeth, grabbed his knapsack and stuffed the lunch that his mom still made for him. I mean, he let her do that because she was having problems letting go, you know. Not wanting to acknowledge that he was growing up and that it made her feel old, and Xerxes didn't want his mom to feel bad, so he allowed her to do little things for him. Like make his lunch, tidy his room, make his bed, you know, for her own mental well-being.

His first class that morning was co-op. He loved that class. If it wasn't for co-op, he wouldn't have gotten the TV gig in the first place. He was placed with a company called Parachute Productions where he was learning how to be a videographer. After he had dropped the videocamera five or six times, the owner of the company, Frank Spigoletto, approached.

"Hey, Xerxes," Frank said, noting the eye piece lying by Xerxes right trainer.

"Yes, Mr. Spigoletto?"

"I've been thinking…"

"Uh-huh…"

"I heard about something you might be interested in. There's this new show, you know, something to do with travel and they're looking for teenagers. Why don't you think about trying out?"

"Geez, I dunno…never done anything like that…"

"You got nothing to lose…"

"What would I have to do?"

"Not sure, really, but I've got the producer's name and phone number." Frank dug around in the pocket of his jeans, pulled out a handful of crumpled paper scraps, carefully, unrolled several of them. "Yeah, here it is." He thrust the wad toward him. "Give it a shot." And I'll save wear and tear on my cameras.

Xerxes stared at the paper ball perched in the palm of his hand. Yup, he could see numbers. Wasn't sure if he could read them though. "You know the name of the company?"

"It's on the paper," Frank said, gesturing.

"I know, but…"

Frank Spigoletto sighed. "Okay… okay. It's Random Run Productions and the producer's name is Mira Gottfreund. Happy now?"

Xerxes nodded and gave his patron a goofy grin, the one he used to diffuse anger and tense situations. It usually worked.

So Xerxes thought, why not? He auditioned.

Random Run Productions had its offices in an old warehouse in the west end of the city. Hmm, needed some reclamation work down here, Xerxes thought, as he sprinted up the subway steps and emerged at street level. This was an area in definite need of repair. As he walked north on Downlands Avenue, good name, it fit the neighborhood to a Tee, Xerxes spotted an abandoned transit warehouse across the street. Most of the windows of the old depot were boarded up and those that weren't had about fifty holes drilled through them by rocks, bottles and, he mused, maybe even bullets. That was kind of cool but a little bit scary too, as Xerxes noticed groups of young dudes in huddles on the street corners. They were laughing and shucking and making lots of noise. Xerxes didn't really want to know what they were up to, so he kept up a brisk pace and his eyes focused straight ahead moving with a purpose. No one paid him any mind and that was more than fine with him even though he felt pairs of eyes that followed him along for a while, and then drained away. Two blocks north on Downlands and then a left turn on Malice Avenue, hmm, another good name and he shivered at the thought. Then he watched the numbers as he looked for 206, suite 258. Ah, there it was, Malice Avenue Studios, an ugly, low-rise, two-story wedge of a dirty, brick building with a bunch of loading docks off to the side.

The front door looked like it could withstand an assault from a bazooka and it was tightly locked. There was a buzzer and he buzzed it. A tinny voice screeched out.

"Who is it?"

He gave his name and purpose.

"What?" screeched the voice.

"Xerxes Frankel to see Mira Gottfreund."

"Come again?"

Xerxes fought to control his anger but impatience won out. "XERXES FRANKEL TO SEE MIRA GOTTFREUND!"

"You don't have to yell." And then the door buzzed and Xerxes felt like he was being let into prison. Already, this TV business was strange and getting stranger. He yanked open the door and found it was heavy, must have been fortified with lead, and went inside, the door slammed behind him and he shivered involuntarily. He checked the building marquee just to make sure he was in the right place and there it was, Random Run on the second floor.

He looked around. The lobby was okay. Nice carpeting, clean, and a sweeping receptionist's desk with a humming computer and a small stereo setup behind it. A fax machine buzzed away and a slick espresso machine sat on a wood counter off to the side. The desk wasn't occupied but he saw a doorway with a hand on it pointing, so he went through the looking glass and up a dark set of stairs, through a fire door and down a long hallway with a very tall ceiling. Some sort of crazy, psychedelic pattern was painted on the floor, something from who knows when? He followed the numbers until he found suite 258 and the sign said the right name, Random Run Productions. Now he was faced with a decision. He could never tell which way these sorts of doors opened. There wasn't a push or pull sign and Xerxes always felt foolish when he guessed wrong, which he usually did. And because he was a little superstitious, he was thinking that if he guessed wrong this time, it wouldn't go well with the interview. But then if he guessed right, well, that was another story. He debated with himself and was doing some hard thinking about this when the door suddenly opened, it would have been a "push" decision and a young girl with blondey, ringletty hair and wide eyes looked up at him, a bit startled.

"Hey," he said, just to say something.

"Can I help you?"

"Oh…yeah…I'm here to see Mira Gottfreund…"

"And you are?"

"Xerxes. Xerxes Frankel." And he gave her the thousand-watt smile, but she didn't bite. In fact, she went a little frosty, he thought. "And you are…?"

"Yolanda Stark. Come on in. They're expecting you." She didn't offer to shake hands or anything, which Xerxes thought rude but then, what did he know about etiquette? She stepped back and he cleared the doorway. "This way," she said and turned and disappeared down another long hallway. Stark was right, not just her name but the office as well. Naked wooden floors, bare furniture, white walls with a few prints and plaques and posters, that was it. The place was clean-looking, though, a bit too hospital-like for him. Xerxes didn't like hospitals and did whatever he could to avoid them at all cost. But given the number of accidents he'd had over the years starting from when he broke two knucklebones in his right hand playing hockey, and then his clavicle, and then his ankle and well, he'd seen his share of emergency-room time, enough to last him for a while longer.

Yolanda stopped in front of a set of double wooden doors, rapped sharply, heard some sort of muffled reply, and went in, holding the door for Xerxes, who suddenly became nervous and when he became nervous, he threw up his smile. Not the thousand-watt one but a look that was slightly dimmer, say 750 watts, instead. It showed friendly tentativeness, like he was a bit unsure of the situation but ready to try anything.

The room was vast and also empty except for a wooden trestle table and a few hard-backed chairs. Seated at the table were four people and they were all staring at him.

"Xerxes, come on in," said a shrill but friendly voice belonging to a woman with the wildest, frizzy red hair he'd ever seen. She got up from the table and walked over to him. "I'm Mira," she said and smiled and shook his hand. Mira looked to be about his mom's age, whatever that was, but she wore a silky sort of blouse over extremely tight jeans and leather boots with the sharpest heels he'd ever seen. You could puncture metal with those heels.

"Hey, nice to meet you," he said.

Then the guy with the salt-and-pepper hair and goatee and wire-rims stood up and reached out. "I'm Max Schafer," he said softly and shook Xerxes' hand so lightly he wasn't even sure if they'd touched skin. Max was dressed all in black, loafers, slacks, jersey and an unconstructed jacket. The other guy was tall and reedy and dressed like he'd stumbled out of the Ozarks wearing a John Deere cap, plaid shirt, fluorescent hunting vest and khakis with more pockets than Xerxes had seen on a bevy of kangaroos.

"Rufus Bickle," he said, "director and camera operator."

Last was a young oriental woman with sleek hair, wearing what looked like a designer dress to Xerxes. She touched her fingertips to his. "Stephanie Chu," she said in a friendly voice. "Field producer."

"Thanks for coming out," Mira trilled. "Have a seat. Can we get you anything? Water? Pop? Doughnut?"

"No, I'm fine, thanks."

"Okay," Mira said. "Good. Let's begin. Tell us about yourself Xerxes. Five strongest points, then the five weakest."

So, this is what the hot seat felt like. "Uh, funny, energetic, good-natured, patient and open-minded. Hmm, impulsive, immature—at times, perfectionist, tell bad jokes, laugh at the same bad jokes." Xerxes rattled it off without thinking too much.

There was silence around the table. Xerxes was afraid they were going to ask him to tell a bad joke and he wasn't sure if even he could stomach that. "Xerxes," Rufus said. "How do you feel about the following things, okay. I'm just going to mention a few." Rufus talked through his nose a little.

"Sure."

"Snowboarding."

"Fun."

"Parasailing."

"Sounds like a lot of fun."

"Hang gliding."

"Cool."

"Rappelling."

"Scary...but in a good way."

"Canopying."

"Can of peeing?"

Rufus laughed. "No, canopying. It's going up into the trees in the rainforest and sliding along a metal cable from tree to tree about 30 to 40 feet in the air."

"Never done it," said Xerxes. "But it sounds like something I could get into."

"Canyoning?" Xerxes shook his head. "Canyoning," Rufus said, "is sliding down a waterfall hooked to a harness so you don't get carried away but the current."

"Well, as long as it isn't in the winter, then no problem."

"Whitewater rafting?"

"A blast."

"Skateboarding?"

"Hey, I'm a pro."

"Surfing?"

"Tried it once and thought it was very cool but it's harder than it looks."

"Heli-skiing?"

"Again, I've never tried it but I'd give it a shot. Definitely. Anything else?"

Rufus lifted his John Deere cap and scratched his head. "Don't think so."

"Any food allergies?" Stephanie asked.

"Nope?"

"Phobias?"

"Well, I'm not crazy about poisonous snakes or black widow spiders, otherwise, I don't get too rattled by stuff."

"Good," Mira said. "This show travels, as you know all over the world to some pretty exotic places and some interesting situations. That's part of the adventure of it all and gives the show it's zing, if you know what I mean."

"Sure."

Max whispered in Mira's ear, after parting a hunk of

frizzy hair. Mira nodded. "Okay." She turned to Xerxes and handed him a sheaf of papers. "Xerxes…"

"Call me X, it's easier and that's what my friends do."

"Oh, okay…X. This is a script. We'd like you to climb to the top of that scaffold there and say it for us a few different ways. Is that okay?"

Xerxes checked out the scaffold. It looked a bit rickety and was about 16 feet high. Fortunately, heights didn't bother him much. "Sure thing. Can I take a minute to read this through?"

"Absolutely," Mira replied.

A minute or two later, Xerxes looked up. "I think I'm ready now."

"Okay," Mira said. "Away you go."

Xerxes left the script on the table, stood up and went around to the side of the scaffolding where he could see a way up. He climbed it easily—it reminded him of the jungle gym in the schoolyard, something he'd conquered when he was seven. Xerxes reached the top and surveyed the scene below. Everyone looked quite a bit smaller. All eyes were on him.

"Okay now, Xerxes," Mira began. "Say the opening intro as if you were drunk."

Xerxes' knees buckled and he swayed over the side: "Get Outta Town! takes you all over the world…" and then he lurched forward tumbling over the side; the onlookers gasped but Xerxes hung on to the railing with his feet and grinned at them upside down. "…and shows you how teens live, love, eat, work, think and have fun. Watch out, Paris, we're cycling on down." Then he hauled himself up, waved and waited.

"Do the intro like you're a monkey," Stephanie said.

Xerxes hesitated, thinking, what was this, humiliate-the-teenager time? But what the heck. He went into his crouch and larked around, let out a few screeches and did the lines. Then he was asked to do the lines like he was going on a first date, as if he were an angry parent and then as an old-age pensioner. After the last one, the group below, clapped and Mira told him to climb on down. Seconds later, his feet touched the floor.

"That was pretty good," Mira said. "No fear, huh."

Xerxes shrugged. "I like to try new things." He put his hands on his hips and looked at the faces around the trestle table, a table, he was thinking, that if he jumped up on it, would probably collapse. So, a good reason not to, though he was tempted. Xerxes felt like he didn't have anything to lose so why not go for it all?

Mira pushed another piece of paper toward him. "Here's a list of questions, Xerxes…uh, …X. You're going to interview Stephanie. I want you to pretend that you're in front of the Arc de Triomphe in Paris, okay?"

"Sure." Xerxes took the paper from her and glanced at the questions.

"Rufus is going to tape this, just like he would for the show on location."

"Fine, that's cool. Makes it seem more real."

Stephanie walked into the center of the room and turned, waiting for him. Xerxes walked toward her, and then turned back to the others. "Ah, Paris," he said, "the most romantic and artistic city in the world. There's the Eiffel Tower, the Louvre, the Right Bank, the Left Bank, a cool music and art scene. Man, if my homies could see me now. Hey, I'm in Paris, France. I'm going to hook up with Stephanie Chu, who's going to be my love guide in the city of romance." He turned toward Stephanie. "Stephanie?"

"Xerxes?"

"That's right, how are you?" And he kissed her on the right, then the left cheek.

"I am fine. Welcome to Paris."

"Thank you. I love everything I've seen so far. You can feel the history and culture in this city."

"That's right. It is alive everywhere you go, everywhere you look."

"But you're an artist and a dancer and a singer, right?"

"Yes, that's right, Xerxes."

"Call me X."

"Okay, X."

"So, you've got some really cool places to show me, things that teens like to do in this town? Things that only you can show and no one else?"

"You took the words right out of my mouth. We shall see Paris, like you've never seen it before and if it's your first time, you won't be able to wait until you come back again."

"We better get started, time's a'wastin'"

"Okay."

Xerxes took Stephanie's hand and they walked out of shot together.

"Cut," Rufus said. "Pretty nice. Looked quite good, actually. I could almost see the Seine and hear the traffic in the background, not to mention that music, that distinctly Parisian music."

Mira looked around the table. "Anyone got anything else?" There were some subtle head shakes. "X, how are your parents with this? Do they understand that you'd be away for weeks at a time? Do they have concerns? Will you be able to keep up with your schoolwork?"

"My parents are very cool with this whole thing. They think it's great, you know, a wonderful opportunity. See the world and all that. They've very open-minded and flexible, you know? I couldn't ask for a better set, believe me. I tried trading them in once, but realized I had it pretty good to start." Actually, Xerxes hadn't said anything to his parents and wasn't sure how they'd react, especially his dad, Darius, who was prone to blow his stack, very much like Mount Etna, from time to time. Very volatile dude, was Darius. "And I'm a whiz kid, pick stuff up pretty easily. I don't think I'll have a problem with school. I mean, I could work the show in as a large homework assignment, you know?" Xerxes wasn't bad in school but was too often distracted by other things and could be doing a lot better academically. Still, he was managing pretty well.

"Okay, that's great then," Mira said and laughed shrilly.

She stood up and reached out. Xerxes took her hand. "Great meeting you. We'll be in touch…and I'm not just saying that, we will."

"When do you expect to make a decision?" Xerxes asked.

"Within the next week probably. The schedule is pretty tight and we need to get a move on, so it won't be too long, okay?"

"Absolutely. Great meeting you all." Xerxes made certain to smile at each person in the room. When he came to Yolanda and her disdainful expression, it made his smile even brighter. What was it with that girl? So pretty and yet very negative.

Xerxes backed his way out with Yolanda showing him the way. Before he could turn and say a special goodbye to her, she closed the door in his face. Xerxes shrugged and then smiled to himself. Not everybody was lucky in love, he thought.

Back inside Random Run, Mira turned to the group and exclaimed, "I think he's our guy." Everyone but Yolanda seemed pleased at the thought.

Three days later, Xerxes took a call at home.

"Hello?"

"Is this Xerxes?" said a vaguely familiar female voice.

"Yeah, that's right."

"You thieving, conniving little rat!"

"Huh? Who is this?"

"I hate you."

"Hey, I don't even know you..." The phone was slammed down and Xerxes looked at the receiver as if the answer would crawl out, then he shrugged and hung up.

The phone rang again. Tentatively, he picked it up. "Hello?"

"I'm going to make sure you fail so bad you won't know what hit you."

"What?" But the caller had hung up again. Xerxes thought a minute and wondered if it had something to do with one of his school projects or an upcoming test maybe. The voice had sounded familiar but he wasn't quite sure why and he couldn't put a face to it. Well. No use worrying about it.

Five minutes later, the phone rang again. Xerxes stared at it for a long moment. He wasn't sure what to do but curiosity got the better of him.

"Hello?"

"Xerxes?"

"Yes."

"Mira Gottfreund here."

"Oh, hi Mira..." and he was prepared to hear bad news because he'd told himself it was all a long shot but when he came back to his senses he heard Mira say, "And we'd love to have you on the show. Thought your audition was great, just the sort of quality we're looking for, so are you interested?"

"Interested?"

"Yes, in being on the show."

"On the show?" And then it hit him. "On the show... oh my God... of course I'm interested. Man, this is way too cool.

Thank you. Man, this is great, really great. I never…I mean….
I never…well, it was a long shot, right? But then I thought,
nothing to lose, so go for it and…"

"…the rest is history, Xerxes. Now listen, we've got a lot
of work to do ahead of time and much planning. Tell me
about your schedule, when are you free to come in for
meetings. We've got a number of production and script
meetings and we want your input on these, make sure you
know what's going on, get you comfortable. We'll need to
get you a contract…who's your agent?"

"Agent? Don't have one."

"Okay, well you'll need a lawyer probably to look everything over. I'm sure your parents have a lawyer so you'll
need to talk to them obviously and considering they're
already onside with this, it shouldn't be a problem?"

"Right, no problem. No problem at all."

"Well, that's a relief but, no disrespect intended and I
don't even know your parents but some of them can be a
serious pain to deal with, you know?"

"Yes," Xerxes replied. "I completely understand. Some
parents can be like that but mine are very cool." And he
looked down at his crossed fingers and wondered if he'd
survive his father's explosion. "Tell me again where we're
going?"

"Oh sure," Mira said. "That's easy. London, Paris,
Lucerne, Munich, Washington, New York, Mexico City,
Costa Rica, Sydney, Shanghai, Rome, Madrid and Athens."

Xerxes whistled into the phone. "Wow."

"That's some kind of great job you've got, you know that, kid?"

"I have a feeling it will be. It just hasn't sunk in yet."

"Okay, first meeting is next Tuesday at 4:30. Does that work for you?"

Xerxes thought for a moment. "Uh yeah, my last class is 3:30, so it should be fine."

"Good. Great. In the meantime, I'll organize the contracts and get them over to your house. Have a lawyer look them over; you need to sign, your parents or one of your parents needs to sign because you're still underage and then you can send them back or bring them back with you on Tuesday. How's that sound?"

"Great. Excellent in fact."

"Good. Congratulations. We know you are going to be fabulous and this series is going to be a big hit." Mira hung up. Xerxes did a cartwheel knocking over some of his mother's cookbooks and kicking the coffee carafe to the tile floor where it shattered into a gazillion pieces. Damn. Xerxes hopped around the slivers, went to the closet and pulled out a broom and dustpan. He wasn't entirely conscious of what he was doing, sweeping up the pieces automatically. Xerxes saw himself on an airplane, traveling to exotic cities around the world, a harem of beautiful girls at his side.

A door slammed. "What the hell!?" Darius Frankel stood in the middle of the kitchen and surveyed the mess. "What'd you do?"

Xerxes looked at his father and the permanent scowl that always seemed etched on his face. Wasn't it obvious? "I broke the coffee pot. It was an accident."

Darius' face darkened. "You'll replace it then out of your allowance."

Xerxes nodded. "Sure thing, Pop. Like I said…"

But Darius wasn't listening. He'd already left the kitchen and Xerxes heard his footsteps stomping on the stairs. Hmm, not the best time to let out the good news. Probably better to do that when his mom was home. She was the calming influence on the mad bull.

That evening at dinner, Xerxes decided he had to spring the news on his parents because time was tight. Hilka, his mom, was a leggy, blonde woman with a calm demeanor in direct contrast to his father, who was large and dark-complexioned, and a man who always seemed ticked off. Xerxes didn't know why but he did know that much of that anger seemed to be directed at him and that it was difficult for his father to vent at work. They lived in a decent neighborhood and had a nice house. His mother was a child psychologist and operated her own clinic, while Darius was an accountant with a large firm in the city. He became very edgy around tax time. Now it's true that Xerxes thought accounting was tedious and boring and he did let that slip one time and that didn't go down too well with Darius but that had been five years earlier and he figured it was time for him to get over it. Darius seemed most relaxed in the kitchen and in fact was a pretty decent cook. Hilka could barely boil water but Darius seemed right at home there. And tonight he'd whipped up a pretty mean jerk chicken with dirty rice and organic salad.

"Killer chicken, Dad," Xerxes said, thinking butter him up a bit first.

"Hey thanks," Darius said and actually smiled. He was already on his third piece of chicken. Darius could pack it away, as much as Xerxes, who was still growing, and then some.

"Yes, it's excellent," Hilka said in a trilly way, still retaining traces of her youth growing up in Oslo. "But then it's always good. Xerxes, I get the feeling you want to tell us something."

That always knocked him off his perch, like his mom was psychic or something. "Well, yeah, I do. In fact, I've got some pretty exciting news actually. Very cool…"

Darius looked apprehensive, his expression verging on a scowl as he set the half-eaten piece of chicken down on his plate, wiped his hands on the paper napkin and sighed. "All right," he said. "Let's hear it." He was thinking to himself, another hare-brained scheme and there'd been more than a few.

"Okay. Well…I'm going to be the host of a TV show and travel the world," he exclaimed. Xerxes looked from one to the other but there was no reaction. His mother's face was expressionless, a total, utter blank while his father looked puzzled. Then Darius banged his hand down on the table and barked out a laugh.

"That was a good one, son. Tell us another."

"But it's true," Xerxes stammered. "It's the real deal."

"Can it be?" asked Hilka. "Can it really?" And her eyes widened.

"Yes," said Xerxes. "It can." He told them about his co-op and Mr. Spigoletto and heading down to Random Run productions and his audition and what he was asked to do and then about the phone call from Mira Gottfreund.

"Oh my God," said Hilka. "That is wonderful news." She rose from the table and went round and gave her son a big hug. "I am so proud of you, really. When does it start?"

"Soon."

"What about school?" Darius boomed. "You are not missing any school, do you hear?"

"Oh Darius," said Hilka. "Relax. Let him tell us what will happen. Don't jump to conclusions…not yet anyway."

Darius' face clamped shut. He wanted to say more but choked it off. His face went darker, almost purple.

"But Dad, I really won't be missing much in the way of school. The production schedule doesn't start until the end of June and we'll be shooting most of the show through the summer. At least, that's what I think is going to happen."

"I'm not sure about this," his father declared. "What do you know about being on television anyway? How did you become an expert all of a sudden?"

"I'm not an expert but I'll learn. I'm a quick learner."

"That's not what your marks say," his father replied.

"Oh come on, Darius. That's not fair. His marks aren't terrible," Hilka said and Darius flushed again.

"But they could be a lot better if he tried harder, if he applied himself more."

"But just think of what he'll be learning as he travels around the world. That is an invaluable education, something he could never find in a classroom. Oh, it's a marvelous opportunity."

"I suppose you aren't getting paid to do this, either," Darius grumbled.

"Well, as a matter of fact, they're sending over the contract and we have to get a lawyer to look at it."

"Contract?" Darius said. "You're damn right we'll have a lawyer look at it. No shark is going to take advantage of my son. How do we know these people are legitimate anyway? What do we know about them?"

Xerxes reeled off the list of credits that Mira and Max had produced and even Darius had to admit he'd seen some of them, even though he mumbled, "Doesn't mean anything you know, they could still be crooks. I hear they all are in that business." But when Darius heard how much Xerxes was going to earn, his jaw dropped.

"That's almost as much as me. And all that in two, three months . . . ?"

"Well," Xerxes replied, trying not to be smug or grin, "there will be some post-production stuff through the fall for sure but just here and there and they'll work around my school schedule."

"Damn right they will. Last year of high school is very important," Darius said, somewhat appeased but still suspicious of the entire venture. It was too good to be true.

"Hey, lighten up, Dad, this is going to be a blast. You'll see. I'll prove it to you and it will be educational too." Xerxes had his fingers crossed behind his back just like he used to do when he was little. He'd be happy to learn stuff but it was all about fun, wasn't it? And the money wouldn't hurt.

"Well, any money you make will go right into your college fund. We'll put it to good use, believe me."

Xerxes' face fell. "But we'll make sure you have some spending money, too," Hilka said. "Don't worry. There's time enough for work and school when you get older. You need to have a little fun, too. Oh, I am so envious of you, Xerxes. To be your age and traveling the world, it's marvelous. I'm thrilled for you, simply thrilled."

Noting his father's less than thrilled expression, Xerxes figured it was decent to have at least one of his parents rooting for him. Darius was going to be a tough turnaround situation, that's for sure. Like turning the Titanic with a spoon. But he'd give it a shot. If he was anything, Xerxes was persistent, and he knew that in time he could wear even his principled, uptight father down.

Darius excused himself to wash his hands. Xerxes leaned toward his mother. "Was he always like this? I mean, so down on everything? How do you stand it?"

Hilka frowned. "I'm not sure you should be talking about your father that way...but...he used to be a lot more fun. Before you were born, we went dancing every weekend. And when you were small, we took loads of day trips to the lake and went on picnics in the conservation area. We spent a lot of time together as a family and they were good times, very good times. I think your father is just unhappy and maybe a little jealous too but don't say I said so, will you? He's burdened with responsibilities and has a job that is filled with pressures. If he makes a tiny mistake, the consequences could be huge, don't you see? Sometimes, it's millions of dollars and he is very meticulous and takes a lot of pride in doing a good job. Lately, though, you know, he hasn't been happy at his work and he's working harder than he ever has."

"Why doesn't he just quit?"

"Oh, it's his pride I think. He doesn't like the idea of being a quitter. And I think he's afraid to. He thinks he'll give up everything he's earned. I also don't know if he's thought of something else to do. He used to be quite a dreamer, your father, believe it or not. Sometimes, I thought he'd spend his whole life dreaming."

"What did he dream about?"

"You'll have to ask him. And that's why I'm saying to you, Xerxes, that if you have this opportunity, you should take it, whether it works out or not. And it may not but at least you'll have tried to do something a bit different. It seems like this is special, so I say, jump at it and have no regrets."

Sometimes, his mom could be pretty cool. She often said a lot of stuff he couldn't understand or just didn't care about, but from time to time she could hit the target.

That evening, Xerxes lay in bed listening to his MP3 player and reading *Sports Illustrated* and he realized that leaving home, at times, wasn't such a bad thing.

Early the next morning, Xerxes pushed his bike through the doorway, holding the screen as he went. He propped his bike against the side of the house and turned to pull the door closed behind him. He turned back to his bike, stopped, thought for a second and turned back to the door one more time. Something weird had happened. Someone had egged his house and it wasn't even Halloween.

"Whoa," said a voice. "What happened, dog?"

Xerxes turned and saw his buddy, Lionel Schlump, standing there, agog, all five foot three inches of flabby sinew, myriad freckles and wavy orange hair.

"We got egged."

"No kidding. A whole frickin' omelette is more like it."

"The question is, why?"

Lionel shrugged his skinny shoulders. "Maybe it was Brutal. It's not beneath him to do something like this."

"Except…"

"Except what?"

"...he wouldn't want to waste the eggs, not if he could eat them first."

"Good point," Lionel said. "He might even get his mom to fry them up. Well, if it wasn't Brutal, and it still could be, then someone's got it out for you, man, and I mean big time. This stuff is murder to clean once it's dried."

Xerxes poked his finger at a gummy patch. "Yeah, tell me about it. Well, maybe my folks won't think it has anything to do with me and I won't get stuck scraping it off the walls."

Lionel laughed. "Dream on, dude."

As usual, Lionel was lugging his double bass, an instrument twice the size, if not more, than he was. Fortunately, it came with a case that had wheels on the bottom so he could push it along. Still, it was pretty awkward.

"Don't know why you bother," Xerxes said.

"'Cause I dig the sound," Lionel replied.

"Yeah, well, when I hear you play, it makes me want to dig up the yard and look for buried bones."

"Har. Har. Not funny," Lionel said. "I'm into a Latin hip-hop fusion sort of thing."

"Easy for you to say. You're not the one listening." Lionel didn't reply but dug his heels in and kept on rolling down the street toward the school. "You think that wailing on this thing the way you do is going to make you more popular?"

Lionel paused in his labors. "Couldn't hurt. Besides, Lisa 'Babes' Babbitch plays the cello and I get to sit right beside her in practice and for my money, you can't beat that."

"Who's talking about dreaming now, man? Come on down from the fifth dimension and touch your toes on reality sidewalk right here." And Xerxes pointed down at the concrete. "Babes Babbitch goes out with some guy from college. She doesn't even know high-schoolers exist, so forget that fantasy, brother."

"Hey, I know it's a fantasy but it's mine and I'll do whatever I want with it, okay?"

Xerxes put up his hands laughing. "Whatever you say, dude. It's your unreal life, not mine."

"Guys, what's up?" Lionel and Xerxes turned. Maya Langlois was bearing down on them atop her ten-speed. Tall, graceful, athletic and popular, they couldn't figure out why Maya hung out with them but she did. They'd all known each other since they were about six and that was probably the reason but lots of kids they knew who grew up together didn't hang anymore. Maya coasted up and hit the brakes. Xerxes was walking his bike, so Maya got off and did the same. Boy's bike too. No gender stuff for Maya, she could do everything the guys could, which in Xerxes' and Lionel's case, wasn't all that much really.

"My house got egged," Xerxes said.

"This time of year?" Maya exclaimed. "Wow, that's strange. Who'd you tick off now?"

"Nobody. At least I don't think so. Well, I don't remember anything recently."

"It wasn't Brutal?"

"Don't know. Might have been but we just don't think he would have wasted the eggs, you know?"

Maya thought for a second. "Yeah, you're probably right about that. He'd just twist the door off the frame or put his fist through a window if he was angry about something."

They walked on in silence. "Hey, how'd you guys make out on the Geography assignment, you know the mapping project on France?"

Lionel's face went red. "Haven't finished it yet."

"It's due today." Maya looked at him in surprise.

"I'm going to ask for an extension…extenuating circumstances."

"What circumstances that are so extenuating."

"Me being too lazy to finish for one thing."

"Oh that," Maya said. "For a minute there I thought it might be something new and important."

"Not really," Lionel replied.

"You'll lose marks," She said.

"I know that." They hit a slight incline and Lionel had to really dig in his heels to push the bass forward. Without speaking, and on either side of him, Xerxes and Maya each put a hand on the instrument case and pushed, helping their diminutive friend over the hump.

Xerxes stopped moving and for some reason the back of his jersey was bunched up and something or someone was breathing hard down his neck. He half turned.

"Hey, Brutal. How you doin'?"

Bruno Bakisse grinned maliciously. He always enjoyed hammering his good friend, Xerxes. Brutal was about as wide as he was tall, which meant he looked like a large stump. He had dark, woolly hair down to his massive shoulders and a swathe covered his forehead to one thick eyebrow. He didn't appear to have a neck but was all jaw and cheek-bones and protruding brow and a surprisingly small and delicate mouth. Like the rest of him, his arms and legs were stumpy but those powerful, large, scary hands with slabs of flesh for fingers could pull apart steel. Xerxes figured he was something that crawled out of a swamp except with clothes that were not quite tattered but never clean, either. Brutal knew that kids would laugh at him if he didn't terror-ize them all and that became his mission in life.

"I feel good now that I've got your scrawny neck in reach. I can snap it like a twig. Like this." And he demonstrated let-ting go of Xerxes' jersey, who quickly spun around, hopped on his bike and pedaled furiously away. "Hey, I've got your friends," he yelled and Xerxes screeched to a stop and slowly pedaled back. "Thought that'd stop you."

"So what do you want?" Xerxes asked.

"Lunch money."

Xerxes shook his head. "No."

"Give me your bike."

"No."

"You want to live, fool?"

"Absolutely."

"Then you gotta give me somethin'."

"I'll think about it."

Brutal placed his hands under Xerxes' handlebars and lifted the front of the bike straight into the air with him on it. "Think about it now," he hissed.

"Okay. Okay. I'll help you with your homework."

"Huh?" Brutal let the bike drop and Xerxes rocked forward. He stared suspiciously. "What homework?"

"Physics."

"I take Physics?"

"You're in my class."

"What else?"

"Math?"

Brutal scratched his head. "Yeah, I remember taking Math. I don't like it." He yawned. "I'd rather have your lunch money."

"Don't have any," Xerxes replied. "Hey, you didn't egg my house, did you?"

Brutal looked at him in surprise and the expression on his face was one of hurt. "Why would I waste good eggs on your house, huh?"

"Told you," Lionel said triumphantly.

Xerxes shot Lionel a disgusted look. "So, it wasn't you?"

"Nah." And the shaggy head quivered. "But maybe it's not a bad idea if we got some rotten ones. Thanks for the tip."

Great, Xerxes thought. How to instruct your worst enemy on how to torture you. "Don't mention it. So listen, we gotta go, class is starting in a couple of minutes. You coming?"

Brutal seemed particularly benevolent this day and he thought about it for a long second, and then shook his head. "Naw, you go ahead. I'll see you at lunch, all right?" And to those who knew all about him or thought they did, this was a surprise.

The trio of friends walked on. Then something pinged off Xerxes bike. He looked around. Something else got him in the back of the head. A stone. Brutal was whipping stuff at them.

"Better walk fast," Brutal called and scooped up a handful of pebbles and began zinging them.

"Ouch," Lionel yelled.

"Come on," Maya said. She put her shoulder to the double bass and pushed while holding her bike.

As the three made tracks as fast as they could, Brutal's maniacal cackle cut through the air. "The guy's seriously demented," Lionel said miserably, a cut had opened up his cheek and a trickle of blood ran along his jaw line. He dug into his pocket and pulled out a tissue which he held to his face while they scrambled forward.

Finally, they were out of range of Brutal, who had exhausted his supply of pebbles anyway. Brutal yelled and danced at them from afar.

Xerxes glanced at his watch. "We've got five minutes before the bell."

They slowed down a bit to take a breather, getting away from Brutal had been hard work. "I think you need a motorized cart for this thing," Maya said.

"My mom would drive me but it won't fit into the back of our minivan."

Xerxes clamped a hand on his friend's shoulder as they approached the front doors of St. Bartholomew High School, affectionately known as St. Batty. "Time to down-size, buddy. That's my advice."

Lionel gave him a rueful smile. "Thanks. I'll take that under advisement."

Maya and Xerxes chained their bikes up in the rack by the front of the school.

Once inside, the three friends split up and headed into different teeming tributaries toward their lockers. Lionel bulldozed a path using the double bass as a pile driver and left a lot of angry teenagers in his wake.

Xerxes first class of the day was English. Miss Petty was the teacher, which was perfect because that's what she was. They were reading *Twelfth Night*, which Xerxes actually thought was kind of cool with the characters in disguises and other characters making fun of them. Miss Petty, however, turned it all into drudgery, droning on in a high, nasal voice that gave Xerxes a headache. Her voice was like a gnat you wanted to swat but couldn't because it hovered just out of range. Maybe we should just try and read her thoughts instead?

10

Xerxes sat in Miss Petty's class while her voice drilled into his skull. School was winding down for the year and he glanced out the window. It was a beautiful day, bright, warm and sunny and he chafed at the confines of his desk. In fact, he wanted to pick it up and heave it through the glass, then make a daring escape, lead the class out of boredom into adventure. He couldn't stop his feet from tapping, his legs from shaking, his hands from drumming. Energy spurted out of him and listening to Miss Petty was like Chinese water torture; he wanted to scream...but he didn't. Darius would flip. Hilka would double-flip and he couldn't jeopardize anything now because of the show. *Get Outta Town!* Man, he liked the sound of that.

"Xerxes. Xerxes!"

"Huh?" He looked up to see Miss Petty's bespectacled face inches from his own. He heard the stifled chortles and spurts of laughter of his classmates.

"Daydreaming again?"

Miss Petty had rather nice blue eyes and many freckles, he noticed for the first time. "Uh, yeah, I guess." He reddened.

"So, where were you, Xerxes, climbing a mountain? Fighting pirates? Jumping out of jets?"

"Uh, no, Miss. It's just that…well…it's such a nice day…it's hard being cooped up inside, you know?"

"Yes, I do know, Xerxes." She had the tiniest nostrils and they flared, like miniature flanges, when she was angry. "There will always be distractions. You have to concentrate, and if you don't what will happen?"

Xerxes, although smart in many ways, had difficulty recognizing a rhetorical question. "Uh, nothing?"

Miss Petty stepped back as if she had been slapped. "Nothing? Nothing indeed. I think you should gather your books…" and she straightened to her full height, which was considerable "…and see Mr. Hammerschlager in the office…"

"But Miss, I …"

"Now!"

"But…"

"No buts…just go…"

Xerxes could see no point in arguing further. You couldn't win, anyway. He felt that way about arguing with Darius most of the time. You just couldn't win. No matter what tack you took, somehow it got twisted and he was always in the wrong. He stood up, scraping the chair as loudly as he could, gathered his books in one arm, and with as much dignity as he could muster, slouched out of the room. He closed the door forcefully behind him. Well, he had to go and see old Hammerschlager anyway, so this was convenient in a way.

As his footsteps echoed down the empty corridor, he heard drones emanating from the classrooms that he passed. The hall monitor, Mrs. Drudge, sat in a chair outside room 211 and dozed, but even if she'd been awake, she'd have nodded at Xerxes and gave him that knowing look, like she was saying, what have you done this time? So, he tiptoed past her. He knew that Maya was in Geography and Lionel was in the Music Room and he wondered, briefly, if he could break them out. It was tempting, very tempting, to reverse his steps, head out the front doors and cycle away to freedom. But he gave himself a mental slap. Snap out of it. There was more at stake now.

The glass rattled as he opened the door to the principal's office. Mr. Hammerschlager, that is. His secretary Mrs. Shawarma sat behind the counter typing like a fiend, her fingers a blur on the keyboard. She was the most frighteningly efficient person in the universe. I guess you had to be. Everyone knew she really ran the show at St. Batty. Mrs. Shawarma looked up over her bifocals that had slipped down her nose. Her dark eyebrows went up and an amused smile formed on her thin lips. The fingers froze in mid-flight.

"Ah, Xerxes. What is it you have done now? What flight of fancy has taken you over this time?"

"Nothing really."

"And that is why Miss Petty has sent you down here in the middle of her class? For nothing?"

"Yeah, basically."

"You didn't do anything?"

"No."

"Perhaps, it was more a matter of what you were supposed to be doing, rather than what you weren't doing?"

Her logic escaped him but it sounded plausible. "Yeah...whatever. Uh, anyway, I need to speak to Mr. Hammerschlager. Is he free?"

"Pick a number and wait." She pointed to a chair. He sat down. "Ah Xerxes, if you don't mind my saying, you need to get your head out of the clouds. You are a first-class dreamer, you. Just like my son. He too, dreams all the time. He dreams so much, he does nothing else. Don't let that happen to you. Come down to earth, Xerxes, and that is where you can make things happen. Like in Miss Petty's class. If you want to go to college, then you will need a good mark in English, am I right?" Xerxes nodded. "Then what is the point in making her upset? Just do what she asks. It is the simplest and easiest way to get ahead. A no-brainer, right? There is plenty of time still for dreaming but school is for learning not fantasizing, do you see?"

"Uh, yeah, sure."

"He'll be with you shortly." And Mrs. Shawarma, having said her piece, turned back to the keys and began again.

Xerxes guessed that Mrs. Shawarma meant well but he'd had his fill of such pronouncements for the time being. Everyone had their opinion and wanted to force it on him, it seemed.

Hammerschlager's door opened and the principal stepped out. He was a rotund man with a florid face, a bulbous nose and a fringe of ginger hair that wrapped itself around his skull just above the ears. He crooked a thick forefinger in Xerxes direction. Xerxes stepped in. Hammerschlager thrust a dish at him. "Mint?" he asked.

Xerxes shook his head. "No thanks."

Hammerschlager sighed and went behind his desk and sat in his chair burdening the springs as Xerxes heard them squeal. "So, what's the problem between you and Miss Petty?"

"No problem, really. Just a misunderstanding. I didn't mean to upset her. I was just feeling a bit restless and…"

"Weren't paying attention?"

"Yeah, that's about it."

Hammerschlager unwrapped the mint and popped it into his mouth. "You know, Xerxes, compared to most problems I deal with, I do have to say, this isn't over the top. However, you've got to understand that nobody likes to be ignored or spend time talking to people who don't listen. I mean, how would you feel if everybody you tried to talk to didn't pay any attention? It would be frustrating as heck, wouldn't it? That's all I'm saying. Just show Miss Petty a little courtesy and be done with it. It's no big deal and doesn't require much effort now, does it?"

"No, not really."

"There you see? I know you are a bright lad and I know you're not a troublemaker like your buddy Bruno Bakisse…"

"He's not my buddy, believe me."

"Well, uh, neighbor then. Anyway, the point is, I have more serious issues to deal with and I don't appreciate these petty, excuse the pun, interruptions, okay?"

"Yeah, sure."

"How's your dad?" Hammerschlager and Darius played high school football together.

"Good. Busy, you know."

"Best damn high school tight end I ever saw. Xerxes, I'd be lying if I didn't say that he could have gone all the way to the NFL."

Xerxes groaned inwardly. How many times had he heard this? "Yes sir, so you've said."

Hammerschlager looked at him sharply. "Doesn't make it any less true, does it?"

"No sir."

"Well, you give him my regards, will you, and your mom, of course." He shook his head. "Lucky man, Darius. Always was. Okay, now, get out of here, I got other matters to attend to."

Xerxes rose, "Uh, sir…?"

Hammerschlager had already dismissed him in his own mind and was bent over a sheaf of papers. "What? You haven't left yet?"

"There is something else?"

"Well, out with it then."

Xerxes told him about the show and that he'd be missing a few weeks of school and wanted to make sure he could make it up and not fall behind because he was concerned about college and keeping his marks up.

After he finished, Hammerschlager sat back in his chair. "Well, I'll be. Sounds like a great opportunity, really. You are a lucky son of a gun. Just like your old man. Okay, here's what we'll do. We'll get your teachers together and they'll come up with a bunch of assignments for you, but we'll make sure it's something that fits with what you're doing, okay? Maybe it's a video diary or something on French culture or a city tour of Paris. Anyway, we'll figure it out. Just remember to send me a postcard, all right?" And Hammerschlager flashed him a grin and a thumbs up. "Way too cool, dude."

Xerxes stared at him in disbelief. "Uh, thanks...I think." He backed out of the office. As the door closed behind him, he shook his head. "Wow."

He glanced at his watch. Lunchtime. Thank God. As he rattled the glass door, he heard Mrs. Shawarma mutter, "Better keep those feet on the ground if you know what's good for you."

Xerxes looked down at his feet. They only left the ground when he lifted them up to take a step forward.

He pushed out into the sunshine. The halls were buzzing with the usual hubbub, kids freed from the shackles of the classroom, and their energy bubbled over as lockers slammed, books and binders dropped, hands slapped and voices rose and echoed off the ceiling. Xerxes had stopped by his locker, grabbed his lunch and headed for the picnic tables on the school grounds where he'd meet Lionel and Maya.

Something nagged at him. Before veering around the side of the building, he took a deep breath and saw Brutal over by the bike rack. He was tossing something into the air. Xerxes went to investigate.

"Hey... what the... that's my rear wheel."

"I know," Brutal smirked as he tossed it into the air like a Frisbee and deftly caught it with one hand.

Xerxes took a closer look at his bike. The front tire was flattened and jam had been smeared all over the seat. Long, ragged grooves had been chiseled into the frame. "What'd you do that for?" It took a lot to get Xerxes riled and he was riled.

"Do what?" Brutal asked mildly.

"Trash my bike."

"Hey, beanpole, I didn't do nothin'. I found it like this, okay?"

"You're telling me... hey, stop that..." and he grabbed the wheel out of Brutal's hands, "you didn't do this?"

Brutal waggled his shaggy head. Tufts of hair floated up around his face. "Nope. But I thought it was pretty funny. Made me laugh." Xerxes gave him a penetrating look. "Okay, don't believe me, I don't give a rat's ass, right? It's the truth."

"Why should I believe you, you hairy dork."

"Ooohhh, you're going to hurt me feelings. I tell you why... because if I did trash your bike, I'd make sure you knew I did it, right? It would have been fun, okay Frankel? But someone beat me to it. Besides…" and then he mumbled something.

"What?" Xerxes cupped a hand to his ear.

"I said…I need to pass Physics…okay?"

"Why?"

Brutal made a show of cracking his knuckles, then flexing his biceps. "Because I got to graduate from high school or my old man's gonna kick me out of the house, that's why. And then I can't go work in his garage, which is all I wanted to do anyway but he's got it in his head that I have to finish because he never did. It's a crazy thing with him, you know? The guy's as stubborn as a rock, can't budge him…so, if you can help me do that, then it will save you from being kicked around for a while. Not a long time but some time. So, I didn't trash the bike, got it? And I don't know who did, neither."

Xerxes shook his head, turned and walked away carrying the wheel with him.

"Hey, maggot. What about that Physics, huh?"

"After school," he barked. "One half-hour. That's it, man, and I mean it."

Brutal laughed. "Good. I'll be waiting."

Xerxes spotted Lionel and Maya munching away, seated at one of the tables.

"Hey, what took you?" Lionel asked. "And what's with the wheel?"

Xerxes lowered himself onto the bench. "Someone trashed my bike. At first I thought it was Brutal."

"Why did you think that?" Maya asked.

"Because he was playing with this when I got there." And he indicated the bike wheel. "But he said he didn't do it and I think I believe him."

"Why would you believe that maniac?" Lionel asked in mid-chew.

"Because he said he'd want to take credit for it, that's why. And he couldn't because he didn't do it. Somebody beat him to it. Besides, he needs help with Physics..."

Maya's eyes widened. "He asked you for help?"

"Yeah."

"Well, that's too weird."

"Yeah. Something about needing to graduate from high school or his old man won't let him work in the garage. I don't know, maybe it's true."

Lionel slurped his juice box. "Well, if it wasn't Brutal, then who was it?"

"Beats me, man. Beats me." Xerxes shook his head. Just when things were going so well. He hadn't told his friends yet about the show; he was waiting for the right time so maybe this was it and the thousand-watt smile lit up. Minor setbacks after all, nothing fatal, right? "So, listen, I have some news..."

Lionel smiled faintly, crumbs sticking to his cheeks. "Yeah? What's up?" Maya didn't say anything, just looked at him expectantly. To her, news wasn't always a good thing.

Xerxes hesitated, then thought, what the heck, and launched into the story, told them about the audition and the crazy stuff he had to do and then the call from Mira and the reaction of his parents. When he finished, he was greeted with another deafening silence.

"Wow," Maya said finally.

"Yeah, that's cool," Lionel said in a tone that communicated the opposite.

Xerxes looked from one to the other. "What's wrong?"

Maya shrugged. "Nothing. We're happy for you. That's great news, really."

"That's right," Lionel said. "Pound it." And he put his hand up and they touched knuckles.

"Well…thanks. I mean, I am a little nervous about this whole thing. It's not like I've got a lot of experience, you know?"

"We know," Maya said. Xerxes looked at her. "Just kidding, you dope. You'll do fine. You always do. You've got the charm."

"That's right, bro'. You are the charm-er."

The bell rang and they packed up. Lionel and Maya walked on ahead. Xerxes wondered if his bike wheel would fit in his locker but decided he could lock it to the frame instead. As he walked away, he glanced back at his buds and wondered what was wrong and why he was disappointed in their reaction.

After school, Xerxes sat with Brutal in the Caf for forty-five minutes going over Physics formulas. Xerxes put down his pen and looked at his adversary.

"Man, I don't get it," he said.

"What?" Brutal replied gruffly.

"This stuff."

"What stuff?"

"This…you're not conning me, man. You're understanding this stuff and don't tell me you aren't, okay?"

"Yeah? So what, jerk face?"

"So, why…" and Xerxes hesitated here because he knew he could be on dangerous ground and didn't want to get a pounding, "…why do you like to have everyone think you're stupid?"

"It's a family thing."

"What? I don't get it."

"That's our rep, right? That's who we are, see? Big, mean and stupid but not stupid enough that we can't figure things out, see?"

"You want people to think you are stupid? You mean, like a cover?"

Brutal knew he was on new ground here, with one of his adversaries yet. But he didn't really hate Xerxes one way or the other. He treated it like a job, what he was supposed to do. And he was supposed to treat everybody badly and in that way, they were all equal in his eyes. "Somethin' like that."

"If you went to class once in a while, you wouldn't even need tutoring."

"Tell me somethin' I don't know, maggot face." And he sneered.

Xerxes put his hands up. "Excuse me for stating the obvious, okay?"

Brutal sat back. Normally, people didn't talk to him that way and he'd have to think of something good to get back at him but he was in a benevolent mood today. "It's okay. You can't help it if you're dumb, right? And just for the record, I didn't trash your bike, okay?"

Xerxes nodded. "Okay. I believe you."

"And I didn't egg your house. Waste of perfectly good eggs."

"I believe that too."

"You'd better, if you know what's good for you…maggot."

"Okay, Brutal. You got me." He glanced at his watch. "Listen, time for me to hit the road and it's going to take a while because I've got to carry my bike." He stood up. "See you in class?"

"Yeah, whatever," Brutal replied sullenly. "And, uh, thanks, all right but don't tell anyone I said so or you're a carcass that I'm going to feed to the squirrels, got it?"

"Got it."

"Remember, I can twist your head off, snap it like a twig and spin it like a top on this table here."

Xerxes laughed. The image of it was funny. As he was laughing, Brutal looked at him and then cracked a smile. Then he broke out in a harsh, braying noise. The two of them laughed like sick idiots, but Xerxes kept a wary eye on Brutal, just in case.

U

Xerxes unlocked his bike and surveyed the damage. Nothing that new tires and some metallic paint wouldn't fix, so the vandalism wasn't fatal. He'd looked around for Maya and Lionel but guessed they didn't hang around after school while he spent time with Brutal. Not that he could blame them for that, of course. The front wheel was wobbly; he lifted the frame from the back and rolled it forward while he held the back wheel in his left hand. It was awkward but doable.

After six blocks, his arms were aching and he decided to take a break. He was about halfway to his house and stopped in the park. He leaned the bike up against the back of a bench, unslung his knapsack and sat down. He sat under a sign that read, "No Golfing. No Ball Playing. No Frisbee Tossing. No Bare Feet! Dogs Must Be Kept Leashed!"

He should be feeling better about things but for some reason, he wasn't and he wondered why. Maybe the strange reaction from his friends? The lack of support from Darius?

Xerxes slapped at his neck. A little early for mosquitoes but man, did that sting. Then he felt another sting against his cheek.

"Geez, that hurt. What the…?" He looked around. Something zinged by his ear.

Holy moly, someone was shooting pellets at him. And they were a pretty good shot. He ducked behind the bench and scanned the surroundings. About 40 meters away stood a thick stand of oak trees and at the perimeter grew a lush hedge. The city parks staff had done a good job with the old green thumb, he couldn't see a thing. Peering through the slats, Xerxes thought he saw some rustling in the branches, a small bit of movement. A pellet pinged off the bench and he dropped on all fours. Then something ricocheted off the handlebars of his bike. Wait a second… that projectile came from the other direction. Jeepers, he was caught in a crossfire! Then things just erupted, spurts of dirt kicking up around him, pieces of bench fragmenting splinters catching in his hair, dirt kicking up over his shoes… all of a sudden, he felt a white heat rising within him. He'd had enough of this. He was fed up.

Crouching low and using the bench for cover, Xerxes scooted over to the next bench and then the next one. He made a dash for a group of poplars thinking maybe he was out of range but then something nicked his earlobe and he knew that was a miscalculation. He had the hedgerow in clear sight and decided to just go for it… and summoning it all up, he charged, bellowing, yelling, screaming, not caring what happened or what he might find.

"YYYaaggghhhh!"

His legs pumped and he grew closer. There was a wavering in the hedge and he tried to follow it. But finding an opening or a way around was no small task. It must be three-feet thick, maybe more. Just a dense wall of prickly branches and green leaves. He skirted the edge, lashing and kicking and shouting out as he went.

"I know you're in there. Come on out and face me, you SOB. You freaking coward. Come On. Bring It ON."

No reply. He jogged around the end of the hedge and peered down the row. Nothing. Then he turned suddenly and squinted... off in the distance he saw the back of a running figure, moving fast and too far to make out, too fuzzy to get any details. "Geez," he said. "Foiled." And he kicked a divot out of the wet grass.

He walked back slowly to the bench. When he got there, he stopped. The contents of his knapsack were dumped on the ground and someone had had a good time booting his stuff all over the park. A note was taped to the handlebars of his bike. "SUCKER!" it read. Xerxes smiled grimly to himself and nodded. He ripped the note into a hundred little pieces and threw them up into the air, swiping viciously as they fluttered around him. This is war, he said silently.

Someone tapped him on the shoulder. He jumped around, arms up, hands balled into fists. Before him, or rather below him, stood an elderly lady with an angry look on her wizened face.

"Didn't your parents teach you not to litter, young man?"

"Er…"

"Now, pick up all these bits of paper, immediately, and put them where they belong!"

"Ah…right," he said sheepishly, the heat draining out of him. The elderly lady in the sun hat and baggy pantyhose watched him carefully until he'd picked up every scrap and deposited each into the waste bin.

"Now, that's better," she said. "I hope you've learned a lesson."

Xerxes kept his jaw clenched shut but nodded to her as pleasantly as he could under the circumstances. Really, he wanted to scream to the heavens but a supreme Frankel effort prevailed. What a dude had to do sometimes.

When Darius pulled into the driveway, he saw Xerxes up on a ladder with a bucket and a sponge. Whoa. Not like his son to do chores without being asked. Not like him to do anything responsible without being asked. Xerxes heard his father pull up but didn't turn at the sound of the car door slamming or the heavy tread of heels on pavement.

"What's going on?" Darius asked.

"Nothing really."

"Well then, what are you doing?"

"Cleaning. I thought I'd do my bit for spring, you know?"

"It's the middle of May. We do our spring cleaning in April. Aren't you just a little late?"

"Better late than never," Xerxes called. "Right?"

"Yeah. Sure." Darius shook his head and went on into the house. He needed to get changed before getting dinner started. And before he got dinner started, he needed a tall, cool drink, just to help him chill a little from the rigors of the day.

Xerxes heaved a sigh of relief. Got away with that one. He didn't want his dad to know about the egging or any of the other stuff. He just wanted to figure this thing out on his own. Must be a Frankel trait, being strong and silent, unable to seek help when required. They'd have to work on that.

"Hey," a voice called.

Xerxes twisted around and saw Maya straddling her bike.

"Hey," he replied.

"Need any help?"

"Naw, I'm almost done." Carefully, he descended the ladder, until he was standing in front of her. "What's up?"

"Not much…hey, how'd it go with Brutal? You know, the tutoring thing."

Xerxes smiled. "Well, it was less painful than getting my head bashed in, that's for sure." He hesitated. "Uh, you want a soda or something?"

"No…thanks."

"Everything okay?"

"Yeah…listen. I just wanted to apologize for before, you know, when you told us about the show? I mean, that's great news and we're happy for you and I mean that. It's just that…"

"What?"

"Well, we thought we'd all be hanging together this summer, right? Probably our last summer to do that and I guess your news took us both by surprise, kinda…so in a way, I was disappointed and Lionel was too. We didn't mean to make you think that we aren't being supportive or anything, you know?"

"Oh. Sure. I understand. I did think about that too you know and it was a hard decision…really. But this is a great opportunity and I still can't believe it's happening…"

"Yeah, I guess it seems pretty unreal."

"It does, it really does."

"Anyway, I felt bad and Lionel felt bad, so I just wanted to tell you, okay?"

"Sure. Thanks. I appreciate it, I really do."

Maya smiled and when she did, the atmosphere seemed to brighten all around her. "Well, that's all I wanted to say. I'll see you tomorrow, okay?"

"Right. Later."

Maya hopped up on her seat and pushed off. After a few strong pedals, she looked back to see if he was watching her and he was, with a puzzled expression on his face.

"Pretty girl," Darius said. He'd crept up behind him without Xerxes hearing a thing.

"Jeepers, man, you scared me."

"Sorry." Darius nodded in Maya's direction. "So . . . am I right?"

Xerxes shrugged. "I guess so. We're just friends, Dad."

Darius took a heavy sip of the long, cool drink he held in his right hand. He smacked his lips. "If you say so, Son."

Xerxes rang the buzzer to Random Run Productions. Yolanda opened the door and his heart fluttered—just for a second. She was wearing a denim miniskirt and a tank top. Xerxes gulped.

"Oh, it's you," she said letting him in, then turned on her heel but just as suddenly turned back. "What happened to your neck?"

Xerxes grinned sheepishly and felt the spot where he'd been pelted. "Uh, oh, mosquitoes."

Yolanda looked puzzled. "If you say so," she said. "We're all in the studio."

Xerxes followed her in and saw everyone seated at the same rickety, trestle table. Mira was writing something vigorously on a pad and the table shook. Rufus held on to his coffee to stop it from spilling. "Hey X," he said and doffed his cap.

"Hey," Xerxes said and went round shaking hands and smiling and saying his various "Heys" and slapping palms and pounding knuckles and the like. "What's that?"

Behind the table hung a gargantuan chart with days and months marked off and stuff scrawled all over it up and down and sideways and every line was color-coded.

"That's just the schedule," Stephanie Chu said matter-of-factly. "Don't worry about it, that's my job. I'll organize you. You just have to remember what I tell you, that's all, couldn't be simpler, sweetie."

Xerxes sat down. "If you say so, Stephanie."

"Don't worry about it," Mira said. "We're used to it.

Things always seem a little crazy...because they are..." and she let loose a high-pitched cackle. "But you'll get used to it." She looked around the table. "Okay, let's get started because we've got a lot to cover."

Stephanie handed out folders to everyone. "Here's the skinny on our Paris co-host."

"Kind of like a dossier?" Xerxes said. "If you choose to accept this mission, this DVD will self-destruct in five seconds?"

Yolanda rolled her eyes and snorted. Stephanie smiled indulgently. "Kind of." She opened her folder, which was everyone else's cue to do the same and the swishing of cardboard was heard. "Okay, his name is Octave Pompidou and he is eighteen years old. We've got his photo..." Xerxes glanced at the smiling visage in the photo. Good-looking guy. Excellent teeth, probably capped or something, long wavy hair in the Bohemian style. Movie star looks. Xerxes didn't like him already. "As you can see, he should play well for the young girls in our audience...he is a mad cyclist. That is his thing. Crazy about it. His goal is to compete in the Tour de France...you know about that, Xerxes?"

Xerxes laughed. "Uh, yeah. Only the biggest, hardest, toughest, most excruciating cycling race on the planet. Grueling beyond belief. Lance Armstrong dog, he's my hero, oh yeah."

"Okay," Stephanie said. "You get it."

"He gets it, he gets it," Mira said.

"And do you cycle?" Stephanie asked.

"Oh yeah, for sure. My butt is glued to that seat. Always."

"Good, because cycling is going to feature very prominently in the Paris episode. In fact, you and Octave are going to be cycling everywhere in Paris … all of the sites … through the streets and the parks … you name it. Of course, there's a bit of a wrinkle."

"Wrinkle?" Xerxes had a bit of a moment when he heard the tone in her voice and it was, uncertainty. He glanced at Yolanda, who was grinning broadly ear-to-ear, and that alarmed him even more. "Okay. Shoot."

"You see, Xerxes," Mira said. "Built into every show is a kind of a quest or a challenge. We try to find co-hosts who have a special skill or talent, like Octave with his cycling …"

"Okay …" Did his voice really sound quivery or was it just his imagination?

" … so," Mira continued, "the cycling theme works out very well … that is if you don't get run over in the crazy traffic over there, but of course we'll try our best to make sure that doesn't happen but if it does, do you have enough insurance?"

"Huh?"

Mira cackled again. "Sorry. Just kidding. TV humor. Okay," and she slapped her palm on the table, "here's the thing. We'll be going over the script in a minute and the idea is to set up a kind of rivalry between you and Octave, okay?" Xerxes nodded. He didn't think that would be a problem. "Makes the show more interesting, we think, and sets you up too and what I mean by that is, you're going up against experts and trying to outdo them and part of the suspense of the show is to see how well you do. That's why we asked you about all that stuff earlier and whether you had any fears or concerns or phobias."

"Or allergies?"

"Right. Or allergies. And keep your sense of humor. We'll need that, big time. Anyway, here's the thing in Paris. You and Octave are going to have this challenge race, right? And it's going to be very cool but not exactly simple or easy."

"What is it?" Thinking, cycling through the Champs Elysées at rush hour on a Friday afternoon or climbing the Alps or what?

"The Eiffel Tower," Mira said and leveled him with a steady stare.

"The Eiffel Tower?" Xerxes, feeling and looking confused, glanced around the table.

"As in riding down it," Stephanie said.

"The outside?" And he was thinking how that was possible.

The table erupted in laughter, hoots and hollers and thigh-slapping. These TV people were a raucous bunch. "No, no," said Mira gasping for breath. "No, inside, down the stairs, from the top, or really, the second level, the highest level tourists are allowed to go."

"Oh." Relief flooded through him and here he'd thought they'd be flying him down the side somehow hooked on to his bike. "You mean…down some stairs right?" Mira nodded. "Okay. No problem…for a minute, I thought, well, you know…it's just…stairs? Piece of cake. Heck, I do that all the time."

"Eleven hundred stairs?" Yolanda sneered. "Ten stories up?"

Xerxes really didn't like her tone. "Hey, twenty stories if need be."

"It's going to be really cool," Rufus said. "We've got a mini-cam rigged up for your helmet and you'll be miked, of course, so we can catch the view from your angle as you're riding, not just down the Eiffel Tower but for the whole trip and we'll be able to cut that footage in. Here's the best part too…"

"There's a better part?"

"Oh yeah. We've also got this…" And from his vest pocket he whipped out a small rectangle and slid it across the table to Xerxes, who picked it up and stared. "It's a miniature keyboard, wireless of course. It straps to your wrist, right?"

"What's it for?" Xerxes asked.

"Blogs," Rufus said.

"Blogs? I'll be blogging as I'm riding?"

"You got it," Rufus grinned.

Xerxes nodded, turning the wee keyboard over in his fingers. "That is very cool…but…"

"Yes," Mira said. "You'll have to practice. So you should take that with you when you're riding around town, especially if you're on rough terrain…"

"Like going down steps?"

"Exactly," Mira said. "Then see what you can do about messaging. Keep it simple though."

"How about…help!"

"That's good," Mira said.

Yolanda looked glum; the easy banter was getting to her. "Here are the scripts," she said and stood up to pass them around.

Xerxes looked at his copy curiously. He flipped through the pages. "Hey, there's no dialogue."

"That's right," Stephanie said. "We don't want to script this too tightly. After all, it's a reality-based show, right? And we have to allow for spontaneous things to happen. It's what keeps everything fresh and new."

"So I can say what I want?"

"Not exactly," Mira said.

"Rufus and I will let you take the lead," Stephanie said, "but where necessary, we'll feed you lines to say or questions to ask and we have to keep our sponsor happy too."

"Sponsor?"

"That's right," Mira said. "And that's very important because without them we wouldn't have a show. So, there are a few things we need to do to help them."

"Who's the sponsor?" Xerxes asked.

"Global Tour Travel. They specialize in school tours and they are a very large company with offices just about everywhere. They're number one in the school-tour travel market."

"Hey, I took a tour with them two years ago. We went to San Francisco. Man, that was crazy. We had a blast."

"Good," said Mira. "Part of our deal with them is to put you in their gear, you know T-Shirt, sweatshirt, backpack and so on, in front of some of the major attractions, Eiffel

Tower, Arc de Triomphe, the Louvre, to do what we call a stand-up."

"Okay."

"A stand-up," Mira continued, "is like a minicommercial for the company. You'll be talking about how great it is to be in Paris and to see these amazing sites and it's a wonderful trip just like the one you'd experience if you took a Global Tour Travel trip . . . that sort of thing. It won't take too long to do but under our existing contract, we're obligated to do this for them."

"No problem. Happy to do it. Like I said, I had a blast on that San Francisco trip."

"Good. Stephanie is writing the script now for it and once it gets approved, we'll get you a copy."

"Groovy." Yolanda shook her head at him, as if saying, how lame could you be? He gave her his biggest grin back.

Quickly, Stephanie went over the script, which, to Xerxes' eyes, was basically a list of all the places they were going to see in Paris. Octave had given them a list of things he liked to do and some of his favorite haunts and these were included too. So, to his inexperienced eyes, the script looked more like a shopping list than a script but he didn't say anything because he didn't want to betray his ignorance. After all, he was the newbie of the bunch.

"For example," Stephanie was saying, "you're standing in front of the Louvre, right? And you can ask Octave a question or say something like, "Doesn't the Louvre have the largest collection of European artwork in the world?" And then he can go on about how many rooms there are and how many hundreds of thousands of art pieces it has and that there isn't enough room to put everything on display, and the halls are so long and wide that King Phillip II and his son used to ride their horses up and down them…that sort of thing. It's meant to be a spontaneous sort of commentary and also make Octave look like he is knowledgeable even if he isn't. If he knows this stuff, great. If he doesn't, that's okay because we have a crack research team that is doing all the fact-checking and everything is verified over and over again."

"Great. Got it. But still, it wouldn't be a bad thing if I read up a little?" Xerxes asked.

"No, that'd be great, actually," Mira said. "And once we've got the fact-checking done, we'll send you the finished research too and you can work from that. So, go over the script and work out your dialogue a bit. Now, we don't know Octave really. He's not a professionally trained actor or had much in the way of on-camera experience and we're hoping he comes across as being natural and energetic, but if he isn't, then you'll have to make up for it, okay?"

This was getting serious now. Up to this point, it was all a bit of a lark. Like, yeah, cool, I'm going to be a TV star but he realized that all these people were counting on him and that their jobs and livelihoods depended on it. If he screwed up, that could cause them problems. There was a lot at stake here and Xerxes was just beginning to figure it out. "I'll do my best. I'll never not try," he replied.

"Then, that's all we can ask," Mira replied. "So take the script home and go over it. We should have the research finished off any day now and we'll email that to you. We've got everybody's email addresses, right, Yolanda?"

"Right," Yolanda replied, startled that someone had addressed her personally.

The discussion then broke down into logistics. Stephanie was finalizing the travel arrangements and the hotel, liaising with the Paris Film Commission and hiring a local "fixer." The fixer was a local dogsbody who acted as guide, chauffeur and interpreter, getting them to their locations quickly, someone who knew the local customs and routes and locales and how to get there quickly and efficiently. There were also the permits to nail down. A television crew couldn't just march into a city, set up their cameras on street corners or in front of world famous icons and begin shooting. Proper channels had to be worked through or the crew could find itself facing a hefty fine or even hauled off to jail and that would put a bit of a damper on the shooting schedule, which, like most shooting schedules, was tight to begin with. There was never a lot of extra time especially when the production operated on a limited budget. So, there were permits to be obtained for every major site they were to visit and even a general permit to shoot the Paris streets and skyline. The airline, which had agreed to comp their tickets for a mention on the show, had to have passport numbers and information. And Xerxes didn't even have a passport. He hadn't needed one before because he'd never traveled overseas and this was going to be his first time.

"You're going to have to take care of this right away," Stephanie said. "We're leaving in about three weeks. Now I'll give you a letter you can take it to the passport office and you should be able to get it in a week. Normally, it takes a minimum of ten days to get one, but we're in a bit of a hurry. I'll tell the airline, your passport information is coming because your passport is being processed but we can't hold up the arrangements or well lose the bookings we've got." From a file folder, Stephanie removed some government forms and slid them over to him.

"There's the address for the passport office, you'll need to get photos taken first and signed by someone who has known you for at least five years and they must be a pro-fessional person like a doctor, lawyer or accountant, even a chiropractor will do. Then you can take everything into the passport office and it will cost eighty-five dollars to have it all processed. The office opens at eight a.m. but I'd suggest you get there by seven-thirty at the latest. There's a big demand for passports and there will be a line-up, but it moves pretty quickly. Fortunately, you don't have to return to pick up your passport like you used to. They send them out by courier now, directly to your home. Any questions?"

Xerxes was a bit overwhelmed and just shook his head. "Don't think so."

"Okay, good," Stephanie replied. "It would be good if you could get this done tomorrow morning. I know a number of places that do passport photos and are open later, until eight or nine o'clock. The photos should cost about fifteen bucks." Stephanie reached into another folder and slid two fifty-dollar bills across to him. "That's for the passport stuff and the photos. Make sure you get a receipt and turn it in to me, okay? This is our petty cash account and we need to keep track of it for the auditors."

"Auditors?"

"Yes, auditors," Mira said. "In order for the show to qualify for the tax credits offered by the government, all our finances have to be audited by an accountant every year. If they're not, we may not get the tax credit and if we don't, it could have a serious impact on our finances. It's all a pain but the government is concerned that everything be squeaky clean and there's no hint of taint or scandal. They need to ensure that taxpayers' money, which is essentially a tax credit, is well and properly spent. So, we do everything by the book to keep everybody happy. It's a bit of a nightmare and a lot of work, but it's better for everyone in the end. Now, there's your first lesson on the glamorous behind-the-scenes world of television production. Exciting, huh?"

"Confusing," Xerxes admitted. "I never knew so much had to happen before the cameras even started to roll. I've got a lot to learn, I guess."

"It's okay," Max said softly. Xerxes had almost forgotten he was there. "Everyone has a job to do and if it's done well, then it all works together and runs very smoothly. It's when somebody doesn't pull his weight, that it could all start to fall apart and it's our job to ensure that doesn't happen. We provide the glue that sticks everything in place."

"I'm beginning to understand that."

The meeting broke about half an hour later and Xerxes' head was spinning with all of the details. Cripes, it was almost as bad as school, having to sit in one place and not fidget and look like he was paying attention when he just wanted to put his head down and close his eyes. On his way out, he saw Yolanda, tidying up the table. "See you, Yolanda."

She gave him a disdainful smile. "Yes, of course." And she turned back to her menial work. Well, he reasoned, you had to start somewhere and if this was something she really wanted to do, then eventually, it should be worth it. Or why bother?

Xerxes stood there for a moment watching her while she ignored him, and then he zipped up his jacket and left the Random Run Productions offices.

UI

Xerxes stopped by his favorite bookstore in the mall and picked up a couple of travel guides and street maps of Paris. He figured he should have some basic knowledge of the city and be able to recognize some of the more obvious icons, buildings and monuments. He didn't want to seem like a complete tourista dork, looking bewildered, standing on the corner with his jaw hanging down to his knees or anything. So, check that.

There was a photo retailer in the mall who was still open and they did passport photos, so he was in luck. He told the chap behind the counter what he wanted.

"Color or black and white?" he was asked.

"What's the difference?"

The guy hesitated. "Well, you know, color has the colors in it while black and white is simply that, black and white."

Xerxes shook his head, and then gave himself a shake. "No, that's not what I meant. What's the difference in price?"

"Ah, I understand," the chap said, touching the sides of his sleek, dark hair with his fingertips. "About five dollars, that is all. So, it's better to get color, don't you think?"

"Oh yeah. Definitely."

The store wasn't busy, so the guy took him back to the darkroom in the back. "Won't take long," he said, fussing with the camera set-up. "Just take a seat on the stool and face me, please." Xerxes sat on the stool in front of a white backdrop. "Now, remember, your expression must be very neutral. No smiling. No smirking. No funny faces at all, okay?"

"Sure.

"Because if you make even a small expression, it will be rejected by the authorities. Everyone must be the same. Sad. Dour. Unhappy-looking."

"Why?"

The fellow made a gesture and Xerxes found it hard to look at his crisp, white shirt. It was too bright for him. "Oh you know. It is because of the security situation in the world today. Apparently, we are all supposed to look like convicts in these photos but somehow they will be able to tell the real criminals from the rest of us. I don't know how they figure it. I do know that they reject a lot of these photos and we must do them over again. So, there is no point in not doing it right the first time. Saves you some time, do you see? We don't charge anything extra, of course, but it is the time required. It is a hassle, isn't it?"

"Do you mind if we just take the shot? I've got homework to do."

The fellow fussed around the lights for a moment. "Yes, yes, yes. Just another quick adjustment and we'll be ready to go." He went back to the camera, peered through the viewfinder and said, "Ready? Don't smile, please. Thank you." And the flash went off, dazzling Xerxes eyes. "That looked good. One more, for luck, all right? Ready?" And the lights popped and flashed in front of him. He could barely see and couldn't bring himself to get off that hard stool. "Thank you. Just hold your position just for a moment. And… all right, you can get up now."

Xerxes slumped a bit. He hadn't realized how much work it took to sit up straight. He should try it more often. The fellow took the film pack off the back of the camera. "Give me about ten minutes and these should be developed and we'll see what we've got, all right? Back into the storefront, if you please."

Xerxes ambled to the front and browsed the small photography shop. He checked out albums and frames and batteries and memory sticks for his digital camera, which he got for his birthday and figured he'd take with him on the trip. That way, he'd have some memories too and put the camera to good use. His dad complained he wasn't using it or just using it to take stupid pictures of himself dunking the basketball in the driveway or he and Lionel shooting very crude home videos doing the same thing. The thing was, neither of them could dunk. Lionel was way too short. Even if Xerxes gave him a big boost, he probably couldn't dunk the ball. And Xerxes just wasn't quite there yet. He thought about trying out for the St. Batty team but they had the worst record in the district and he didn't need to embarrass himself anymore than he already did on his own.

The chap in the white shirt came out from the back waving the photos. "These have turned out very well." And he laid them on the counter. "See? You look like a true criminal, don't you think?"

Xerxes looked at the pictures. It was true. He did look kind of surly. Put a stubble on him and it could have been a jailhouse shot. "I've looked better, that's for sure."

"You don't like it?"

"Not especially."

"Then that means it is perfect."

"Huh?"

"When the customer does not like the passport photograph, it means the authorities will. Congratulations." And the small man shook his head. "It will pass muster very well."

"Okay."

"That will be eighteen dollars, please." Xerxes gave the fellow a twenty-dollar bill. "And don't forget, you must sign there in the space at the bottom, all right?"

"Right."

"And you must get someone who has known you for at least five years and who is a professional to sign your application form."

"Right."

"I would do it for you but we have just met, you see."

"That's okay. I'll find someone."

"I give you my regrets."

"No problem. Just bag it, please, and I'll be on my way."

With a flourish, the fellow pulled a bag from behind the counter and snapped it open in one fluid motion. He slipped the photos inside and handed Xerxes his change. "Thank you for your business and I hope you have a pleasant trip. Stop in again, perhaps after you have all of your photos back? We also provide CDs and DVDs for digital photos as well. We have many bases covered."

"Uh, thanks again and I'll remember that. Bye." Xerxes practically fled the store. But at least, he had his passport photos done. One thing down, a few more to go.

He was late for dinner but Darius kept a plate for him which he warmed up in the microwave. Not bad. Chicken breasts Cajun style, vermicelli noodles and fresh peas. His dad could be surly at the best of times, but his cooking was usually inspired.

After dinner, he called up Maya.

"Hey," he said.

"What's up?"

"Nothing much. Actually. Is your dad at home?"

"Yeah."

"I just need someone to sign my passport application. It has to be someone who's known me for at least five years and is a professional and since your dad's a dentist, I thought I'd see if he'd do it."

"Want me to ask him?"

"Sure."

Maya dropped the phone and then came back a minute later. "No problem."

"Can I come over now?"

"Sure."

"See you in a minute."

"Bye."

Xerxes told his mom where he was going. Darius was up in his study working, as usual. The deal was he did all the cooking and Hilka and Xerxes did the washing up. While he was drying the dishes, Xerxes asked Hilka if he could borrow the car in the morning so he could drop off his passport application and photos, then take his bike in for repairs.

"What about school?" she asked.

"Umm, I've got a spare first thing and I should be able to make it in by second period."

"All right. I'll catch a lift with you to the subway then."

"Great." He gave her a kiss on the cheek. "And I have to zip over to Maya's for a second, to get her dad to sign my passport application."

"Oh," Hilka said. "That's a good idea. He's known you long enough, hasn't he?"

"Yeah." And he turned to go.

"I like Maya. Always have."

He turned back. "We're just friends, Mom. You know, hang out together, et cetera."

"If you say so."

"I do. What's with you guys?"

"What do you mean?" Her pale face had a puzzled look, well, more blank really. Even her freckles were pale.

"Dad was ragging on about it too."

"He was?"

"Yes. He was."

"Don't get snippy. We're just interested, that's all."

"Nosy you mean."

Hilka shrugged. "That's a parent's prerogative, mister."

"I wouldn't know." He tossed the dishtowel over the back of a chair. "See ya. I won't be long."

Xerxes grabbed a windbreaker from the closet. Maya's house was just a five-minute walk up the street. They had met at daycare, just after Xerxes and his family moved into the neighborhood. They didn't get along in the early days. Maya used to pick on him all the time. But eventually that changed, although there was still that sense of rivalry, like they were competing for something or against each other all the time. It was just something they understood.

He pushed open the screen door, skipped down the porch steps whistling, then started down the walk, hooked his toe and went sprawling onto the concrete, skinning his palms. "Damn! What the heck was that?" He rolled over and stood up, brushing the dirt off his shirt and pants and jacket sleeve. He bent down to examine something. Someone had cleverly strung some wire across the walk, staking it into the grass on either side, just low and taut enough to send him flying. He looked around quickly but it was dusk and nothing seemed out of the ordinary. Geez, it was like he was getting punked all the time and he didn't know by whom. He had to admit, whoever it was, was pretty darn clever. This told him he needed to keep his wits about him.

During the three-block walk to Maya's house, he kept his eyes peeled, looked behind him frequently and scanned his surroundings. He spotted two cats, a dog walker and three kids playing 21 in their driveway. He knocked on Maya's door. A second later, she opened it, the light flooding out from behind her.

"Hey." She took a closer look. "What happened to you?"

"Uh, tripped on the stairs."

"Really?" She narrowed her eyes suspiciously. "That's not like you... being clumsy like that. Was it another practical joke?"

"Seems like it."

"Wow. They're really out to get you."

"Can I come in?" He didn't bother mentioning the rifle practice in the park earlier that day.

"Oh, yeah. Sorry." And she stepped back. Maya wore a pair of cut-offs, a tank top and was barefoot. Xerxes squeezed by. Maya seemed to take some pleasure from his discomfort. "Want a drink or anything?" He shook his head. "I'll go get my dad."

"Thanks."

Xerxes liked Maya's house. The front door led right into the kitchen and it was one of those rooms that just welcomed you in. It had long sweeping counters and a breakfast nook, which Xerxes thought, but would never admit openly, was just the coolest thing. Maya had a younger brother who was doing his homework there. He had a glass of chocolate milk in front of him. "Hey, Brad."

Brad looked up. "Hey."

"What you doing?"

"French."

"How's it going?"

"Crap. I hate French."

"It's a beautiful language."

"It's crap."

"You like french fries, don't you?"

"Yeah, so?"

"So, not everything French is bad, is it?"

Brad, who was nine, looked at him. "You're really lame, you know that."

"Hey, thanks."

"Cool it, Bradley," Maya said.

"Don't call me Bradley. You know I don't like it."

"That's why I said it . . . Bradley."

"Shut up. Go play dolls with your boyfriend."

Maya and Xerxes exchanged looks and muffled laughter. "Brad. That's the best you can do?" Xerxes asked him. "You gotta work on that."

Dr. Langlois stepped into the kitchen. He was a tall man

with kinky, blond hair and dazzling teeth. "Hey, Xerxes. Everything all right in here? How's the French coming, Bradley?"

Bradley made a sour face. "It's crap." He slammed the text shut, downed the milk, slammed the glass on the table and stood up. "I'm gonna play video games." Then he stalked out of the room.

Dr. Langlois shook his kinky head sadly. "Future generations," he murmured.

"Don't take it so hard, Dad. He'll shape up. You did."

"You know how to make a guy feel better," her father replied. He took a good look at Xerxes. "What happened to you?"

"Uh, tripped on the stairs."

"Well…make sure you protect those teeth. I spent a lot of time and effort making them what they are today. And now that you're a TV star, you can't underestimate what a good set of teeth will do for your career."

"I'll take your word for it, Dr. Langlois."

"Okay. You've got some papers for me to sign?"

"Yup. Here they are." Xerxes handed him the application. Dr. Langlois slid into Bradley's spot at the breakfast nook, extracted a pen from his shirt pocket, quickly perused the form and murmured, "Seems in order." Then he signed his name and dated it. He took another look. "I think that's it. I see you've already filled in the other information."

"Thanks a lot. I really appreciate it."

Dr. Langlois stood up and handed the forms back to

him. "Glad to be of help. We've known you a long time. Ever since the two of you were in daycare together…"

"Dad…"

Dr. Langlois held his hands up. "Okay, okay. Don't want to be too predictable." He held out his hand and Xerxes shook it. "Listen. Good luck with the show. And don't miss your next appointment. No excuses, got it?"

"Got it," Xerxes said.

"And keep flossing…especially in the back, those molars on the bottom…"

"Dad." More insistent this time. Dr. Langlois held up his hands, grinned foolishly and left the room. Maya shook her head. "God, my family is crazy…between my brother and my father…"

"Your dad takes his work pretty seriously."

"You don't know the half of it…" She stopped and suddenly they both could feel this tension between them.

"Uh, listen, I better get going. I've got a lot of things to do and I've got to be out early tomorrow to get this application in."

"Oh sure. Thanks for stopping by."

"Thank your dad again."

"I don't think so."

Xerxes grinned. "Okay. Have it your way." He was halfway down the walk before he turned back, but Maya had already closed the door. Ah, stupid idea, he said to himself. She's probably busy first thing tomorrow anyway. No point in her missing school if she doesn't have to.

Having talked himself out of it, he turned around and headed back home. Meanwhile, Maya had been watching him through a crack in the door, which she finally closed, feeling disappointed, even a bit sad and she didn't really know why.

UII

Hilka nattered on her cell phone while Xerxes drove to the subway. She had received a call from a panicked patient, something about a fear of flushing toilets, at least that's what Xerxes picked up from the scraps of the conversation.

"Of course, you must try, Eric," she said. "You have to use the toilet and so it must be flushed sometime, no? You don't like the odor when it isn't flushed, do you? Well, I understand that but your mother isn't going to be around forever. At some point, in your life, you will have to take the plunge...if you get my meaning...no, sorry, I wasn't making fun of you...but having a sense of humor about this may not be a bad strategy, you know. If you can laugh at it, then you have won, yes? Don't you think so?"

Xerxes was trying to keep his mind on the road while listening to his mother's dialogue. He'd even turned down the radio to hear better. When he glanced at her, Hilka rolled her eyes. Xerxes could see she was exasperated but at the same time, he knew his mother was one for making the best of a situation. She would say that this was her chosen profession, that she knew what it was all about when she went into it and some days were better than others. The satisfaction of helping others made it all worthwhile. Xerxes didn't want to think about that stuff, too much a grownup thing. He was willing to take on a measure of responsibility but didn't want to feel suffocated by it and there were times when he thought both his parents were gasping for air.

Hilka finished her conversation. "I'll be in my office in about twenty minutes, Eric. You're my first patient and we'll continue our talk then. I must go. Bye." And without waiting for him to answer, she snapped the phone shut and emitted a deep sigh. "Not the way I'd have chosen to start the day."

"Problems?"

Hilka looked at him and laughed. "Don't be so clever, you heard all about it. It's sad really, but I'm not going to talk about it with you anyway. I have my patient's privacy to protect, you understand?"

"Sure." And he respected his mother for her professionalism. It was unshakeable, always undeterred, she bent her head to the wind and moved forward. For her, there was no going back to anything. One direction was darkness, the other, light. Xerxes shook his head, thoughts far too deep for this early in the morning. "I don't care because I know how to flush the toilet, most of the time."

"Yes, for you, it is unclogging it that seems lost in your vocabulary somewhere."

Xerxes shrugged, signaled right, pulled up to the curb and stopped. "That'll be five dollars and fifty cents plus tip," he said.

"At least I let you drive the car, not like your father."

"He doesn't trust me yet," Xerxes replied mournfully.

"He doesn't trust me, either," she said.

"Some people," and he shook his head slowly.

Hilka laughed, and then she leaned over and kissed him on the cheek. "Have a good day, darling, and I'll see you this evening, all right, my TV star?"

"Aw, Mom. Yeah, okay. See you later."

"Thanks for the lift," she said as she got out and slammed the door behind her. Xerxes tried to look at her objectively and he saw a tall, slim woman with shoulder-length blonde hair in a tailored suit and expensive shoes, who walked gracefully. She still had a good figure, he thought, then felt ashamed for even thinking it but he told himself he was trying to be dispassionate. She strode purposefully forward and then marched down the stairs into the bowels of the subway. He just hoped Darius appreciated what he had, but he wasn't sure if that was the case.

Xerxes parked his mother's Toyota Camry in a paid lot across the street from the passport office. He took the elevator up to the third floor and then followed a series of twisting corridors until he was stopped by a long line. He glanced at his watch: 7:33 a.m.

"Is this the line for the passport office?" he asked the lady in front of him.

"That's right. The doors open at eight," she said sourly.

"Thank you," he said lightly. It was a good thing he'd brought along a couple of *Spiderman* comics, just so he could pass the time.

When he next looked up the line was moving in. The doors were open and they were directed into a series of hard plastic chairs. There were at least ten wickets and each had an electronic display overhead that flashed numbers. Xerxes glanced at the ticket in his hand, 10001, which seemed kind of far away. He couldn't figure out the numbering system at all but dutifully looked up when a new number flashed up on one of the displays. Finally, his number came up.

He handed his documents and photos to the clerk, a middle-aged East Indian lady with a weary smile and grey strands of hair floating behind her ears. She glanced at the photo and then looked at Xerxes, presumably, he figured, to verify it was really him and not some imposter. "These will do," she said. "Everything is in order."

"Is it possible to put a rush on this, please?"

"Are you leaving the country?"

"Yes."

"When."

"About two to three weeks."

"Where are you going?" When he told her, her eyes opened wide. The production schedule for *Get Outta Town!* called for Xerxes to travel all over the world, thirteen destinations in all over the next three to four months. It was a lot of air miles. Her eyes narrowed for a moment, then widened. "I'll put this in the rush pile for you. You should have it by next week. The passport will be delivered to your house by courier."

"Thank you."

"No problem. Good luck and enjoy your travels."

"Don't worry, I will."

Next stop, Al's Pedal Place. Xerxes had managed to stuff the bike into the trunk of the car. Al's was about four blocks from his house and a twenty-minute drive from the passport office, even in rush hour. It was a misty day that cast a shadow on the city. Everything seemed to have slowed down. Certainly the traffic had.

Xerxes carried the bike into the shop, a tight space with the walls and ceiling crammed with bikes of all makes and sizes. Xerxes ducked a few swinging handlebars. Another wall was plastered with bike accessories; helmets, tubes, tape, pumps, racks, pedals, gears, water bottles, whistles, everything the serious or pleasure cyclist could ever want.

Al himself presided behind the counter. A giant of a man in his sixties with a white beard and reddish-gray hair, he was a Philosophy professor who opened his shop on the first of April and closed it on Halloween, juggling his teaching and publishing load all the while. His wife, Gabby, and some of their four children pitched in. Al had been a cycling enthusiast who got frustrated having his bike serviced at some of the more established shops, not to mention the rates he was charged. So, twenty years earlier, he opened his own. Al didn't own a car; he cycled everywhere no matter the weather.

"Hey, Al," Xerxes said.

Al's red-tinged brows shot up. "Were you in a train wreck?" he asked, as Xerxes set the bike down in front of the counter. Al teetered perilously over it to take a better look.

"Nope. Vandalized."

"Now, who'd want to do that? I can understand vandalizing a car, which pollutes the atmosphere, but a clean and wholesome bike? Outrageous."

"I know what you mean. Can you fix it?"

Al stomped around the counter. He was dressed in spandex cycling pants, a Shimano jersey and cycling shoes. He peered and squinted. "Sure, most of it is cosmetic anyway. They could have stomped your gears and cut the cables but they didn't do that. Just slashed the tires and scratched the heck out of the paint. Tubes no problem, eight bucks each. The frame will need to be repainted and we'll have to true the wheels too. Your back rim seems a bit wonky."

"Someone was playing catch with it."

"I see," Al said in a tone that implied he didn't at all and how dare someone even think of doing something like that. To him, bikes were sacred ground.

"Well, you're looking at about seventy-five bucks total and I can have it back to you tomorrow afternoon."

"Great. I'll pick it up after school."

"Do you want it the same color?"

"Yeah, if you can."

Al rubbed his chin. "Might be a challenge to match it up, but I'll check with the manufacturer on the paint code and see if we have it in stock. If not, I'll have to order it, which might take another day but I'm pretty sure I have something that's close. Will that be okay?"

"No, that's fine. I'll trust your judgment on this."

Al snorted. "I wish the dean of my department was so trusting. If there's a hitch, I'll give you a call, okay?" The door jangled and two cyclists came in limping, their bikes in tow. "Uh-oh, what have we got here?"

"Train wreck," the lead cyclist said.

Xerxes drove his mom's car and parked it in the St. Batty's parking lot. They'd reserved about twenty spots for students, just barely enough, and Xerxes got the last one. He checked his watch, five minutes until Geography class. He rushed inside and signed in at the office. It was the end of class change and the halls were draining fast. He made it just as Mr. Flook, the Geography teacher, was about to close the door.

"Good timing," Mr. Flook said and closed the door after Xerxes slid in. Maya was in this class and Xerxes took a seat behind her. She turned and glanced at him, arched her eyebrows, then turned back as Mr. Flook, acknowledged as one of the most boring teachers in the school—and that was saying something—droned on.

Finally, the bell rang and it was lunchtime. Xerxes tried to pay attention in Geography. They were studying elevation and population maps of Europe, and since he was going to be there soon, this was actually relevant to him. But it was a struggle to keep his eyes open. When the class ended, he gave a silent thank you to the gods for delivering him from this boredom.

"How'd it go this morning?" Maya asked him, falling into step, swinging her long hair behind her.

"Pretty good. The passport office was crazy busy. Big lineup at 7:30 and I've never been anywhere that early before. But it moved fast and they're putting a rush on my passport so I should get it in about a week or so."

"That's cool. Then you can travel the world hassle-free."

"Hope so," he replied and again, for some reason, he was feeling this awkwardness between them but decided to ignore it. "Then I took my bike to Al's and he asked me if I'd been in a train wreck."

"He says that to everybody," Maya said. "He's a Philosophy professor...not too imaginative."

"Ah...right. Anyway, I should be able to pick it up tomorrow after school but it's going to cost me seventy-five bucks, which isn't terrible, I guess."

"Maybe you should have called the police."

"I don't think there's much they could have done. I mean, nobody saw anything and it's hardly major crime. They've got serious stuff to look after."

Maya split off to her locker. "Meet you outside, okay?"

"Sure." Xerxes went to get his lunch too.

Lionel was already seated at the picnic table. "Man, don't you love this weather," he said as he watched a trio of girls in short skirts walk by without giving him a glance.

"Is it the weather or the view?"

"Both. Both, my friend."

"What's that you're eating?"

Lionel looked down at his sandwich. "My mom's on this holistic vegetarian kick. So, it's flax bread, alfalfa sprouts, been sprouts and watercress."

Xerxes examined his peanut butter and banana and honey sandwich on a whole wheat bagel and figured he got the best of the deal. "They must be talking to each other," he said.

"Why don't you make your own lunch?" Maya said, sliding onto the bench. "You two are just lazy. You're mama's boys, letting your moms still do everything for you. I bet you don't even make your beds in the morning." She looked at them as Xerxes and Lionel exchanged sheepish looks. "See? I was right."

"It'll happen soon enough," Lionel said.

"Why put off the inevitable," Maya replied. "Take some responsibility, the two of you or you'll never get anywhere."

"Whoa," Lionel said. "Where's all this coming from?"

"What?"

"The sharp critique is what I'm talking about."

"Nowhere. Nothing," she said and dug out an apple, a small bunch of grapes, a tub of yogurt, three lettuce leaves, a chunk of cheddar cheese and some multigrain crackers.

"That looks wholesome," Lionel said.

"And filling," Xerxes added.

"Guys," Maya said giving each of them a penetrating look. "Just lay off the lunch, okay?"

Lionel and Xerxes reeled back, raising their hands in the air. "Surrender, surrender," they chorused.

They looked so stupid that Maya had to laugh. "Forget it. You guys just aren't with it. Too immature."

"Us? Immature?" Lionel asked. A shadow fell across the picnic table. Lionel looked up at the sudden absence of light, and then gulped.

"Hey, Brutal," Xerxes said, feeling less confident than he looked.

"Brutal," the others murmured in acknowledgment.

Brutal didn't respond but kept his brows pressed together and his face in a permanent scowl. He jerked his head at Xerxes, who sighed, and then got up from the bench and moved toward him. Brutal turned and strode off without looking back. Kids parted in his wake, some dove out of his way and the air suddenly became thick with tension as he crossed the field and came around the side of the school toward the parking lot. Xerxes noticed the curious and fearful looks darting in his direction. A small crowd trailed them, thinking that perhaps there was going to be a fight of some kind. Maybe there'd be blood?

Just as they reached the parking lot, Brutal stopped, swiveled and pointed a thick forefinger at the crowd. "Scram," he snarled, and the group dissipated fast. He laid a hand across Xerxes back and steered him toward his mom's car.

"What the...?" The car was splattered with paint. Gobs of bright color on the windshield, the trunk, the doors, the hood, even the rims.

"Just so you know, "Brutal said. "Wasn't me...again...but it's a pretty cool idea. I like it. These people are creative." He nodded his shaggy head in appreciation.

"Wasn't you?"

"No." Hair flew across his face. "Someone's out to get you."

"Looks like it."

"I could watch your back."

"What do you mean?"

"What I said, find them...for a price."

"What price?"

"A hundred bucks."

"Oh...that kind of price."

"What else? More homework?" He spat mightily onto the tarmac. "Don't think so."

"Let me think about it."

"Sure. If you want to stay a chump and let people crap all over you that's your decision." And he stomped off.

"I'll get back to you," Xerxes called. Now he really had to get his mom's car cleaned off and fast.

Maya and Lionel came running up, and then put on the brakes. "Whoa," Lionel squawked. "What happened?"

"Paint happened," Xerxes said dully. "I gotta go wash it off. I can't take the car home like this."

"We'll give you a hand," Maya said, turning to Lionel. "Right?" No response. She dug her elbow into his ribs. "Right?"

"Yeah, right. Geez, right, right, right."

"Thanks guys." Good friends were hard to find, he thought. Xerxes went off to the maintenance room to get a bucket of hot water, soap and some brushes. When he found the caretaker and told him what happened, Xerxes was directed to drive the car carefully around the side where they could hook up a hose to rinse the car off.

"I'll leave all the stuff you need by the side door there; just put it back when you're done," the caretaker said.

"Thanks, man. I really appreciate it." Xerxes bounded off to get the car.

Xerxes hosed the car down and some of the paint began to run right away. "You're in luck," Lionel said. "It's water-based. Should clean off pretty easy."

"Hey, what's with you and Brutal, all of a sudden?" Maya asked, scrubbing a glob of Day-Glo orange off the rear bumper.

"What do you mean?"

"I dunno. You guys seem like, well, like you're almost friends…"

"Yeah," Lionel chimed in emphatically.

"I wouldn't go that far, I mean, we'll never be friends. He still scares the heck out of me."

"Well?" Maya asked.

"I don't know, for some reason, he's decided to temporarily suspend torturing me. I'm not sure why and I don't care. I'm just glad it's happened, so I'm not going to look for any deep meaning in this, you know? The dude's laying off me for a bit and that's okay by me. Then, if my luck holds, I won't run into him at all during the summer and who knows where he'll be next September, right?"

"Great," said Lionel in disgust, pitching a sponge into the bucket. "That means, he'll have lots of time to go after me instead. That's it. The summer is ruined. I'm dead meat."

"Lionel, don't be so melodramatic," Maya said. "It's not that bad."

"Oh yeah? He's never bothered you..."

"Tied my pigtails together in grade four. Put crazy glue on my seat in grade five. Burned my English notebook in grade six. Regularly hit me with spitballs in grade seven...shall I go on?" And she put her hands on her hips defiantly.

"Okay, okay," Lionel said irritably. "But that's almost normal stuff. I'm mean, it's not like it was anything really bad or harmful..."

"I almost had to repeat English..."

"But no real physical threat is what Lionel means, Maya, nothing that caused you any actual pain, you know?"

Maya resumed scrubbing, kneeling down by the bumper, her short skirt riding up her thighs. Xerxes averted his eyes. "Well, you might have a point," she conceded. "But he's never been what I call nice or considerate."

"Not in this guy's vocabulary, believe me." Lionel dropped the sponge in the bucket, and then wiped his hands on the butt of his jeans. "That's it, I think. Mission completed."

"Almost finished the bumper," Maya said and then tossed the sponge at Lionel, who jumped out of the way.

"Hey."

"Chicken," Maya called.

"I'm going to hose this baby down," Xerxes said. "Stand back unless you want a car wash too." He turned on the hose and when he turned around Maya was holding the nozzle. Xerxes stopped. "You wouldn't." Then he eyed the tap, calculating how quickly he could get to it and turn it off before Maya could soak him.

"Wrong," Maya said and let it rip. Xerxes was hit by a cold blast of water. He dove for the tap, laughing, but Maya had followed him and was keeping the spray on him. He jumped up, grabbed at the nozzle but Maya was strong and quick and she jumped out of the way, then shrieked, dropped the hose and took off. Xerxes picked it up and played the hose out as far as it would go, then hit the trigger. He got her square in the back and she doubled up from the wet and the cold.

"Ha. Ha. Got you good," Xerxes called. But Maya had stopped for some reason and was looking at him or past him; he slowly released the trigger and the spray fizzled. Then he turned slowly around and came almost nose-to-nose with Principal Hammerschlager. "Whoops. Hi." And he grinned weakly. "I was just washing off my mom's car, heh, heh."

"So, I see," Hammerschlager said. "You got a little wet."

"Uh, yuh. The hose slipped."

"I see that too." He glared at Lionel. "Shouldn't you be in class?"

"Yes sir," Lionel replied vociferously, spun around and marched away.

Xerxes wanted to cringe. "Mr. Frankel, you look a little wet. As do you Ms. Langlois."

"Yes sir," they said in unison.

"In that case..." and he glanced at his watch and saw it was after 2:30, "you'd better call it a day. You can't sit in class dripping water on the floor. Go home. The two of you. And let's start again tomorrow, shall we?"

"Yes sir," they said and watched as Hammerschlager shook his head and seemed to visibly age right in front of them. Then mumbling something, he walked across the field.

"How does he do that?" Xerxes asked.

"I really don't know," Maya replied. She shivered, a pulse coursing up and down her body.

Xerxes turned to her. "Want a lift?"

"Sure."

"Are you cold?"

"No, not really. Just got a sudden chill. I'm fine."

They grabbed their knapsacks and put them in the back of the Toyota. Xerxes opened the passenger side door first and then walked around to the driver's side.

Maya got in, looked around the inside of the car and said, "Hmm, freedom."

"Where do you want to go?"

"Well, I need to go home first and get changed."

"You got it."

Xerxes started the engine and then backed carefully out and around, bumping along the field until he arrived at the edge of the parking lot where he eased the car gently onto the pavement. As he pulled out of the parking lot, Xerxes saw Brutal leaning up against Principal Hammerschlager's Buick, smoking a cigarette. He looked in their direction but seemed to be seeing right through them. He didn't acknowledge their presence or change his posture, expression or demeanor in the slightest. As Xerxes made his turn, Brutal flicked the cigarette butt into the air and blew a long stream of smoke, tilting his head back and working his jaw mechanically.

Ten minutes later, Xerxes arrived at Maya's house. They got out, Maya unlocked the door and they went in. "I'll just be a second," she said and he heard her pounding up the stairs. Come to think of it, he was pretty soaked too and the driver's seat of his mom's car was a little more than damp and his boxers were a bit clingy. He took a step, and then looked down. Wet footprints were embedded in the carpet. Xerxes panicked. Damn. He whipped off his T-shirt and started sopping them up.

When Maya came back down she froze. She'd changed into a pair of hip-huggers and an overlarge T-shirt. She saw him on his hands and knees desperately rubbing away. "What are you doing?"

"I forgot my shoes were soaked." He stood up and swayed side to side. They both heard the squishing.

"Get those shoes off," she said. "Just a second." And she disappeared again, only to reappear holding up a pair of leather sandals.

"You've got to be kidding."

"Nope. Put them on and take those off." Then she held out a plastic bag. Sighing, Xerxes removed his shoes and socks and dropped them into the bag.

"Here," she said and tossed something at him. Instinctively, he reached out and caught it. "It's my dad's." And then she actually blushed.

Xerxes held up a T-Shirt with a Motley Crue logo plastered on it. "Your dad's?"

Maya nodded. "I know, it's embarrassing. And, uh, I thought these might fit too."

Xerxes took a look at the pair of Jockeys she'd tossed him. "Also your dad's?"

"Well, they're not my mom's and they're a little big for Bradley."

"You think it'll be okay?"

"I won't tell him. Just throw them in the wash when you're done and I'll slip them back into his drawer. I'll get some dishtowels for the carpet."

"Okay." Xerxes knew where the downstairs washroom was. "Just be a sec," he said and slipped inside. Quickly, he stripped out of his jeans, removed the wet boxers and stuffed them in the bag along with his T-shirt, shoes and socks, grabbed a towel and carefully dried himself as best he could, pulled on the dry Jockeys, the jeans and the Motley Crue T-shirt. Not bad, he thought, checking it out in the mirror. I'd be right at home in the seventies. Even the sandals didn't look terrible but Xerxes thought he had funny-looking toes.

"Very retro," Maya observed when he stepped out. "We'll make a head banger out of you yet."

"You sure your dad won't mind?"

"Not if we don't tell him. Besides, it's not like he counts his underwear and I can't remember the last time he wore that T-shirt. He bought it at some concert or something eons ago."

"A Motley Crue concert?"

"Must have been. Are those guys still alive?"

"For sure, they've just started a new tour."

"Oh yeah? Do they take their respirators on stage with them?

"They're not that old…"

"Hey listen, want to go to the Burger Shack? I could do with something."

"Thought you were watching what you eat, organic and natural stuff only."

"Yeah…well…I can get a veggie burger."

Xerxes made a show of scratching his head. "It's a deal."

They were seated in a corner booth. Xerxes was demolishing a cheeseburger while Maya took demure bites out of her veggie burger. They shared a plate of french fries between them. The Shack was fairly empty at that time; it got busy when school let out. An older guy sat at the counter drinking coffee and reading the paper.

"So I guess you're excited," Maya said. "About the show and traveling, I mean."

"Oh yeah. It's going to be an adventure, all right. But I've never done this before and a lot of people are counting on me and if I screw it up, jobs are at stake."

"Stage fright already," she teased. "You haven't even started yet."

"Pretty lame, huh?"

"No, not really. It's a normal reaction."

"Well, thank you. Xerxes Frankel is normal as declared by Maya Langlois," he said in a fake announcer's voice.

She threw a fry at him. "You know what I mean."

Xerxes picked the fry off the Motley Crue T-shirt, held it up to the light and said, "Ah, a very good year." Then he ate it.

"Seriously," Maya said. "It'll be cool watching you on TV." She thought for a moment. "You're going to have to get yourself an agent."

"Why?"

"Because every TV star has one."

"Why?"

"To handle all of the business stuff."

"I can handle that myself."

"Oh really? How much money do you have in your bank account?"

"What's that got to do with anything?"

"Just answer the question."

"Since when did you get so practical?"

"Answer."

"Okay, okay. Uh, let me think...about one hundred and seventy-five dollars."

"That's it?"

"Well...yeah."

"That's pathetic."

"Okay, Ms. Einstein Wall Street entrepreneur, how much you got?"

"Like five thousand dollars."

"What?"

"Oh yeah..."

"How'd you get so much?" he asked.

"Saving all my birthday money, Christmas money, money I earned babysitting, working part-time. I'm going to need money when I go to college after next year. I don't want to be totally broke, do I?"

"I guess not. Aren't your parents going to pay for tuition?"

"They're going to help but I can't expect them to pay for everything."

Xerxes sat back. "Man, I never really thought about that..."

Maya sighed. "Typical. Typical. Typical."

"But you spend some money right?"

"Of course. I give myself an allowance."

"You mean like your parents give you?"

Maya screwed up her face. "Hello. My parents don't give me an allowance anymore."

"They don't?"

"No. Why? Do yours?"

Xerxes looked down at his plate, which he suddenly realized was empty. He drained the soda. "Uh, no they don't."

"Then I'm surprised you even have a hundred and seventy-five dollars in the bank."

He thought about it. "Yeah, me too. And after tomorrow, it's only going to be a hundred dollars. I've got to pay for the repairs to my bike."

Maya pointed another fry at him. "The bottom line is, buddy, you've got to get your affairs in order. If you're going to be making some serious cash here, you don't want to blow it. You want to save something for later."

"Yeah, but a car would be nice. Having wheels would be very cool."

"Don't waste your cash on a car."

"Why not?" And now, he was indignant. Maya was trying to tell him how to run his life all of a sudden. Like, where did this come from?

"Chill," she said, then smiled like a conspirator. "Get your parents to buy you one. That's what I'm going to do."

"Aha. Clever, but Darius will never go for it. He's so hard-nosed about everything."

Maya sat back in the booth pressing her back against the fake leather. "You are so dumb sometimes." And she shook her head.

Now what? "What do you mean?" he asked.

"Get your dad to manage your finances for you. He's an accountant. Who better? It'll be like a project between you, a father-and-son thing…"

"Accounting? A father-and-son thing? Baseball is a father-and-son thing. Watching the basketball play-offs, heaving a football in the backyard, that's what fathers and sons are supposed to do."

"Don't be so stereotypical. Okay, so that's most people. In this case, it's something a little different. Be open-minded, Xerxes. It'll give you something to do together."

"Counting money?"

"Why not?" she asked emphatically. "Especially if it's your money. After all, who are you going to trust?"

Hmm, maybe she had a point. Maybe it wasn't such a bad idea. He needed to get on Darius' good side for once. He took a good look at Maya. Tousled brown hair and lightly tanned complexion. Deep dark eyes you could sort of lose yourself in. Tall and athletic. And then the perky image of Yolanda muscled its way in and he felt confused.

Maya gave him an inquiring look, the sort of look that seemed beyond her years, sophisticated and knowing. "What?" she asked softly, leaning in to him.

"I…uh….."

"Hey guys!"

Xerxes and Maya sprang apart.

"Lionel," Maya said.

"I've been looking for you. Where'd you go?" Maya explained what happened. "Hammerschlager let you go? I can't believe it?" Lionel exclaimed. "Wish I'd gotten soaked. "Man, Bio was the beast, man, and I don't mean because we were dissecting pig fetuses either."

"Lionel," Maya said. "We're eating here."

Lionel held up a hand. "Sorry. No offense. Man, I'm starved." He slid in beside Maya and picked up a menu.

Sally, the waitress, came over. "I don't know why you bother with the menu," she said. "You order the same thing every day."

"I know what I like," Lionel said defensively.

"Well, that makes you different from most men," Sally said. "Okay, banquet burger, double mayo, extra bacon and a chocolate shake. Right?"

"Right," Lionel said sheepishly.

"You'd think putting all that food into you, you'd be twice the size," Sally said. "Wish I could eat like that and get away with it."

"Yeah, me too," Maya said.

Sally eyed her up and down. "You got nothin' to worry about, honey." Then she sashayed off to put in the order.

"She likes you," Maya said to Lionel.

"Go on, she's old enough to be my mother," he said.

"So?"

"And she looks like one of the lady wrestlers on *Slammin'*."

Maya shook her head, looked up at the ceiling and said, "Hopeless. You're both hopeless."

"Hey," Xerxes said. "Why am I hopeless?"

"What's that supposed to mean?" Lionel asked.

"Er, nothing," Xerxes said, then turned back to Maya. "So?"

"You know…"

"I don't."

"Yes, you do."

"But I don't. Really."

"I'll tell you later."

Sally brought Lionel's order and set it down in front of him. She patted his cheek. "*Bon appétit,*" she said.

"See?" Maya said with a triumphant look.

"My aunt Sadie does the same thing. All that's missing is the great big pinch she gives me." And without further ado, he attacked the food.

"You did eat today, right?" Maya asked.

"Yeah, I had lunch, so?"

"Just wondering."

"Why?" his cheeks bulged.

"Slow down before you do yourself an injury," Xerxes said. "That's what Darius says when I'm throwing it back, and then he gets angry because I'm not appreciating his cooking."

"Is he a good cook?" Maya asked.

"Yeah. Pretty good actually."

"So, there's another thing."

She was really confusing him now. "What?"

"Cooking. Get him to teach you. It's a great life skill to

have. One of the things I look for in a man is his cooking ability."

Lionel and Xerxes looked at each other and grinned. "Since when are you looking for a man?" Xerxes asked.

"I'm always looking."

"You are?" This surprised and shocked him. He'd never thought about Maya as being on the prowl.

"No one, as of yet, has met my standards."

"Guess, that means us," Lionel said, laughing, bits of food falling onto his plate.

"Gross," Maya said.

"Stick with Sally," Xerxes told him.

"Mind you…" Maya began, "Rick Oswald is kind of cute."

Xerxes was stunned. "That guy? Mr. Jock with no brains?"

"Who needs brains? Easier to control that way," she teased.

"Really?" Lionel gaped. "Girls really think that way?"

"Of course."

"Then I'm banished for good," he said miserably. "I'm nothing but brains…"

"You forgot…winning personality," Xerxes said. "And excellent eating habits."

"That too." And he crammed the rest of the burger into his mouth and chewed heavily.

Sally cleared away the dirty dishes. "Anything else, kids?" They all shook their heads. She wrote out the bill and slapped it on the table. "Have a great day," she said.

"Hey, you guys want to see something cool?" Xerxes

began digging around in his knapsack until he found what he was looking for.

"What is that?" Lionel asked.

"It's a miniature keyboard," Xerxes said.

"What's it for?" asked Maya.

"Watch." Xerxes unhooked the straps, then wrapped them around his left wrist, then held it up and with his free hand, began to type. "It's wireless. See, I can cycle and post blogs at the same time."

"Get out of here," Lionel said. "Let me see." Xerxes held his wrist out. Maya peered in. "That's really cool."

"How are you going to do that without crashing?" Maya asked.

"I'm practicing," he said. "It's going to be tricky but I think I can do it."

"It's different, that's for sure," said Lionel and whistled.

"What are you going to say?" Maya asked him.

"When?"

"When you're cycling."

"I don't know. Depends on what's happening, I guess, but you guys can log on and check it out. It's all going to be live and interactive."

"Get outta here," Lionel said again.

"I've even got a handicam in my cycling helmet so the show and the website will have that right-on-the-spot feel to it."

"Very cool," Maya said. "Hey listen. Let's split, okay? I've got a ton of homework due for tomorrow and a science quiz."

They paid the bill and said their goodbyes to Sally, who glanced up and gave them a brief wave as they left. Xerxes drove Maya home first because it was on the way.

"Later," she said and hopped out of the car. The two guys watched her as she strode up the driveway and went inside. She didn't look back.

There was a moment of silence while they continued to look.

"She's actually a real babe, you know that?" Lionel said.

"Yeah."

"So, why's she hanging out with us?"

"What do you mean? We're friends. Have been for years."

"But that changes," Lionel said. "When your friend ends up looking like that." Lionel groaned softly. "This is not going to be a good summer for me."

"What are you talking about?"

Lionel turned to him. "Think about it, genius. You're off being a TV star all summer and Maya's got Rick Oswald or some other mutant drooling after her. So where does that leave me? Nowhere, that's where."

"Lionel, you're exaggerating."

Lionel shook his head. "Don't think so."

"It'll be fine."

"Easy for you to say. You'll be in Paris and other points meeting sophisticated French chicks, hitting the cafés, having a great time in the City of Love while old Lionel will be working his butt off as a courier with nothing to do other than that."

"You're feeling sorry for yourself—not an attractive quality."

"Well, right now, it feels like the only one I've got."

"Get real, will you? You've got a lot to offer."

"Okay," Lionel said. "Start the car. We're not having this discussion. Too touchy-feely, too girly, okay?"

"Yeah. Maybe you're right. Sorry."

"Just drive."

Before he put the car in gear, Xerxes said, "Rick Oswald? You sure about that?" But he was thinking, man, I'd hate to see Maya dating Rick Oswald.

 UIIII

The clock radio buzzed. Xerxes groaned, reached out from under the covers and swatted at it. He missed and knocked the radio off the side table onto the floor where it continued to buzz. God, that was annoying. He opened one eye and tried to angle it so he could see the time. Five-fifteen a.m. Man, the sacrifices some TV stars had to make. Xerxes pushed back the covers, shivered, swung out of bed and padded to the bathroom where he turned on the tap and splashed cold water on his face. He peed mightily, washed his hands, went to his minifridge, took out a juice box and sucked it back. He tossed the container into the recycling bin, and then began pulling on his cycling gear. Five minutes later, he was ready to go. He unhooked his bike from the rack and set it down. Al had done a great job on the repairs. It looked practically new and was worth the seventy-five bucks. The man was a genius with bikes…as a philosopher, Xerxes wasn't so sure, but as a pedaler, Al was tops.

Xerxes strapped on the keyboard and powered it up. He filled his water bottle with Super-Ade and opened the door. He looked down at the sidewalk, catching the glint of something metallic by the light of the street lamps. Dawn was a good thirty minutes away. Setting his bike carefully against the side of the house, Xerxes crouched down to take a look, and then nodded to himself. Clever, man, clever. A series of mousetraps, big ones, had been set in a staggered pattern all the way down the walk to the street. Well, he'd deal with them later. Heh-heh. He rolled his bike through the damp grass skirting the walk…then his foot slid out from under him and he went down hard on his rump. What the…? He touched the ground gingerly around him…something wet and viscous…his fingers came away oily and he brought them to his face and took a tentative sniff, hmm, some kind of vegetable oil, he thought, quite a lot of it. The traps were a blind to force him off the sidewalk and guess what? The ruse worked. Someone somewhere was having a good laugh at his expense. Again.

He stood up cautiously and took a few careful steps and then moved more quickly to the street. At last, solid ground. He wiped his hands on a towel he kept stuffed under the bike seat and scraped his shoe on the grass, then on the curb and finally on the road. Well, they wouldn't stop him, he told himself as he mounted the bike and set off on his practice ride. No way.

He glanced down. He noticed that the tiny keyboard lit up in the dark. As he rolled along on flat terrain, he tried typing a "Hello and How are you?" Before he knew it, he'd careened to the side of the road, bouncing off the curb. Whoa, need to try that again. Okay, mount up. Eyes straight. Xerxes had taken keyboarding in school so he knew where the keys were and he'd been practicing typing on this thing with his eyes closed for a while now. Rolling along the quiet street, he typed away. "Maya, I do not want you to date Rick Oswald. I do not want you to date Rick Oswald. I do not want you to date anyone . . ." Okay, he'd better get off that trip. Even though he'd emailed it to his own address, you had to be careful these days. You'd send a message thinking it was private and before you knew it, the whole world had it in their inbox. He pressed delete, just to be sure.

Even though he hated getting up early, Xerxes liked these early-morning rides. The streets were quiet, the houses dark, he'd see the occasional light on or hear a solitary dog bark in the distance. In a way, he felt like he owned these streets, the lonely road warrior keeping the neighborhood safe while citizens slept soundly in their warm beds.

Xerxes rode along feeling nothing but peace and goodwill.

Something or someone stepped out from behind a tree. A hand gripped his shoulder and wrenched him off the bike tossing him effortlessly to the ground. When he looked up, Xerxes saw a wide shadow and the glow of a cigarette . . . then, heavy exhaling.

"Told you I'd watch your back."

"Brutal, what the heck . . . ?"

"You're an easy mark, you know that? Even your jersey is fluorescent. It makes a great target." And he held out what looked like a pistol, pointing it at Xerxes' chest. Instinctively, Xerxes held his hands up. He saw the cigarette move to the side as Brutal twisted his lips into an evil grin. He pulled the trigger. Xerxes closed his eyes. He felt the impact of a projectile. He opened his eyes, one eye at a time. He wasn't dead. Not even maimed. A rubber dart protruded from his chest and a noise like rusty pipes clogged with gurgling water filled his ears. It was Brutal laughing. "Got you there, huh? Bet you thought I was going to do something bad, didn't you? I'm just teaching you a lesson for a change. Kinda like Physics but opposite, right? These people know every move you make. They know your routine. They're always gonna get you."

"So what do I do?"

"Change your habits."

"I'm leaving town in two weeks."

"That's a good change," Brutal conceded. "Until then, I'd try and be a little harder to spot, know what I mean? Don't be predictable. Take 'em off guard. Right?"

"Yeah, sure."

"Okay, I gotta split. Gotta get to work. My dad's garage opens at six and I'm not supposed to be late."

"What about school?"

"What about it?"

"Are you going?"

"Oh yeah. I told you I need to graduate and this is the moment. No more wasting time. Now or never, right?"

"See you, Brutal."

Brutal reached down and pulled the dart from his shirt that bunched up from the suction. "Easy target," Brutal said, as he headed off into the semi-darkness and snorted through his nose. He disappeared over and beyond the crest of a hill.

The world is a strange place, Xerxes thought, as he got up, brushed himself off and remounted the bike. Fortunately, this didn't really faze him. Weirdness, he could deal with.

He cycled past Maya's house and wondered if she were sleeping. Stupid question. Of course she was. What else would she be doing? He glanced at his watch. Hard to believe, it was 5:35 and he'd only been on the road for ten minutes. He'd better step it up.

An hour later, Xerxes had sent thirty-five messages and worked up a good sweat traveling the streets. He'd logged over twenty miles and he was still feeling fresh, even though he'd climbed hills and crossed ravines and plowed through gravel and grass. Next up was the Boulevard of Broken Dreams. And then, it is Paris here I come.

Xerxes rode up to his door, snapping off the mousetraps clickety-clack. He saw a light come on in his parents' room. Quickly, he carried his bike inside, hung it on the rack, stripped off his gear, stuffed it into the laundry bin, grabbed a T-shirt, briefs and shorts, then hustled into the shower as he heard heavy footsteps crashing down the stairs. As he heard the door to his room open, Xerxes hit the taps on the shower and stepped in, pulling the curtain behind him. Darius knocked on the bathroom door.

"Xerxes?" He knocked again, louder this time. "Xerxes?"

"Yeah, Dad?"

"What are you doing?"

"Taking a shower."

"Not now. I meant…before."

"Before what?"

"Before you were taking a shower."

"Uh, nothing. I wasn't doing anything. Just getting up."

Darius opened the bathroom door, bracing himself for the blast of steam. "You didn't hear that noise?"

Xerxes poked his head out, dripping water. "What noise?"

"That clattering sound…like a bunch of castanets or something."

"You think there are flamenco dancers outside our house?"

"No, I never said that."

"Well, you implied it."

Darius steeled himself. Why was it always an ordeal talking to this kid? "Did you hear that noise?"

"No."

"Did you make that noise?"

"No."

"Well, who did?"

"Dad, I don't know, okay? Can I finish my shower now?"

Darius hesitated. He knew he should be angry. He wanted to be angry but Xerxes gave him this goofy smile and, well, it reminded him of when his son was little and the stupid things he'd do but he'd had a hard time getting angry because he always knew how to make him laugh somehow. "Okay…see you at breakfast."

"Cool." Xerxes popped his head back in and began lathering up in earnest.

Darius insisted on making breakfast every morning and got up early to do it. It had become a tradition and he felt strongly that everybody should have a good breakfast to start the day. Today, he'd made waffles, home fries, fresh squeezed juice and fruit salad.

Xerxes sliced into the waffle. It was hot and soft and steam rose up—Darius bought maple syrup right from the farm. "Man, this is good," and Xerxes stuffed another forkful into his mouth and then slurped some orange juice. "I am hungry."

Hilka smiled at her son and then drank some juice. "It is good to see you with an appetite."

"Slow down," Darius said. "It's not a race." Something he said every morning.

"You say that every morning," Xerxes said.

"I like being consistent."

Sensing danger in his father's tone, Xerxes changed tack. "Say listen, uh, Dad. I had this idea, you know…"

Darius' fork paused in mid-air and he was thinking, oh

no, what scheme has he got going now and what will it cost me? "Yes?"

"Now, don't look like that…"

"Like what?"

"Like you think I'm going to come up with some dumb idea that is going to end up costing you money."

"You'll forgive me but it's happened before."

"Look, I said I was sorry about renting out your tuxedo. How was I supposed to know that spaghetti sauce doesn't come out of silk? Besides, that was last year."

"Why don't you just tell us what you're thinking of?" Hilka said.

"Okay. Well, you know I'm going to be making some money this summer, with the show and all, and I was wondering if, uh, maybe you could help me, like, manage the money I'm earning a little bit, you know?"

"That's a wonderful idea," Hilka exclaimed.

Darius cleared his throat. His son was asking for his help? "Well…I, uh…"

"Well, you're good with money and it doesn't seem like I am but maybe I could learn, you know? And I was also thinking that maybe I'd like to buy a car…someday, I mean, not right away because most of that money should be put away as an investment or for college but at the same time, I thought, my dad is good with this stuff and if we could invest it and make it grow, then out of that part of the money, I could see if I could afford to buy a car. So, what do you say?"

Darius put his fork down; his brows came together. He cleared his throat. "I . . . think . . . it's a good idea. Probably the most sensible thing I've heard you say in years. I'd be pleased to help you, son. It would give me great pleasure actually." And for the first time in what seemed a long while, Darius smiled.

Xerxes sat back in his chair and silently thanked Maya for her wisdom. "Well, all right then. My people will contact your people . . ."

"Don't push it," Darius said.

"Okay, I won't. Promise."

The next two weeks were a blur. There were meetings at Random Run Productions to cover all of the ongoing and last-minute details. He received his passport just like he was told he would. School seemed like something he sandwiched in between everything else. Little time was spent with Lionel and Maya apart from walking to school and home again. Xerxes went shopping with Hilka to get him some traveling gear. He didn't have a suitcase or even a travel kit of any kind. Darius helped him sort out some money and the conversion of dollars to euros, the currency in most of Europe.

Xerxes kept his cycling routine, up pedaling early in the mornings. Finally, he figured he was ready for the Boulevard of Broken Dreams. He strapped the keyboard to his wrist, pulled on his helmet, lifted the bike off its rack, took a deep breath and opened the door to the wider world. He was cautious, looking down, then up, and in every direction for some kind of booby-trap. He'd become skilled at spotting the pranks; he'd been doused by a bucket of water once and had his cycling shoes crazy-glued to his pedals. Since then, the attacks had been random, even sporadic. Xerxes figured that maybe he'd worn the attackers out or they'd just gotten bored, or something. It was no big deal now. He'd learned to roll with it.

Still, on this morning, he wasn't taking any chances. He tiptoed out cautiously, easing his bike out of the door. Xerxes caught the screen before it slammed and closed the inner door behind him. He took a look at the walk, then the grass. He leaned the bike up against the house and stepped carefully around, probing with his toes. No darts flying at him. No ground giving way. No slime on the walk. Suspicious, but slowly gaining confidence, he rolled the bike on the walk and moved toward the road, making it there without incident. He checked the road. Clear.

Hmm, maybe the tide had changed after all, he thought, as he pedaled smoothly along. He glanced at the fluorescent keys outlined against his wrist, then sent a quick email to himself: You are now the cycle king. Paris, here we come.

Fifteen minutes later, he'd climbed the vertical hill and straddled his bike, overlooking the Boulevard of Broken Dreams. He'd ridden these steps a hundred times and sensed all of the nuances, the creaky ones, the tilt in the first hairpin, the sway of the banister, when to stand up and when to sit down in the saddle, all of it blazed in his memory.

Now, with this new wrinkle, essentially, for part of the ride, he'd have one hand to steer, his left, while he typed with his right, and this could be a little bit tricky.

Xerxes drew on his martial arts training, breathing deeply, concentrating his mind, visualizing the ride, the bumps, the rhythm of the bike, how he would hold his balance, the feel of the pedals and the restraint of the stirrups, he saw it all flicker before him. Okay, he thought, enough of the deep breathing, or I'm going to pass out.

He figured he could begin a message while on a straight downward section. If he was still typing as he went into a turn then he was toast for sure, so that was the key. Look for the space and keep the messages short. He'd even figured out what he would say in advance, even though you lost some of the spontaneity that way. But, hey, it was television and even reality shows are scripted . . . at least he thought so.

Xerxes rocked back and forth on the bike, psyching himself up. On the third rock he shot forward and, after negotiating the actual BBD, he hit the first flight of stairs. He'd counted them; there were fifty-six steps from the top. Time for a quick message: Hello, it is bumpy up here. Xerxes relaxed. That had been easy. His fingers had missed a bit since the keys were so small and he'd been bumping around a bit, but still, not bad. Then another: I think I have to pee. Also, good. No hesitation, found the keys right away. Into the first turn, both hands on the handlebars, slowing down the pace but not squeezing the brakes too hard, the second time around and down the next series of steps, only thirty-four in this one: School sucks always.

Xerxes grinned. He was getting the hang of this and right now, it was a piece of cake. If he could handle the Boulevard of Broken Dreams, man, he could handle it all. Then suddenly, his thoughts turned to Maya and his misgivings about taking off for the summer and leaving her behind. He didn't feel quite the same way about Lionel. Lionel would always be Lionel, creating his own situations, and besides, his courier job would keep him busy enough and out of trouble. But his thoughts strayed back to Maya and this image he had in his mind, a 3D holographic image that rotated before him, floating in his inner space, of Maya and Rick Oswald kissing, like he was a video camera circling them, circling, circling, spinning around and around and around as the kiss grew a little more intense, a little more intimate as their bodies seemed to meld together and Xerxes felt this fear and rage well up inside of him, then…whoa!

The bike rattled off the railing, veered sharply to the right and hit the opposite railing as Xerxes fought for control. He'd let loose of the brakes and the bike had picked up speed—he'd given up his mastery of the machine, like it had a mind of its own and had gone berserk. He looked wildly down, then around…pads and helmet, thank God for that as the front wheel twisted to the left, then the right, then the left again and Xerxes found his weight shifting off

the seat just as he went into the longest down section of
104 steps . . .

"Yyyyeeeooooowwwww!"

Xerxes missed the curve at the bottom. The bike had
picked up so much momentum he couldn't wrench it
around, and he hit the corner flat out. The handlebars
dipped and then jammed under the railing, the front tire
hanging over the edge. Xerxes left the seat. With his left
hand, he held on to the handlebars and with his right he
scrabbled, then dug his nails into the railing—thank good-
ness he hadn't trimmed them,—and clung on . . . but was
left dangling over the edge some two stories up, legs kicking out, heart acting up, pulse jumping up around his ears.

He looked down. Yikes. A long way. Funny, looking up,
it never seemed so bad but looking down . . . different story.
Too far to drop without breaking something he cherished.
Pain licked his fingers; flames of torment oozed into his
wrists and forearms. The bike was wedged securely and
through gritted teeth Xerxes sucked air in and puffed air
out, and bit by bit, he solidified a grip with his right hand
and began to pull himself up. Again, he visualized. The
image of Maya and Rick Oswald had vaporized in his
panic-stricken mood but he clearly saw himself nearer and
nearer the railing. Xerxes then managed to sling his arms
over and hang by his armpits, still dangling but a little more
stable, though not ideal. With an elongated grunt he gave
a surging heave and swung his legs over the railing and toppled
onto the platform; then he rolled onto his back, panting for

air. "Geez, that was close," he exclaimed to no one, the sky, the curious birds pecking away at the bark of the trees, the squirrels jumping from branch to branch. "Oh man, you guys don't even care. Why should you?" Still panting, he sat up supporting himself from behind. "That'll teach you to lose concentration. Man, was that ever stupid, stupidest thing you've ever done." And he gave himself ten mental kicks in the butt.

Xerxes stood up and unjammed his bike. He took a quick look, no visible damage, so he was lucky there. "Okay," he said. "Stay focused." He got back on, steadied himself and took in the dizzying view of the steps before him, one melding into the next, practically an optical illusion where they stretched out seemingly forever. "It's okay," he said. "I'm on this. Must complete the mission." Then he took off bumping forward to do just that.

IX

The day before he was to jet off for Paris, Xerxes' parents offered to take him and his buds, Lionel and Maya, out for dinner, a farewell event.

"You mean, they didn't invite Brutal too?" Lionel asked, straining against the double bass. "This is the last day I take this thing home. That's it. I've had it."

"Yeah, you're funny, Lionel. Brutal? Get real," Xerxes said. He walked alongside his friend while Maya was on the other side.

"Well, I think it's very nice of them," she said.

"We'll pick you guys up around six, okay?"

"And we're going to the Manchu Buffet?" Lionel panted.

"Right."

"Excellent. I might even skip lunch for that."

"You? Skip lunch? That's a first," Maya said.

"No, it's not. There was that time about five years ago...I had stomach flu."

"Right," Maya and Xerxes both said.

"You finish packing yet?" Maya asked.

"Finish? I haven't even started."

"You're kidding."

"No. I've got all day tomorrow. I don't have to be at the airport until dinnertime, around six o'clock."

"I'd be packed and have my luggage waiting at the door already," Maya said.

"I know you would."

"I'm with X," Lionel said. "Packing's no big deal. Throw a bunch of stuff in a suitcase. What could be easier? It's a no-brainer." Sweat dripped off his forehead. It was a warm day and the sun was hot already and it was only 8 a.m.

"That's because you haven't been anywhere," Maya said. "If you had, you would know that packing is essential to a successful trip. You really have to plan what clothes to take and know how to pack them properly."

Lionel was wounded. He showed her his cow eyes. "I took a bus trip to Detroit last year."

"That was just for a weekend. So you could sneak into the casino."

"They busted us anyway," Lionel said. "It wasn't that much fun."

"And you never even got to wear the clothes you packed, right?"

"Not really. Anyway, that's just my take on the subject."

Xerxes laughed. "Thanks for the insight. Not to worry, my mom has been making lists and then I make a list and we compare the lists and I argue for what I want and she wins. So, it's been pretty simple really."

Lionel paused to catch his breath and leaned up against the massive instrument. "You think I'd be in better shape after pushing this thing all over town."

"You'd think," Maya said. "Better cut out the bacon burgers and chocolate shakes." And she poked a finger into his midriff.

Lionel recoiled. "Hey," They were standing at the bottom of a small hill and Lionel tripped. The double bass slid backward, hit the bottoms of his feet, and began to teeter. "Grab it," he screamed.

Maya and Xerxes jumped forward, grabbing at the case. Xerxes snagged the zipper but didn't have enough of a grip to hold on. Maya just plain missed and the towering instrument came crashing down on top of Lionel, who shrieked. The resonating tones of the protesting bass echoed up and down. Xerxes saw Lionel's outstretched arms and legs pinned to the sidewalk. Then a spasmodic quiver.

"Oh my God," Maya said. "He's been killed, crushed or brain-damaged. Maybe all three . . . we'd better call 911."

"Lionel . . . Lionel . . . can you hear me?" There was a feeble response. "What?" Xerxes bent down a bit. "What? I can't hear you?"

"I said, get this thing off of me, you idiot!"

Xerxes turned to Maya. "I don't think he's dead . . . not yet." Together they bent down and each seized a handle, hefting the stringed monstrosity up, steadying it on its pins.

Lionel sat up shaking his head. "My life passed before me."

"That should have taken all of a millisecond," Xerxes said.

Lionel gave him a sour look. "You're not funny. But wow, that was pretty amazing. Maybe I'll become religious."

Xerxes put a hand down and hauled Lionel to his feet. "You could become a Buddhist. That's a cool religion."

"I'll check it out."

"But you can't eat meat. No more burgers."

"Ah…" Lionel was thinking. He put his palms flat against the double bass and pushed. "I wouldn't want to make a hasty decision . . . not before the Manchu Buffet."

"You just flunked the piety test," Xerxes said.

"Add it to the list," Lionel replied.

The Manchu Buffet was one of the busiest restaurants in town. It was enormous and constantly busy. From Darius' point of view, it was also the perfect place to take teenagers: a fixed price, all-you-can-eat extravaganza where bottomless stomachs could be filled without costing you a small fortune.

As they were being shown to their table, Lionel inhaled deeply and rubbed his hands together. "Ah, I love this place. Nothing like the smell of peanut oil in the early evening."

"You're such a dork," Maya said.

"Second that," Xerxes said.

"I don't care. This is nirvana." Lionel rubbed his palms so hard Xerxes thought he was going to start a fire.

Hilka smiled indulgently at them while Darius forged a

path to their table, following behind the petite Asian waitress who had introduced herself as Sheryl. They sat and then ordered their drinks. No sooner had they ordered than Lionel and Xerxes took off.

Hilka placed her hand over Maya's. "That's okay; you don't have to wait with us. If you're hungry, why not start?"

"I can wait," she replied and glanced in the direction where the guys had disappeared. "Typical."

"They're just boys," Hilka laughed. "This is like being in the candy shop."

"I guess."

"Busy tonight," Darius said, so he wouldn't seem rude. He wasn't a great conversationalist and had considered it a character flaw, but he liked Maya and didn't want her to feel ill at ease for any reason.

Sheryl, the waitress, brought their drinks. Maya then excused herself and went off to join the guys. "I like her," Darius said. "Always have and she's blossomed into a lovely young woman."

Hilka looked at her taciturn husband in surprise. "I haven't heard you speak like that for a long time."

"I know. But it's what I think."

"Care to throw any compliments my way?"

Darius looked at his wife appraisingly. "None that would do you justice and I mean that too." He looked at her and then broke away. He cleared his throat. "Listen, I know I've been kind of moody lately and I'm sorry about that. You know, it's just the usual pressures."

"Maybe you need a change?"

He shrugged his massive shoulders, shoulders that used to take out linebackers and defensive ends. "I don't know. Probably, but I don't know what to change to, that's the problem."

"One thing you can change is easing off Xerxes, he is a good kid, it's just that … things seem to happen around him."

"He gets these crazy ideas."

"Yes he does, but that is what is wonderful about him too. He is open to just about anything. He has a spirit of adventure … you used to have that once, Darius. I wonder what happened to it."

Darius looked down into the glass of iced tea he was holding. Then he drank about half of it. "I wonder about that too," he replied quietly.

The three teenagers returned to the table, their plates heaped with food. Lionel had roast beef, mashed potatoes and gravy and peas. "This is supposed to be a Chinese buffet," Xerxes said.

"They do nice roast beef here," Lionel said and tucked in.

Xerxes had sushi, oysters on the shell and a heap of shelled shrimp, while Maya started with a salad.

"Nothing changes with you two," Maya said.

Hilka laughed and then she and Darius went up to fill their plates.

The Manchu Buffet parking lot was located on the roof. A long, windy, gut-wrenching drive whirled you up and spun you down. It made Xerxes' head ache each time, especially the way Darius drove.

"I think I'm going to hurl," Lionel whispered to Xerxes. "Quick, open a window."

Xerxes and Maya, who were in the back seat with Lionel, looked at him and laughed. He did look kind of green. "Must have been those ten plates you packed away."

"Yeah," he replied weakly. "Please...I don't feel well..."

Xerxes powered down the window. He caught Darius' look in the rearview mirror and in that instant, Xerxes saw the momentary sympathy on his father's face.

"Just a couple more turns," Darius said in a reassuring tone as the tires squealed like a frightened animal. At the bottom of the drive, he stopped the car and turned. "Do you want me to pull over so you can get out for a second?"

Lionel had his head half out the window and drew in deep breaths. "Ah, sweet, fresh air," he exclaimed and then he pulled his head back in. "No, that's okay Mr. Frankel, I'm feeling better now."

"Good," said Darius and turned back. "I'll take it slow."

Darius loved this time of year—the warm nights, spring slipping into summer, even the buzz of lawnmowers on Saturday mornings didn't bother him. It brought him back to a carefree time in his life, when he was young and had no worries or responsibilities. He wondered what happened to all of that.

The car stopped in front of Lionel's house. Lionel and Xerxes got out.

"Have a great summer, man," Lionel said and put his hand out.

Xerxes took it and pulled Lionel to him quickly in a short but manly hug. "You too, man. I'll email you, no problem. I'll give you the inside scoop."

"Yeah, sure. Eat a few baguettes on me."

"Enjoy the courier thing."

Lionel rolled his eyes. "Yeah. Right."

Xerxes leaned toward him. "And if Rick Oswald is hanging around Maya, sick Brutal on him…okay?"

Lionel snorted. "Yeah, sure." He leaned toward Darius. "Thanks for dinner Mr. Frankel, Ms. Frankel. It was great…especially the up and down to the parking lot."

"You're welcome, Lionel. Say hello to your folks," Darius said.

"Nice to see you, Lionel. Don't be a stranger over the summer," Hilka added.

"Sure thing," Lionel replied and stepped back onto the curb. Xerxes got back into the car and Lionel lifted a hand in farewell. Xerxes looked back as Lionel grew smaller and smaller and he didn't move until Lionel was out of sight.

"I feel bad," Xerxes said.

"Don't," Maya said. "He'll be okay. He's got to learn to look after himself." "Yeah, I guess…still…"

"Lionel is a character…" Hilka said from the front seat. "I don't suppose he'll grow much more."

"You wouldn't know it from the amount he eats," Darius said. "Does he always eat like that?"

"Uh-huh," Xerxes and Maya said in unison and then laughed.

"Just watching him made me feel like I was putting on weight," Darius said.

Hilka patted his hand. "Don't worry, you aren't. You're still the sleek, handsome man I married." Darius shot her a grateful look.

"Whoa," Xerxes said to Maya. "Not sure I want to take this in."

"Hey, it's nice," Maya replied. "Even older people can be romantic, you know."

"Uh, right." And he was thinking maybe there was a message there somewhere?

Xerxes insisted on walking Maya home. Darius and Hilka wished her a good summer and told her to stop by anytime. She thanked them for dinner. Maya walked on ahead for a moment—she was wearing a sleeveless top, a short, print skirt and sandals, and Xerxes took a good look and liked what he saw.

Maya turned. "What?"

He gave her the thousand-watt smile. "Nothing. Uh, you look nice, by the way. I should have mentioned it before."

"Thanks." She took his arm as they strolled. "I like your parents. Your dad looks all stern and gruff, but he's really a pussycat."

Xerxes sighed. "If you say so. He's got this death stare though. Something he learned playing football. Very effective."

"I'll bet." They walked on a moment in silence. About a block from Maya's house, she stopped suddenly and cleared her throat. "I'm going to miss you X," she said softly.

For some reason, Xerxes had a hard time hearing over the pounding of his heart and he strained to listen. "Thanks. I'm going to miss you too."

Maya started up again. "No, you won't. You'll be so busy being a TV star, you won't even have time."

"Hey this isn't like *CSI* you know. It's not that big a deal."

"Yes, it is."

"And the days might be busy but there will be times I'll be on my own and pretty lonely, I'm sure. I could get homesick."

Maya laughed. "I don't think so."

Suddenly, they were outside her house. Even more suddenly, they were at the top of the drive, then on the front step. How did that happen? Xerxes didn't remember how he got there so fast.

"You're wrong," he said.

"Am I?"

"You really going to date Rick Oswald?"

"Why? You jealous?"

He stammered. "Er…no…'course not. It's just that…the guy's just a manikin, preprogrammed to walk and talk and smile. Doesn't have an original thought in his brain, what there is of it."

"You are jealous." And she poked him.

"No." And he shook his head to prove it.

"I don't believe you," she said softly and stepped closer to him.

"Believe it," he said.

She inched in again. "Why should I?"

Their faces were practically touching. Xerxes could feel her light breath. "Because...because..." And she closed her eyes and he felt her hands on his shoulders and his hands went to her waist, which was narrow and taut through the shimmery material of her skirt...

The light snapped on above them and the door wrenched open. Maya jumped back. "Dad!"

Dr. Langlois beamed at them out of the darkness, his perfect teeth on high intensity. "Thought I heard talking out here. Hi, Xerxes."

"Hi, Dr. Langlois," he replied glumly.

"Have a nice dinner?"

"It was great," Maya said. "But I am so full."

"Heh-heh. Got to watch those buffets. They can kill you. Maybe you should come in and floss your teeth?"

"Dad..."

Dr. Langlois offered up a palm. "Okay. Just a suggestion. Coming in, Xerxes?"

The perfect moment had vanished and he saw an anguished look flick across Maya's face, then disappear. "Uh no, Dr. Langlois. I've got a busy day ahead tomorrow. I haven't even started packing yet, you know, so I better go." He gave Maya a brotherly hug but held it just a bit longer than a brother would. "I'll email you, okay?"

"You better," she said and poked him in the stomach.

"Hey..." and he smiled while her father looked on

indulgently. "Well, bye ... I'll give you a call before I leave for the airport, okay?"

"Sure."

"Make sure you wear a mouthguard when you're biking," Dr. Langlois called as he watched Xerxes stride down the driveway to the sidewalk. Xerxes raised a hand in acknowledgment. Maya hadn't moved.

As Xerxes rounded the corner, her father said, "You're going to miss him?"

"Uh-huh." She sounded faraway, even to herself.

"Don't worry. The summer will go quickly. It always does," the wise dentist intoned.

Hilka donated her suitcase to the cause and coached Xerxes in how to pack the right way. That is, to roll up his T-shirts and boxers so they'd use less space. Pick combinations of shirts and pants to wear and instructed him how to use an iron since everything would be wrinkled anyway.

Xerxes lugged the case out to the car and stowed it in the trunk. Hilka was going to drive him to the airport where he'd hook up with the *Get Outta Town!* crew.

"Last-minute check," Hilka said.

"Okay."

"Passport?"

"Check."

"Plane ticket?"

"Check."

"Hotel information?"

"Check."

"Money?"

"Check."

"Toiletries?"

"Check."

"Camera?"

"Check."

Hilka smiled at him. "Good. At least this way, you'll have all of your identification, some cash and you'll still smell good if your luggage gets lost…"

"And I can take pictures of it all…speaking of which…" Darius had sauntered out the front door looking casual in golf shirt, jeans and sandals. "How about a photo of you two?" He took out the Sony 6.5 megapixel he'd been given for his birthday. "Come on, haven't all day, have a plane to catch, assume a pose you two…" Darius put his arm around his wife's shoulders and pulled her in closer. "Good. Got it."

Xerxes looked in the viewfinder, expressed his satisfaction, and then walked over to his parents to show them. He hadn't realized it, but he was looking at his father head on, straight in the face and he saw that Darius recognized it too. "Take a look." They peered in.

"Very nice," Hilka said. "Isn't it?" Darius nodded. She turned to her son. "We'd better get going. You can't be late and there may be traffic."

"Sure." Xerxes stuck out his hand. "See you, Dad. Have a great summer, okay?"

Darius took his son's hand. "You too. Keep in touch. Don't do anything stupid."

Xerxes gave him the thousand-watt. "Who, me? Stupid?" He powered the camera down, stuck it in his knapsack and hefted it up onto his shoulder; then he gave his father a wave.

"I'm not going to wait," Hilka said as she pulled up to the Departures lane at the airport. They'd made the trip in just under twenty minutes. Traffic had been light. It was late Saturday afternoon and the malls hadn't quite emptied yet.

"Okay." He got out as Hilka popped the trunk. The airport was a noisy place, the vehicular traffic never seemed to stop and of course, the drone of airplane engines was constant. Xerxes lifted out the suitcase and set it on its wheels. He raised the handle, checked the tags one more time and pronounced himself ready. Hilka came around and gave him a massive hug that made his bones crack. When she stepped back, he saw she was crying.

"Ah, Mom…"

"I'm just happy for you," she laughed through her tears. "This is such a wonderful opportunity…"

"Okay," he said and he looked around.

"I'm embarrassing you."

"Well…"

"That's okay," she said. "It's what mothers are for. I'm going to miss you so much."

"Yeah, me too." And he gave his mother another hug. "I'll keep in touch, don't you worry. As soon as I land in Paris and get to the hotel, I'll email you, all right?"

"All right." She let him go then and backed away, gave him a small wave and got into the car, then expertly inserted herself into traffic without looking back. For a moment, Xerxes felt a little forlorn. When he came to and sensed the flow of travelers around him, he simply joined them.

Xerxes found the long queue for the check-in counter, which snaked around in a small maze. He felt like a rat.

"Hey X, how ya' doin'?"

Xerxes looked up. There was Rufus Bickle dressed like he was going hunting in the Bayou, combat boots, fatigues and the ever-present John Deere cap perched on his head. "Rufus, what's up, dog?"

Rufus laughed. "We're goin' to Paris, man." Rufus had a cart with him, piled high with bags.

"You look like you're going for a year."

"Naw, that's mainly my camera stuff, I've got a set of lights, microphones, even a fold-down boom so we can set the audio in certain trickier situations. Gotta have the laptop a'course, that's the brain that makes all of this gear run. Really looking forward to this trip, man, it's going to be a blast."

"I feel the same way."

"Hey, we're partners you and I," Rufus said. "Together, we're going to make beautiful video."

They made it through security without having to remove their shoes or pants. Xerxes set off the metal detector when he forgot a pack of gum in his pocket. After that, it was all cool. Rufus took a bit longer because he had more gear to get through. Much of the camera equipment was packed in specially molded cases and sent through as luggage. He carried the camera itself and a small knapsack filled with accessories.

"We also shipped some of the gear on ahead. Should be waiting at the hotel for us," he said.

They found seats in the lounge. Each then whipped out his MP3 player and settled in. Xerxes pulled out his copy of *Catcher in the Rye* and began to read.

"Hey, good book," Rufus exclaimed. "I read that in school too."

"Sure thing. Nothing like Holden Caulfield for a good come-backer," Xerxes said.

Rufus leafed through his copy of *Rolling Stone*. The lounge was beginning to fill up. Xerxes checked his watch. The flight was scheduled to depart at 6:30 p.m. Boarding was to begin at 5:45. It was now 5:30. He glanced up and saw Stephanie walking briskly toward them. She wore a long, stylish, belted raincoat, a pair of Ferragamo pumps and Oakley sunglasses. She could have stepped out of the pages of *Vogue*.

"Hi guys," she chirped. "How are you?"

"Hey Stephanie," Rufus said. "Good. It's all good. Right, X?"

"Right."

Stephanie wheeled her carry-on bag toward them and sat down. "No sign of Yolanda yet?" The other two shook their heads. "Well, I'm sure she'll be along." Stephanie rifled through her Prada bag, checking the essentials; cell phone, makeup, wallet, cosmetics, tickets, passport...

"You got a ham sandwich in there?" Rufus asked and guffawed.

"Nope, but I do have a flashlight and a toolkit."

"You kidding?" Rufus was agape.

"Nope." And she pulled out the flashlight and the toolkit, both miniaturized.

"How'd you get through security with that?" Xerxes asked.

Stephanie shrugged. "Said I needed it for my work."

"And what did you say you did?"

"Told them I was a celebrity plumber."

"Huh?"

"And I was going to fix Jean-Claude van Damme's toilet."

Xerxes laughed. "They believed you?"

"Well, I have the evidence, don't I?" And she held up the objects in question.

"Cool. Very cool."

"Glad you're with us, Stephanie," Rufus replied. "It's good to have someone who can be inventive when we need to be."

"No worries," Stephanie replied calmly, checking herself out in her compact. "Now I wonder where Yolanda's got to?" The agents were calling the first section to board the plane. "Ah, there she is." Xerxes looked over and saw Yolanda just on the other side of the security desk. A guy was with her, a rangy guy with long hair and a scruffy beard. The two were locked in a ferocious embrace, much to the annoyance of other passengers trying to get by and make their flights.

"Geez," said Xerxes. "Who's that?"

"Just one of her many paramours. Yolanda plays the field."

"Pretty intense competitor, I'd say," Rufus remarked, then turned back to *Rolling Stone* where he was reading about 50 Cent and a learn-to-read program he was promoting.

Xerxes watched Yolanda and her boyfriend for a moment feeling, well, feeling confused and jealous. Then he thought about Maya and felt, well, confused and jealous, not able to push the image of Rick Oswald out of his brain. And here, right before him, was another image he couldn't squeeze out either. Finally, Yolanda, stepped back, smiled, and turned toward the security desk. She locked eyes with Xerxes and her expression turned cold, almost icy. Quickly, she emptied her pockets. Xerxes watched her for a moment and then he heard their section being called and got up to join the line. He was supposed to sit beside Yolanda, but Stephanie switched seats with her. Xerxes took the aisle like he requested. That way, he could stretch his long legs and wouldn't be crammed in if he had to go to the bathroom. An important point to remember when flying, especially if it was a long flight. And this one was seven and a half hours. He was going to use the bathroom sometime. Fortunately, their seats, although in Economy, were fairly close to the front of the aircraft. That meant quicker access to the exits on landing and a better view of the large-screen television too.

Stephanie slid into the seat beside him and patted his knee. "This way, there'll be no shenanigans."

"What are you talking about?"

"I'm talking about you being stuck on Yolanda and her not caring."

"Is it that obvious?"

"Pretty much. Remember X, we're working here. Keep it all professional, okay?"

"Sure, you're the boss."

"And don't you forget it," she said, severely, and then smiled to let him know there were no hard feelings. "Relax, it's a long flight." She rooted around in her bag and pulled out an eye mask to cover her face, maneuvered a pillow expertly behind her head, covered herself with a blanket and snuggled into her seat. "Call me when they serve dinner."

"Right." Xerxes figured she had flown a lot and had this routine down pat. But he was too wired to drop off to sleep. The plane hadn't even left the terminal yet and already Stephanie's breathing was slow and regular. Impressive.

Xerxes prepared for take-off. He chewed gum and when the plane was finally airborne, he yawned deeply, letting his ears pop so they could clear by equalizing the pressure. Still, there was the ominous drone to consider. He checked the in-flight magazine. The movie was *Triple X* with Vin Diesel. He'd seen it but wouldn't mind watching it again. He didn't like being cooped up. Too restless. Fortunately, he'd brought his Game Boy Advanced to help kill time until the movie started.

He didn't really see Yolanda the entire flight. He could see the top of her blonde hair up in front, right next to the John Deere cap Rufus wore, even in the plane. Guess he never took it off, maybe his head would come off with it. Still, her coldness really puzzled him. After all, what had he done to her? She didn't have to be out and out rude about it. So, what if the attraction was only one-way?

The plane hit turbulence. Xerxes glanced over at Stephanie. She didn't even stir. Although he found this unsettling, he considered it just another roller-coaster ride, just a lot bigger and a lot longer. The captain came on and apologized, stating that the rough air they were flying through would last about twenty minutes. Xerxes smiled with some satisfaction when he saw Yolanda get up quickly and rush to the bathroom.

Xerxes awoke just as the plane was touching down. He felt groggy and stiff. He looked around. Stephanie, on the other hand, was bright-eyed, rosy-cheeked and fresh-faced. "Welcome to Paris," she said. "We've just landed at Orly."

Xerxes groaned and moved his tongue around inside his mouth. He rooted around inside his knapsack for some gum and popped in a stick. "That was about as uncomfortable as I've ever been. Like sleeping in a closet standing up."

Stephanie laughed. "We'll be at the hotel soon. You can freshen up then."

"What time is it?"

"Nine thirty-five in the morning, Paris time."

"Wow."

Everyone but Stephanie dragged themselves down the long corridor to the luggage carousel. Yolanda's face was puffy and she had a surly expression. Xerxes stayed away from her. It seemed to take an eon before the carousel began to rotate and eventually bags began trickling through. After almost forty minutes, they had all their luggage.

"Okay guys," Stephanie said. "Stay together. We're supposed to meet our fixer on the other side."

"Fixer?" Xerxes asked.

"Yeah," said Rufus laconically. He looked like he could do with a gallon of coffee. "He's the guy who drives us around. We arrange it through the local film office. They give us recommendations. Makes it much easier in a foreign location if you've got someone who knows the city. You don't waste time trying to find things that way."

"Makes sense," Xerxes said, luggage in hand and ready to roll. So far, his impression of Paris was muted. Orly looked like any other big airport, except the dominant language from the announcers was French, of course.

Coming through the exit doors, the *Get Outta Town!* crew were confronted by a crowd of people, all waiting for travelers. Many held up signs. Stephanie scanned the crowd until she spotted something and pointed. "There." A man held up a hand-scrawled sign on a piece of white cardboard that read "God on the Toon." "That must be it," Stephanie said. "Let's go."

Stephanie went right up to the man and began talking with him. He shook her hand and bowed, smiling. The crew learned that his name was Julien and that he was to be their fixer while they were staying in Paris. They all shook hands after the introductions.

"Em, I have a van," Julien said. "It is just outside. Please…to follow me?" Julien was of medium height and middle-aged. His lank brown hair fell across his forehead almost boyishly. He walked quickly taking short steps but kept glancing back to make sure they were following him. "This way, this way," he said, like he was herding a gaggle of ducks.

"This is it?" Yolanda exclaimed. "This rust bucket?" To be fair, the van, a Citroën, had seen better days; rust showed through the paint, what there was of it, and the rear end had been dented badly. The tires didn't appear to have much life or bounce.

"Please…," Julien said. "What is a…rust bucket?"

"A heap. A dud. A clunker," Yolanda said unkindly.

"But it drives very well," Julien said.

"All right," Stephanie said, stepping in. "We're all tired. Let's get our gear stowed and head to the hotel."

Julien obliged, opening up the boot and helping place the luggage, which just managed to fit. They got in. The seats were cracked and the springs showed through.

"Hope I don't snag anything," Stephanie said. "This rain-coat cost a small fortune."

Julien looked up into the rearview mirror. "Welcome to Paris, everyone. I hope you enjoy your stay here."

"Let's go," Yolanda said.

"Of course." Julien turned the key. The engine coughed, sputtered, shook, and then exploded into life. Julien grinned. "You see? I told you. The engine is a thing of beauty."

"Then this guy must be blind," Yolanda muttered. "And deaf."

The Citroën lurched out into traffic to the blare of horns. "This is nothing," Julien assured them. "Just the typical Paris traffic. The drivers here are very rude, you know?"

"Like New York City," Rufus said.

"Oh yes?" Julien responded politely. "It is also like this in New York City?"

"Worse," Rufus said. "Ten times worse."

Xerxes gazed out at the wide streets and buzzing traffic. Motorbikes, more motorbikes than he'd ever seen in his life. And circles, they seemed to be constantly going in circles. He remembered the maps he'd studied and figured he knew exactly where they were in the city.

"To our right is the Arc de Triomphe," Julien said. "You know the Arc de Triomphe?"

"May have heard of it," Xerxes said.

"Yes. Really?"

"He's just kidding," Stephanie said. "Of course he's heard of it. Who hasn't?"

"Yes, of course," Julien replied. "This sense of humor. I am not used to it."

"Neither am I," Stephanie said ruefully and Julien laughed at her in the rearview mirror.

The crew contented themselves with staring out the windows at the City of Light. Suddenly, the van rocked, then stuttered, then rocked again.

"What was that?" Stephanie asked.

"Hmm. Very curious," Julien muttered. "I am not sure."

Then came a loud bang. Yolanda screamed in fright and the Citroën rolled to the curb and stopped. Instantly, a hundred horns blared in anger.

"We have stopped," Julien said incredulously. "I will check the motor."

"We're going to die in here," Yolanda said. "I'm getting out."

"Hold on a second," Stephanie replied. "Don't panic."

"This is killer traffic."

Julien raised the hood and clouds of smoke engulfed him. He waved his arms frantically, and then stepped back hacking and coughing. He came to the driver's side with a handkerchief pressed to his face, eyes streaming. "It appears kaput," he said.

"What?" Yolanda asked.

"It is *mort.* Dead. No life. *Finito.* My sincerest apologies. My friend assured me it was in the most excellent of conditions…"

"Well, your friend lied…get a new friend…"

"Please. I am very sorry…"

Yolanda forced the door open and stepped down to the sidewalk, pacing back and forth rapidly.

"Let's grab a taxi," Rufus said.

"Good idea," Stephanie replied. "Come on, let's get the luggage."

They piled out and stacked the luggage on the sidewalk as pedestrians stared at them curiously. A few smiled sympathetically after glancing at the Citroën in its death throes. Julien, continuing to apologize, managed to flag down two taxicabs so they could get to the hotel.

"The hotel isn't far away...perhaps six blocks or so...again, my profound apologies."

Stephanie patted him on the arm before getting into the second cab. "That's okay. Just make sure you have a reliable vehicle for tomorrow, okay?"

"*Oui. Bien sûr, mademoiselle.* It shall be done, I promise."

"You going to be okay here? Do you need any help?"

"No, no, it is fine. I will call the tow truck to come and take this unfortunate vehicle away. It is beyond repair I think."

"Okay. We'll see you at the hotel tomorrow morning at eight. Okay?"

"I will be there without fail and with reliable transport," he said gravely.

Stephanie nodded, and then slammed the cab door. The taxi sped off into traffic.

L'Hôtel Artiste was just off Square de l'Avenue Foch, which made it well situated for the crew. The taxis dropped them and all their gear off at the front door. The hotel was characterized as a "boutique" hotel, one that was smaller and more intimate and more reasonably priced. But it didn't have certain facilities that larger hotels might. There was no café for breakfast or lunch and no exercise room, pool or equipment. There was, however, a spa and a sauna for those who wished to indulge. It was still early, just after ten in the morning but fortunately the rooms were ready. The concierge was calm and patient, undaunted by the amount of luggage or the exasperation of the guests. Stephanie dealt with the arrangements, checking everybody in. That's what she's good at, dealing with the organizational details. Xerxes caught her in animated conversation at the check-in counter.

"Hope her credit card clears," Rufus said affably. Yolanda gave him a sour look, in a perpetually bad mood, it seemed.

"What do you mean?" Xerxes asked.

"Oh nothing really. We were once stranded in Istanbul because the security code on Stephanie's card set off some sort of alarm bells. Before we knew it, we were surrounded by armed police."

"What happened?"

"Oh, it was just a misunderstanding, really. The hotel guy got the number mixed up and apparently it was a credit card they'd flagged as being used by a wanted terrorist."

"Whoa!"

"But a guy came over from the embassy and vouched for us. We spent about four hours in a concrete room but nothing happened. No strip search or anything."

"Good thing," Xerxes said.

"Really good thing," Rufus replied.

"That would have been gross," Yolanda said.

"For who?" asked Rufus.

Before she could reply, Stephanie marched over in her belted raincoat waving pass keys. "Here are your room keys," she said, and handed them out. "Let's take a bit of a break, say about three hours, to get settled in and catch a nap, get over the hump of jet lag, and then we'll grab some lunch and tour a few sites close by. How does that sound?"

"Sounds good," Xerxes exclaimed. "I've got to send some emails anyway."

"There should be a hookup in each of the rooms," Stephanie said.

"Cool."

They picked up their gear and headed to the elevator. When it opened, Xerxes could see it was the smallest elevator in Western civilization. Only one person could fit in with luggage.

"Figures," Yolanda said, rolling her eyes.

"You go first," Xerxes said to her.

"Thanks." And she marched in and hit the button without saying anything else as the door slid closed. Rufus and Xerxes exchanged looks, while Stephanie tapped the toe of her red Ferragamo.

"Let's take the stairs," Rufus said.

"I'll wait," Stephanie replied.

"See you later, then." Rufus and Xerxes hefted their luggage and headed for the stairs. Xerxes was tired and felt a little light-headed from the lack of sleep and the time change but he was wired too, as if his neurons were firing off erratic pulses of energy.

The stairs were narrow and didn't make for easy passage. The two of them, lugging their gear, chugged up. They met a maid coming down who tried a few angles to get past them. Finally, they cleaved to the wall to let her pass and a bark of language splattered them as she went by.

"That didn't sound too good," Rufus said laconically.

Xerxes was in Room 214. He kicked the door closed behind him and dropped his luggage on the floor. It was a nice room but small, dominated by the double bed. There was a writing table and a chair, a perfect setup for his computer, a wardrobe just opposite the bed and when he opened it, he discovered the television on the top shelf. Curious, he thought, but practical. He closed the wardrobe, snuck a peak into the bathroom and was momentarily baffled. There was no shower or bath, so he thought. He stepped inside the narrow little room. Toilet, sink and then catching something in the mirror, he looked up to his left. Set into the tiled wall jutted a nozzle. Glancing down, he saw a hot and cold water tap. Lowering his gaze to between his feet, there was a drain. It finally hit him. The entire bathroom WAS the shower. Then he noticed the curtain rod and shower curtain above his head. Well, this would be interesting, very interesting indeed. He'd take a shower later.

He unpacked his clothes and stuffed them into the dresser, designating a drawer each for pants and shorts, jockeys and T-shirts, and pajamas and socks. Sounded reasonable to him.

Xerxes plugged in his laptop and fired it up. The hotel boasted a high-speed Internet connection that took him some minutes to figure out since all of the instructions were in French, but he managed to get it going. He sent short "I have arrived and am dead-tired" emails to his parents, Lionel and Maya. He made some early notes about his impressions and what had happened so far and posted them to the *Get Outta Town!* website… "Paris is not only the City of Light, it is the city of smog. Man, the traffic is so bad here that the air is thick with exhaust fumes, guess they don't believe in pollution controls, not yet anyway…looking forward to my first real French croissant and a large café au lait…"

Xerxes' eyes began to droop and his chin hit his chest. He signed off and shut down, and then crawled onto the bed, rearranged the pillows and crashed.

The next thing he knew, the phone was ringing. "What?"

"Time to go, X. You've got half an hour. We'll see you in the lobby, okay?"

"Right. Right. See you then." He hung up and then rolled over, shading his eyes with his arm. "Okay," he said. "Time to check out this shower."

It was a bit weird because you had to stand right under the nozzle while turning on the taps, which meant there was no time to adjust the temperature. Xerxes hit himself with the cold first.

"Yikes." Then he dialed up some hot to even it out. "Better...better...better." But the cold fusion had jolted him awake out of his torpor. The shower thing was a bit weird. At first, he expected all of the water to run down the wall and out the door flooding his room but the drain did the trick, sucking it all in. "Weird but interesting," he said.

Xerxes grabbed his digital camera, shades and knapsack and headed down to the lobby. The others were there waiting for him. Rufus had the video camera with him. Yolanda looked sullen and puffy-eyed. *What is up with her? Xerxes thought to himself. We're in Paris, how great is that?* Stephanie looked cool and calm, checking a clipboard frequently. Xerxes was given an assignment to do a photo diary of his trip and keep a journal too, which would be easy since he'd be blogging every day for the *Get Outta Town!* website. Principal Hammerschlager seemed particularly keen on getting him to write a paper on the history and culture of France. That, Hammerschlager said, would satisfy his academic requirements while he was away and missing the last two weeks of school. Xerxes thought it was a pretty fair deal, all in all.

"Okay guys," Stephanie said, "I've scoped out a café not far from here. We can fuel up there before we do a little sightseeing."

"Great," Xerxes said. "I could eat a dozen croissants." And that's practically what he did.

Café de la Poste turned out to be a homey, cozy little gem with hearty, plentiful food at great prices, even for

Paris. Rufus and Xerxes tucked into a platter of steak and frites and of course, the requisite croissants, which is normally a breakfast food for the French. But the locals were willing to indulge the habits of their foreign clientele.

Xerxes eyes popped when he saw the platter heading his way. "Wow."

"Don't be all day eating it," Stephanie said, picking her way through a substantial Salad Niçoise. "We've got a few locations to scout this afternoon before we meet Octave for dinner later. And I don't want you guys dragging your bellies along the street."

"It's cool," Xerxes said. "This is just a pick-me-up." He glanced up and saw that Rufus was, discreetly, shooting them while they were eating. He waved at the camera. Then Yolanda got up and began taking shots to post on the website.

"Get a shot of the café sign outside too, when we leave," Stephanie said. "It'll be good PR for them and we'll give them a credit on the show. After all, they've agreed to comp the meal, so it's the least we can do."

"You're kidding," Xerxes said. "We're eating for free?"

"Yup," Stephanie replied, with an amused smile.

"But that is so cool."

Yolanda rolled her eyes. "You're such a boy," she said.

Xerxes looked at her calmly, for a moment. "Thank you," he said. "I'll take that as a compliment."

Rufus was ready to go, so they hiked along Avenue Foch to where it intersected Champs Elysées, a long walk along an expansive boulevard. At the end of Avenue Foch stood the Arc de Triomphe; even Xerxes, who wasn't ordinarily taken aback, admitted he was awed by this monument. They gathered at Place Charles de Gaulle and looked up, standing with a crowd of tourists and their cameras and videocams posing their wives, sons, daughters, mothers, fathers, sisters, and husbands to get the perfect shot. Rufus could barely get a clear view until he broke through the crowd and found an open area where he began to set up. The crew huddled around to help.

"Isn't this amazing?" Xerxes asked Yolanda, pointing to the monument.

"Hmmpph," she sniffed. "Just another symbol of death and destruction and the folly of men." And she turned back to take something from Rufus.

"Hey," Xerxes said. "Why don't you lighten up a little?"

Stephanie, sensing the tension, stepped in. "Hey X, come and take a look at these inscriptions. They're very cool. You know, they've got the names of over five hundred French generals on the walls; a lot of them died in battle." And she led him away from Rufus and Yolanda toward the Arc de Triomphe.

"What is the matter with her?" he asked.

"Just grumpy. Maybe lack of sleep, jet lag, who knows?" She stopped him. Pigeons swarmed around them expecting to be fed.

The next stop was Musée d'Orsay, a museum housed in a former railway station built in 1900 and then renovated in 1986. Inside was a spectacular collection of famous French paintings and sculptures produced primarily between 1848 and 1914. Rufus loved the charm of the exterior and shot it from several different angles. He posed Xerxes out front and had him riff off some lines. Mainly, he talked to his mom, Hilka.

"Yo, Mom. I can't believe I'm here in Paris, France. Hey, take a look behind me ... Musée d'Orsay ... very cool place with some amazing art and artists. Mainly Impressionist and Post-Impressionist paintings and sculptures set up inside. Impressed? Have I made an Impression? How about a Post-Impression?" Xerxes bent over laughing, slapping his knees. "Sometimes I kill myself," he said.

"Must be jet lag," Yolanda intoned. She glanced at Stephanie and arched her eyebrows.

"He's having a good time and that's what we want," Stephanie said.

"If you say so."

Stephanie took direct aim at her. "Look Yolanda, I understand why you are angry with X but you've got to get over it and act like a professional ..."

Yolanda squared up and put her hands on her hips. "Or what?"

"Or you'll be on the next plane outta here, that's what? Clear?"

Yolanda held her look for a long moment, and then broke off. She needed this job. She needed the experience and this was her first break in the industry, something she wanted very badly. "Okay," she said, stubbing the toe of her trainer into the cement. "I'll behave."

Stephanie nodded. "Good. Make sure you do." Then she turned and walked away toward Xerxes. While she'd been talking with Yolanda, a crowd had gathered, Asian tourists it looked like, and Xerxes was doing handstands while Rufus improvised some shots. The tourists were snapping away and Stephanie noticed there was quite a crowd of them and they began to press in. Something else she noticed too, they were all guys, young guys, and that seemed a little odd.

"Whoa fellas," Rufus said as he got bumped. He was down on one knee setting up a shot. The tourists kept snapping; the whirr of cameras became constant. Xerxes had a puzzled look on his face as they now formed a perfect square around him but still he smiled and nodded, kept friendly, tried to make conversation with one or two but received a stone-faced silence in return and then the continuation of the cameras whirring. And then suddenly, as if on cue, the tourists dissipated, broke up and melted away.

"That was different," Xerxes said to Stephanie. "Guess I'll be famous in the Orient."

"Guess so," Stephanie said distantly and then snapped out of her reverie. "Let's keep going. There's still lots to cover before we meet up with Octave tonight, and I'm sure everyone would like a little relaxation time too. I know I would."

"Let's do it," Xerxes said.

They strolled the Champs-Elysées and then hiked along the banks of the Seine, taking it all in. Paris in the late spring. Not too shabby.

X

The crew headed back to the hotel after two more hours of trudging the busy but vibrant streets of Paris, to get some relaxation time in and then get ready for dinner. This was something Xerxes needed to get accustomed to, the European lifestyle, which was less hustle and bustle than in North America. Everything had its own time and place and the people seemed more relaxed and very social. Dinner was a big event and was eaten later in the day. It was unusual for Parisians to eat dinner before eight o'clock in the evening. That would be considered early, in fact, if you showed up at a restaurant at that time. Most of the tables would be empty and those that were occupied would be peopled with North American tourists who were stuck in their old habits.

Xerxes carded the door to his room and entered. He stopped in his tracks. Everything was upside down and all over the place. Bedding overturned, drawers pulled out, shirts and pants dumped on the floor. He didn't think this was how the maid service operated. He called Stephanie's room.

"Yes?"

"My room's been trashed, better have a look."

"What?" Xerxes could hear her brain seething over the line. "I'll be right up."

Less than a minute later, Stephanie stood in his doorway. "Wow, you weren't kidding. They did a good job. Is there anything missing?"

Xerxes had placed his valuables and passport in the room safe but his computer still sat at the desk unscathed. "Don't think so. At least not that I could see."

Stephanie called down to the concierge. Within minutes, a man and a woman showed up.

"I am Philippe Leger, the day manager of the hotel," the man said in heavily accented English. He was a tall, slim dude with a pencil moustache and dark hair combed back straight off his forehead. He wore a powerful cologne. Xerxes almost gagged. "And this is my colleague, Marie Bourbon, our chief concierge." Mr. Leger took a look around the room and tsked under his breath, shaking his head as if to say this couldn't be happening. "Ah, Monsieur, is there anything missing?"

"Don't think so," Xerxes said.

"So sorry for the trouble and inconvenience," Ms. Bourbon said.

"Sure."

"How did they get in?" Stephanie asked in a strident

tone. "We were out sightseeing and the room was locked, so how is that possible?" Mr. Leger shrugged and he turned to Marie Bourbon, who, in turn, shrugged back at him.

"Do you want us to call the police?" Leger asked. "We should report it in any case."

"If you must," Stephanie replied.

"We shouldn't touch anything," Marie Bourbon said. "You know, for the fingerprints."

Leger frowned. "Marie, I think you are being melodramatic, yes?" He looked over at Xerxes. "And of course, we will get you a new room while this one is being investigated. He pulled out a cell phone, dialed a number and spoke rapidly into it, then listened. "The police will come but we don't know when. Unfortunately, this is not a serious matter and they will get to it when they can. Perhaps, Monsieur, you could bring some of your clothes and other articles with you and we will take care of this when the police arrive, all right?"

"Sure. Thanks," Xerxes replied.

To compensate for the inconvenience and the obvious security lapse, Xerxes was treated to one of the hotels larger suites on the top floor. "Wow," he said.

"Double wow," said Stephanie, peeking over his shoulder.

"Right this way, Monsieur," Leger said. He was carrying some of Xerxes' clothes in a laundry bag and he placed the bag down in front of the sofa.

"We can hold our production meetings in here," Stephanie exclaimed, walking around the expansive suite. It had a sitting room off to the side with a couch, chaise lounge and three wingback chairs. Then there was a small foyer and a short set of stairs leading to the bedroom area and a four-poster king-sized bed.

Xerxes stared at it. "Just like Louis XIV," he said.

"Just so," said Leger, smiling thinly.

"Hey, Stephanie, check this out." Xerxes was standing by the window taking in the view.

She came up beside him. "Nice," she said. "Even the carpets are really nice, a kind of fluffy Burberry."

"I think this will do," Xerxes said.

"I am pleased to hear it," Leger said. "I hope you continue to enjoy our hospitality. I will let you know when the police arrive and if they will require your presence before them. I will see to the rest of your things."

"Sounds like a plan," Xerxes said.

Leger then gave a short, stiff bow and left the room. Stephanie giggled. "He's something else, isn't he? Right out of the old school."

"I feel sorry for the guy."

"Why?"

"All these situations—none of them his fault and he's stuck with the load."

"Comes with the territory, X. I'm sure he had other choices but he chose this," Stephanie said.

"Very practical," he said. "I guess that's why you're the producer."

"You got it."

"Okay, listen," Xerxes said. "I'm going to send a few emails, then freshen up for dinner. What time are we meeting in the lobby?"

"Seven forty-five, so don't be late. Our reservation is for eight-fifteen."

"I'll be there."

"Don't get kidnapped or anything."

"Heh-heh." He pointed at her as if that was a good one.

Xerxes had changed into a clean pair of khakis he'd just ironed, or the best he could do, never having ironed before—Maya was right, his mom still did all of that stuff for him—and a long-sleeved Shimano cycling jersey, in case the night got a bit chilly. He made the lobby right on time. The others were there and buzzing about the break-in. Only Yolanda asked no questions. She didn't seem concerned or curious.

"Sure nothing was missing?" Rufus asked.

"Yup."

"Weird," Rufus said. "Trashing for kicks. How'd they get in?"

Xerxes shrugged. "Don't know."

"Makes you feel secure, doesn't it?" Rufus snorted.

"It can happen anywhere, Rufus," Stephanie said. "Even the most secure hotels in New York or Washington can be broken into, you know that." She wore an ankle-length peasant dress and had draped a white shawl over her slender shoulders. Her hair was glossy and she'd exchanged contacts for her usual spectacles.

"Hey, you're looking good. Nice outfit," Xerxes said.

Stephanie smiled. "Thank you. Good of you to notice."

"And you look nice too," Xerxes said to Yolanda, who was wearing a pair of tight jeans, a top cut off at the midriff and spiky heels. Not many could get away with dressing that way but Yolanda could. She made a face at him. "No, really, I mean it."

"Thanks," she said curtly.

"You're welcome."

"Here's our taxi," Stephanie called, heading out to the street. Yolanda gave Xerxes a stiff look before following on. Rufus shrugged, took a peek through the viewfinder of the mini-cam he carried with him, and then shook his head.

"Won't work," he said.

"After you, Bro'," said Xerxes.

The restaurant was called La Rue des Trois-Frères and the seating was Breton-style with long tables where everyone cozied up to his or her neighbor. The specialty of the house was crêpes. Xerxes liked the atmosphere; it was friendly and noisy and everyone seemed to get involved with what everyone else was eating and drinking. The waiters were enthusiastic and the company boisterous.

Octave Pompidou met them there. He was a tall, lean dude with long, dark hair and a winning smile, rivaling Xerxes' own thousand-watt model. He sported a wicked scar on his chin, the result of a nasty cycling accident it seemed, and his spoken English was pretty good. Xerxes disliked him on the spot. Octave Pompous Ass is what he thought. Too smooth, too self-assured, too…too…good-looking if he wanted to admit it. Xerxes noticed the way Yolanda stared at Octave from the moment he walked into the restaurant. In fact, a lot of the women sought him out as he made his way over to the table, introduced himself to Stephanie and kissed her liberally on both cheeks. Then he did the same to Yolanda.

"Please," Xerxes said, shaking Octave's hand, "no kissing, all right?"

Octave laughed politely. "Of course, er…"

"X…just call me, X."

"Eeeks?"

"X."

Octave looked puzzled. "That is what I said…Eeeks."

Xerxes laughed. "Right, right. Eeeks, okay, I can dig it. Join the party, my man. Grab a seat." And to his chagrin, Octave plunked himself down beside Yolanda and the quarters were tight. Everyone was sitting shoulder-to-shoulder. Octave engaged Yolanda in conversation right away. Xerxes, who was across from them diagonally, couldn't hear what they were talking about, which was just the way Stephanie liked it. She liked the fact that Octave's English was so good. This way, he'd understand her when she ordered him around, and she was looking forward to doing that.

The food came and everyone dug in. Despite Xerxes' dislike of this Octave character, he had to admit, it had been a pretty good time. The food was great—he loved the chicken and mushroom crêpes he'd ordered, not to mention the chocolate crêpe for dessert. He'd have to blog this meal for sure—make everyone jealous. Rufus snapped some digital stills at the table while everyone was eating and drinking.

"So, Eeeks," Octave called across the table. "You are into cycling too, am I right?"

"Hey, you bet. I live to cycle, man."

"Yes, me too. It is my entire life, cycling. It is all I think about. All I dream about…to be a professional, you know?"

"Well…that's cool. Don't you have any other interests? Like music, or movies or comic books."

"Comic books? Uh, please…"

"You know, like *Spiderman, Superman, Fantastic Four…*"

Recognition washed over Octave's lean face. "Oh yes, of course, I saw the movies. They're okay but still…" And he shrugged.

"Got it," Xerxes replied, thinking man this guy is one-dimensional and right away he flashed to Maya and Rick kissing again. He shook his head to clear the image from his mind. "Lance Armstrong, right?"

Octave's face lit up. "A very great rider…perhaps the best rider in the history of cycling, certainly the Tour de France, the most challenging cycling race…"

"Boring…" Yolanda said.

"Sorry?" Octave was confused. He didn't think anyone could find cycling or anything to do with cycling boring.

"I said it was boring," Yolanda said brightly, enjoying Octave's confusion and Xerxes' consternation. In fact, Xerxes was just beginning to warm up to the Frenchman.

"Is everyone finished?" Stephanie asked. There were nods all around and she signaled for the bill.

Outside on the street, pedestrians strolled arm-in-arm, looking in shop windows, chatting in animated fashion; people called greetings to each other. A number of cafés lined the street and the patios were all full.

"I could get used to this," Xerxes said. "Beats going to high school."

"You are still in school?" Octave asked.

"Yup. How about you?"

"I finish this year," the lanky Frenchman said. "Then I will train full-time." He glanced at Yolanda, not wanting to say much more. Such a pretty girl, he was thinking, but the attitude, it left much to be desired.

"Where are your wheels, man?" Xerxes asked him.

"Wheels?"

"You know, transportation . . . how'd you get here?"

"Oh yes," Octave said nodding. "Over there." And he pointed to a bicycle rack and a mountain bike chained to it.

"You rode here?" Xerxes asked.

"Of course. Why should I pay for a taxi when it is faster this way?"

"Right. Well, that's cool. You walk the talk, I respect that."

"*Bon* . . . Good."

Rufus used the handicam to get a sequence of Xerxes and Octave talking together. Then he took a few digital snaps for the website. "Okay, we're good," he said.

"So Octave," Stephanie said. "We'll see you at the hotel for eight in the morning, right? You'll be there on time?"

Octave smiled and Xerxes had the weird impression that the atmosphere around them brightened up a little. "Of course, I will see you then. I am very prompt." He went around and shook hands with everybody. "Goodbye until tomorrow then." Still, there were the kisses for Yolanda and Stephanie.

Xerxes held up his fist. "Pound it." Then he saw the completely confused look on Octave's face and laughed outright. "Hey man, like this." And he took Octave's hand, formed it into a fist and brought their knuckles together.

"Ah yes…I understand. Pound it." And he held his fist up and Xerxes did the deed. Octave laughed and walked toward his bike, holding his fist up and looking at it as if it were a strange object.

Xerxes shook his head. "So naïve," he said to Stephanie. "I'm going to have to smarten that guy up to the ways of the real world."

Stephanie and Rufus choked back laughter. "If you say so, X." Stephanie put her fingers to her lips and whistled shrilly and a taxi screeched to a halt. "Here's our ride. Hop in."

Back in the hotel lobby, Yolanda was on her cell phone while the others waited for the elevator. "Don't get lost in that suite of yours," Stephanie said to Xerxes.

"Don't worry, I'll find my way around, no problem."

The elevator doors opened and Rufus, Xerxes and Stephanie got on. "Don't wait for me," Yolanda said to them while cradling the phone. "I'm meeting up with some friends." She looked at Xerxes pointedly; light danced in her eyes. "You can't come. You'd be carded."

Xerxes shoved his hands in his pockets. "Whatever," he muttered. Life is cruel when you are just seventeen.

"Don't forget...eight o'clock call," Stephanie said. "Bright-eyed and bushy-tailed."

"Don't worry," Yolanda said. "I know how to do my job."

"Goodnight then." Stephanie hit the Close button. Xerxes caught a glimpse of Yolanda gloating, definitely gloating. "So that went well," Stephanie added.

"Uh, yeah," Xerxes mumbled.

"Octave seems like a good guy," Rufus said.

"Yeah...he's cool..." Xerxes replied in a neutral tone.

The elevator doors opened and Stephanie and Rufus stepped out.

"See you, X," they said.

"Right...later..." Xerxes said. "Bells on." And he gave a little hop, clicking his heels together as the doors closed. The elevator lurched and he staggered back, grabbing onto the bar for support. He got off at the top floor and approached his room gingerly. He carded the door, opened it, and then felt for the light. He flicked it on. The room was perfect, not a thing disturbed since he'd left earlier. He let out a sigh of relief. It was as if the jinx from home had followed him to Paris. Maybe he should have brought Brutal along as his bodyguard. He'd scare off just about anything.

Feeling tired, he went into the bathroom, washed his face and brushed his teeth, got into his PJs, sent a few emails, and then hit the sack. He was asleep almost instantly.

True to his word, Julien was waiting for the crew in the hotel lobby. He had his new ride outside. By eight o'clock, everyone had assembled, even Yolanda, looking puffy-faced and red-eyed. Just before the hour, Octave rode up and his bike was stowed in the back of Julien's van. The crew piled in and headed off to Café Marly on rue Rivoli for an early breakfast of café au lait and fresh-baked croissants.

"Man, I just love these things," X said, downing one and then another one. He slurped up some fresh orange juice.

"They are very good here," Octave said. "How many do you think you could eat, Eeeks?"

"Uh, dunno. Maybe half a dozen."

"That is all? I could eat close to a dozen myself."

Xerxes licked his lips, rubbed his palms and said, "All right, Bro'…bring it on."

"Guys," Stephanie said in an exasperated tone. "We don't have time for this. Besides the two of you will turn into blimps and won't even be able to do the riding scenes."

Rufus was up and filming, having downed his café au lait. "Could be interesting," he said, focusing the camera. "Yolanda, grab the filter there will ya?" Yolanda sighed but jumped to it. This was part of what she was hired to do. "Could provide a little comic relief, here. They're supposed to be having a good time. They're still teenagers," he said, being all of twenty-nine himself.

The waitress brought a dozen steaming croissants. Octave grabbed one. "Excellent with, uh, butter and jam, I think you say..." He buttered one up enthusiastically.

Not to be outdone, Xerxes did the same, wolfing down the croissant. Another kind of race was on.

Yolanda rolled her eyes. Rufus had the videocam rolling and Stephanie looked exasperated. Only Julien sipped his café au lait looking amused, his blue eyes filled with humor.

With Rufus circling around them zooming in on the culinary action, Octave gulped back seven croissants, while Xerxes, not to be outdone, forced eight with butter and jam into his gullet, then threw his hands up in exultation as Octave, smiling weakly, declared defeat.

"Yeah," Xerxes crowed, and then belched. "I think I feel ill," he said.

"Great," Stephanie said.

"So immature," Yolanda muttered.

Xerxes jumped to his feet with a big grin. "Just kidding. I'm ready to go," and then turned to Octave, "...you ready to hit the road?"

Octave patted his belly. "Of course. Now I need to work some of this out of my stomach."

Julien stood up, drained his café ou lait and pronounced, "The van awaits you, *tout le monde.*"

Julien's new wheels, a white Renault van this time, seemed in marginally better condition than the previous one. At least, there were no holes in the body and the tires had some tread left on them. The crew piled in. Julien started the engine and it caught on the second try. Progress. Two bicycles, one for Xerxes and the other, Octave's, were stacked in the back. Julien took a look at his clipboard with the itinerary attached and set out for the first stop of the day: the Eiffel Tower. This is where the show would begin and end.

Julien parked the van on Avenue Gustav Eiffel, named after the man who designed the tower that was completed in 1889. The backdrop was the Seine River. Rufus gave Yolanda brusque instructions and the two hauled out the gear they'd need, microphones, boom mike, umbrellas and shades to help diffuse the bright light a touch. Octave lifted his bicycle out of the back of the van and rode slowly around the square to get limbered up and for something to do. A policeman came up on foot and spoke to Julien quietly. Stephanie had her permit out and ready; the policeman examined the documents, nodded, then said, "*D'accord,*" touched the brim of his helmet and moved on.

"They are very strict in this area," Julien said. "But there should be no problem. I have a good relationship with the police. They know me, so we won't be bothered. You have all the necessary permits?"

"Naturally," Stephanie said, with a hint of disdain.

"Just checking, Mademoiselle. You would be surprised at how unorganized some of your colleagues in the film and television world can be."

"I'm not one of them," Stephanie said curtly.

Julien bowed slightly. "No offense was intended, I assure you."

"None taken," Stephanie replied.

Xerxes stood about 100 meters from the base of the Tower. He was dressed in cycling gear. Rufus had him in a medium tight closeup. "Rolling," Rufus said.

Thousand-watt smile turned on. "Here I am in Paris, standing in front of the Eiffel Tower. I have an amazing day planned. I'm going to hook up with Octave Pompidou, a young Parisian known as the mad cyclist. He is going to take me all over Paris, show me where he likes to hang out, introduce me to some of that fine French cuisine I have heard about, but most of all ... we get to put our feet down and hit the streets ... cycling style."

Octave rode into frame moving fast, then hit the brakes, stood straight up off the seat and on the pedals and stopped right in front of Xerxes, then he sprang lightly off the bike landing on his feet.

"Octave? Octave Pompidou?"

Octave set his bike carefully down on the pavement. "That is right. And you are Eeeks?"

"X, that's right. Pound it." Xerxes holds up his fist and Octave obliges. "So, I hear that you are crazy for cycling, absolutely nuts for it."

"Yes, this is true. I love to cycle; it really is my passion in life."

"So, do you race?"

"Yes, I am always racing, but after this year I hope to compete for the national team of France."

"Wow, that is very cool." Xerxes turns to the camera. "This guy must be good. I hope I'm up to the challenge."

"So, we will do a little cycling together while you are in Paris?" Octave asked.

"Absolutely. What better way to see the sights than from street level, am I right?"

"Yes, definitely. There is no better way to get around. As you can see, the streets are busy with traffic and this goes most of the day here. On a bicycle, you don't have to wait as long and it is good exercise too." Octave, not to be outdone, smiles and looks directly at the camera. "He doesn't know it yet but we are going to have an extra special challenge…a race that is a bit different."

"Well, whatever it is, I'm up for it," Xerxes said. "Let's get started." He reaches out of frame and pulls his bike into view. "Octave," he said. "Mount your steed and off to the races."

Octave followed by Xerxes hopped on their bikes and rode off into the cool morning air and heavy traffic where the blare of horns crashed like an unfinished but cacophonic symphony. Rufus called, "Cut." The two cyclists stopped and rode back smiling.

"That was pretty cool," Xerxes said.

"That was great," Rufus said. "I need to shoot it from another angle. So let's repeat the sequence okay?" Rufus listened to the dialogue on the playback through the headphones he wore. "Sound checks out okay. You good to go?"

Xerxes nodded. "Sure thing."

Xerxes repeated the dialogue and the action went well and within a few minutes, the two were cycling off again. Rufus called them back and said they were done here. He and Yolanda began packing the gear into the back of the van. Octave and Xerxes stowed the bikes and the crew piled in and they were off to the next destinations. This was television, and low-budget television at that, so things had to move fast, very fast.

That morning, the crew passed Place de la Concorde, headed over to Pont Neuf and kept going to the next stop, Pont Alma. Octave and Xerxes, almost literally, along with their bikes, jumped on to one of the *bateaux-mouches*. These touring boats cruise up and down the Seine, and from that vantage point, all the major sights of Paris can be seen. Octave and Xerxes take their places among the tourists taking the picturesque cruise. The rest of the crew managed the equipment while Stephanie helped get them organized. Some of the tourists pointed and whispered and were genuinely interested in the filming taking place. Julien took the van to the end-point of the cruise and would pick them up there. After a few minutes of adjustments, Rufus was ready-to-go.

"This is the best way to see all of the sights of Paris," Octave said. "See, Eeeks, there is the Trocadero, it faces the Eiffel Tower. It is also known as the Palais de Chaillot and it was designed for the 1937 World Exposition."

"Very cool," Xerxes said, enjoying the smooth ride.

Octave gave him a nudge. "Take a look, Eeeks. You see the people resting on the banks of the river over there?"

Xerxes followed Octave's pointing finger where people were congregating on the banks. "Right."

"In the summertime, in August, the Mayor of Paris has a lot of sand trucked in and dumped there…brought in all the way up and down the banks of the Seine. In this way, he creates a beach and people come to lie or play on the beach. It is very hot here in August and for those who cannot take their vacation, they are given their own beach instead."

"Wow, that is very cool. A man-made beach right in the heart of Paris."

"*Oui.* That is right," Octave said, laughing. "It is a lot of fun going to the beach here." He pointed again. "Look, there is the Grand Palais, built for the World Fair in 1900. It was almost torn down afterward but fortunately smarter heads said no, to keep the building, and now it has many galleries and many famous works of art."

Xerxes took in the sun dancing off the surface of the water and the lightness of the day. "This is a great way to travel, almost as good as being on a bike."

"Almost," Octave said. "Now, there is the Hotel des Invalides. This is an area filled with the most famous monuments in Paris. Many years ago, hundreds of years, it was a barracks for army troops. Some four thousand troops quartered there. During the French Revolution, when the Bastille, the famous prison, was stormed by the people of the city, they took arms from the barracks, which helped them to defeat the government. This is also where the burial crypt of the Emperor Napoleon is located." Xerxes assumed the pose, a kind of strut, and pretended to put his right hand inside the folds of a jacket. "Yes," Octave laughed at his impersonation. "That is the one...and of course," he continued. "There is the Louvre, the most famous art museum and gallery in the world. It is where the famous Mona Lisa is kept, painted by Leonardo da Vinci."

The *bateau-mouche* meandered on, passing under bridges, roving close to the banks, navigating around small islands. "And finally," Octave said. "Here is Notre Dame; it is the cathedral, the most important in Paris and perhaps of all France. It was the inspiration for the novel by Victor Hugo, The *Hunchback of Notre Dame*. Did you ever read it?"

Xerxes smiled and shook his head. "No, but I saw the Disney cartoon version."

"Not as good as the book, I don't think," Octave replied.

"Maybe not, but I enjoyed the songs and you don't get that with the book."

Octave laughed and held his hands up in defeat. "You win...this time."

The *bateau-mouche* approached the jetty. "What a great way to see the city," Xerxes said. "Thanks, man. That was really great."

Octave held up his fist. "Pound it."

Xerxes laughed. "Man, you are learning quick."

The *bateau-mouche* completed its docking, and the crew along with the rest of the tourists headed up the ramp to the jetty. Julien was there to meet them.

Stephanie checked her watch. "Let's grab some lunch," she said.

"Thank God," Yolanda exclaimed. "I'm famished."

"I could eat a bite," Xerxes said.

"After all those croissants?"

"That was hours ago and I'm still growing."

"Not mentally," Yolanda muttered.

Xerxes was about to say something but Stephanie stepped in front of him. "Stow your bike in the van, okay? Julien's got a spot for us."

Julien took them to Chez Georges at 1 rue de Mall. It was a traditional Parisian bistro. The crew ate baguettes just freshly baked. Their timing was excellent on the fresh-baked goods front. No eating contest this time. The baguettes and the lightly cured ham and runny brie along with them were quite filling.

Stephanie and Rufus huddled together at their own table comparing notes. They were pleased with the way the shooting had gone. Rufus thought he'd gotten some great shots and the makings of a terrific episode for the show. Stephanie called over to the others where Octave, Xerxes and Yolanda shared a table. Julien was sitting on his own reading *le Figaro*. "Hey guys, after lunch, we're going to get some cycling shots. Julien's going to take us to some of the city's parks and we'll get some action footage, okay?" Octave shrugged and Xerxes grinned, giving the thumbs up. "X, we'll put your helmet cam on and we want to test it out, make sure it's working, that and the mike. Your helmet is wired for sound and has a range up to 500 meters so we can hear what you're saying and Rufus will be recording it, so think about what you're going to say before you say it, right?"

"Right?" Jeepers, he thought. Stephanie really did like to give orders. Glad she wasn't my sister or anything.

"We should be able to pick up Octave too, so you guys can dialogue as you're riding, point out the sights, talk about cycling, anything, and then we'll decide what we can use afterward. Sound good?"

"Yeah sure."

"*Bien sûr*," Octave acknowledged. He downed the orange juice in front of him.

Xerxes strapped on the helmet. "Okay," Rufus said. "Give me a level."

"*Buffalo soldiers…*" Xerxes sang.

Rufus twisted his head. "Too strong. That mike's pretty sensitive. Tone it down a bit, will ya?"

"*One life… one life… let's get together and…*"

"Okay, perfect," Rufus said.

Octave looked at Xerxes curiously as if he were saying What planet are you from? But he smiled, twisting his lips. "I am ready. *Prêt.*"

Xerxes swung his leg over the crossbar. "*Prêt*," he said.

"Okay," Rufus said. "I'm going to set up down the street and get you guys coming toward me. Give me a sec. I'll signal Yolanda when I want you to start." He picked up the camera and set off. The afternoon was still warm; it was alternating between cloud and sun and that made the lighting a challenge. Down the block, Rufus hefted the camera onto his shoulder, set the focus and gave the signal.

Xerxes and Octave set off with Octave in the front setting the pace, pedaling smoothly in a strong, fluid motion. Rufus caught them coming into frame, then swiveled, following them as they whizzed by and then shot them from behind, zooming slowly as they cycled away from him. After a moment, he raised his hand and the van shot forward, stopped in front of him, where Yolanda slid open the side door. Rufus climbed in and sat down holding the camera while Julien signaled then took off from the curb following the two riders who had kept going. This was like a pursuit.

Xerxes and Octave turned from rue de Mall onto des Petits champs and kept on going until they passed Jardin du Palais royale, cut down rue de Richelieu, and then turned onto rue de Rivoli and headed toward Jardin des Tuileries, a large, inner-city park, sort of like Central Park in New York City.

Xerxes gave the route as they went, naming the streets and calling directions. He managed to keep close to Octave's rear wheel.

Octave looked back. "You are okay?"

"Fine, no problem. This is sweet."

"Sweet?"

"Yeah… cool… you know, fun."

"I can dig it, Eeeks."

As Octave turned on to rue de Rivoli taking a tight turn, Xerxes followed focusing on his front wheel and the road. Something appeared in his peripheral vision, a shadow of some kind, then another and another. Xerxes looked at the road surface and suddenly shadows appeared from all directions. He craned his head up, thinking a flock of birds had flown over. The sound of tires spinning and gears clicking snapped him to. A group of black-clad cyclists appeared out of nowhere and surrounded them. What the heck was going on? Xerxes looked around, confused, and then noticed Octave had picked up his speed and took off, the other cyclists in hot pursuit. Wondering what was up, Xerxes put the hammer down and followed. These guys were spooky, dressed in black like that with black helmets and visors—eerie, man. But whatever was going on, he was up for it. Just like cruising down the Boulevard of Broken Dreams. Man, he was missing that ride but now he'd found something to take its place.

Xerxes caught up to Octave. "Stay close to me," Octave hissed through gritted teeth as they whipped into Jardin des Tuileries at top speed, scattering pedestrians who raised fists and cursed at them uttering guttural sounds. Xerxes captured all of this and more on his helmet-cam and deciding not to waste an opportunity, sent an email to Stephanie using the tiny, wireless keyboard strapped to his left wrist. The van had been left behind. Rufus had stopped to set up another shot and was waiting for them to come around again.

The bunched-up cyclists whizzed through the Jardin at high speed, zipping in and out of clumps of trees, skirting bushes, hammering up, then down, footpaths, until finally, Octave pulled in behind a greenhouse, jumped off his bike and stretched out flat on the ground behind some shrubbery. He motioned to Xerxes to do the same. No sooner had he hit the turf, than the black riders zoomed by and kept going, like an elongated blur.

Octave heaved a huge sigh of relief.

"Okay, man, what was that? Who were those guys?" They sat up, panting, leaning with their backs against the wall of the greenhouse.

"Eeeks, they are *les rats d'égouts.*"

"What? Who?"

"Les rats d'égouts."

"What's that?"

Octave gave him a serious look, brows knitted. "In English, you would call them...er...rat bastards...but the name means...sewer rats..."

"Whoa...rat bastards?" Xerxes shook his helmeted head. "Man, that sounds serious...sort of. What they want with you?"

Octave grabbed his water bottle and took a long pull. He swallowed hard. "Okay, I tell you but you must not tell the others, do you promise?"

Xerxes gave this some thought. He wasn't a stoolie but then again he didn't want anything to happen that might harm the show. "Okay…shoot. What's going on?"

"Good…I tell you…about four weeks…a month ago, I was in a cycling race and I was ahead but close behind was one of this, er, group…"

"These *rats d'égouts* guys…"

"*Oui.* Just so. This one tried to pass me on a steep curve…the road was uneven and there was some dirt…sand…on the side. Somehow, I don't know how, really, our pedals locked for a moment and we both were very unstable. I managed to pull loose but this other fellow, he lost his balance and flipped over and he rolled and rolled across the pavement, like the rag doll, you know? His bike went off in the other direction. There was a gash on his leg and his cheeks were scraped and his bike was badly damaged. I went on to win this cycling race. I didn't know *les rats d'égouts*…who they were…a street gang and ever since then, they have been out to get me, you understand? It is a matter of pride and they now want their revenge."

"Man, you'd better be careful. Why don't you call the police?"

"And tell them what? That some crazy guys are following me? I don't know who they are and have never seen their faces? They would just laugh, I think."

Xerxes got up on his haunches and looked right, then left. "All clear," he said, standing up and brushing off his clothes. "I'd consider it if I were you. Maybe they know these guys."

Octave stood up slowly. "I don't think so. The police…here…" and he shrugged.

Julien's van appeared around a corner and stopped with a screech of the brakes. The doors flew open and Stephanie raced out, followed by Yolanda and Rufus, videocam in hand, digital tape rolling. Slowly after, Julien got out and shut his door carefully and sauntered up behind.

"What happened? Where'd you guys get to?" Stephanie called. "Are you all right?"

Xerxes looked sheepish but didn't say anything. "I am sorry," Octave said. "We decided to have a little race…things got a bit…competitive…" Standing behind Stephanie, Xerxes gestured toward his head, distracting Octave, who glanced over. Stephanie swung around but Xerxes had assumed a neutral position. He was trying to remind Octave about the helmet-cam, his eyes lit up as he caught on. "And then, of course, there was this, uh, group of riders who joined in and we all raced together through le jardin as a group…"

"We just got carried away," Xerxes said. "Sorry guys. But I got it all on the helmet-cam, so you should have some good stuff."

"Great," said Rufus enthusiastically. "Excellent. Can't

wait to see it." And he gestured for the helmet. Reluctantly, Xerxes took it off and handed it over. Rufus popped out the mini-disc and pocketed it.

Stephanie looked from one to the other suspiciously. "All right, you two. I know you're up to something. Just don't do it again, all right. We can't afford any accidents, understand?" She gave each of them a death stare and they gulped and then nodded meekly. "Okay, let's go. Back in the van. Rufus can take some shots as we go, for the montage sequence."

The crew headed back to the L'Hôtel Artiste. Before disembarking, Octave said he'd meet up with them around eight. Xerxes headed up to his room and typed up some blogs for the website. Stephanie and Rufus reviewed the helmet-cam footage, which, although jerky, was pretty exciting stuff. Stephanie's eyes narrowed, however. She got on the phone.

"Hello?"

"X, just what was going on there?"

"Huh? What're you talking about Steph?"

"Don't con me, okay? Rufus and I are reviewing the footage and it seemed to me that you were kind of confused, even alarmed about what was going on during the ride."

"Well, you know, those other guys came out of nowhere, took us by surprise…"

"Ever watch cycling on TV, X?"

"Yeah, sure."

"Ever see when a team pools their resources together and goes on the attack, for the good of the team but they are slowing everybody else down so one guy, one of their own guys, can get ahead?"

"Yeah…" he replied tentatively with a sinking feeling. Stephanie sensed something was wrong and he wasn't going to be able to deny it. He'd read a book once about deniability and this was a classic situation where he couldn't deny what he knew. Yikes.

"I'm coming up."

Xerxes gulped. "Okay."

Stephanie rapped sharply on the door. Xerxes opened it and she brushed past him and then turned with her hands on her hips. "Okay," she said. "Give it to me straight and no crapola, okay?"

He sighed. "I promised not to tell."

"Octave is not in charge here, I am, and I need to know for the good of the show and for you too."

Xerxes nodded and then slumped into a chair. Stephanie followed him to the small sitting area and sat down, carefully crossing her legs. She propped her chin up in her hands, elbow balanced on her knee. "I'm listening," she said.

Xerxes told her what he knew, which wasn't much. Stephanie listened carefully, not asking any questions. "We should call the police," she said. "This could be serious."

"He doesn't want us to."

"I don't care what he wants." She thought for a moment. "Maybe it was just a scare tactic, a macho boy thing." She looked up at him. "I'm willing to wait for now but if anything else happens, the hint of anything else, we dial 911 or whatever the French equivalent is, got it?"

"Yeah."

She stood up. "See you downstairs at eight."

"Right." Gucci and Pucci and Prada notwithstanding, Stephanie took no prisoners and he respected that. She had a tough job to do.

Julien showed up promptly at eight to take them to the restaurant.

"Let's go," Stephanie said.

"What about Octave?" Xerxes asked.

"Oh, he phoned and said something came up and he'd meet up with us there. I gave him the name and address. Okay?" Xerxes nodded. Stephanie shooed everyone forward.

La Mascotte was situated at 52 rue des Abbesses in old Montmartre, the artists' area of the city. Even in the fading light, Xerxes saw the area was charming, peopled with artists and artisans selling their work behind stalls or even chairs set up along the street. You could have your portrait sketched for 10 euros, sometimes less. You could buy jewelry, pottery, paintings, sketches, sculptures—a cornucopia of art.

Octave was late and the crew ordered dinner. Dinner was being served and he still hadn't shown up. "Can I borrow your cell phone?" Xerxes asked Stephanie. She rummaged around in her purse, and then handed it over.

"What's Octave's number?" She consulted her notebook, and then read it out. Xerxes dialed the number, it connected and Octave answered.

"*Oui, allo?*"

"Octave? It's X."

"Ah, Eeeks…"

"What are you doin', man? We're waiting on you, having dinner, you know? Everything all right?"

There is a long pause and Xerxes heard some rustling in the background. "Er, yes, everything is fine. Something has come up to delay me, that is all. I have to help my parents with something, so I don't think I will make it but I will see you tomorrow at the hotel, yes? At eight o'clock?"

"Anything you need help with?"

"Er, no, no, it is fine. No problem. Tomorrow…bye." And Octave rang off.

"Everything okay?" Stephanie asked as he handed back the phone.

"Dunno. Sounded a bit weird."

"What do you mean?"

"Not sure, just weird, that's all." Xerxes didn't notice that Julien was looking and listening to him very carefully.

The next morning, as the crew assembled in the lobby waiting for Julien, Octave still hadn't shown up. "Where could he be?" Stephanie asked. "First last night and now this?" She was beginning to get concerned about his reliability. They needed him to show up on time for the shoot or the whole schedule was out of kilter. Julien came through the front doors and indicated the van was ready to go.

"He seemed responsible enough," Yolanda said.

"I can only shoot around him just so much," Rufus stated.

Stephanie's cell phone rang. She answered it but heard only muffled voices talking in the background, nothing clear. She was about to ring off when Xerxes, watching her expression turn to annoyance, grabbed the phone from her and listened. Then he shushed everyone and held up his hands. "Paper...pen..." he hissed. He wrote,

"It's Octave. Being held somewhere. Giving us clues." Xerxes put his hand over the receiver. "Let's go."

The crew piled into the van. Stephanie got out her Paris street map as Octave, mumbling in the background voiced oblique clues to his whereabouts. Undaunted, Rufus kept the videocam rolling as if this is all part of the show. In truth, who knew really?

"Hope his battery doesn't die," Xerxes said. "Before we can figure this out."

Stephanie wrote down all the places Octave mentioned; it seemed like he was having a muttered conversation with someone that was complicated by the fact they were speaking French. Julien translated as best he could but with the poor sound quality from the phone, some of it came out garbled.

"Stop the van," Xerxes screeched. "And follow me." The van skidded to a stop. Horns blared and drivers screamed invective. Xerxes made apologetic gestures and then lifted his bike out of the back and raced off with the van in hot pursuit. He envisioned the map in his head, saw arrows pointing to his final destination. Traffic was heavy, Monday morning rush hour, and Xerxes just decided to go for it. He knew that the wireless mike carried a 500-meter signal radius, so he could afford to zip in and out of traffic while it was stopped and still keep in touch. And that's what he did. He rode up the lanes of traffic, breezing by cars and when the traffic started to move, Xerxes kept up with them. He noticed angry drivers looking at him, gesticulating, yelling things but he didn't care. A blast came behind him. He glanced over his shoulder and a motorbike with two helmeted riders was right on its tail, the driver annoyed that he was being blocked. Xerxes raised his hand, pumped the pedals, saw an opening, and then cut in front of a Smart car. The motorbike tooted then sped ahead. The passenger lifted a hand in salute. Xerxes cut back between the lanes while the Smart-car driver yelled at him. He raised a hand in supplication but it cut no ice with the driver who continued to yell. The traffic had slowed almost to a halt but Xerxes kicked it into high gear. As he turned and twisted, cut corners and rounded intersections, he called out the directions to Stephanie and, although there was no two-way, figured she heard him. All the studying of the street maps back home paid off.

Xerxes zeroed in on his destination, the street traffic thinned out but the noise level ratcheted up. He was heading toward the Foire du Trône, a massive fun fair that dated back to the year 957 and took place every spring. It had a carnival with a Ferris wheel and rides and hundreds of merchants hawking their wares. Xerxes loved the idea of it, a massive street party, what could be cooler? Xerxes looked behind him and saw the van. It had to pull over because vehicular traffic wasn't allowed into the square. Xerxes blasted ahead into the hubbub. Must be hundreds of thousands of people here, he thought but he figured that Octave had to be somewhere nearby, it only made sense.

The crew followed behind. Stephanie had her ultracompact notebook PC with wireless remote and Internet access so she could pick up Xerxes' messages. She accessed satellite photos of Paris and zeroed in on the area where the Foire du Trône was taking place. "Got it," she said. "This is where we're at." The others leaned over her shoulder and peered at her screen.

Xerxes rode slowly, weaving in and out of pedestrian traffic, getting caught up in the sights, the sounds and smells of the fair, losing himself in it momentarily, caught up in the excitement and buzz of the crowd. He took in the arcade games, the penny toss, skeet ball, carts and balloon tying…reminders of his childhood and the carnivals back home. His eye caught something. Moving closer, he dismounted and saw what looked like Octave's bike chained up with a bunch of other bikes—black bikes, a lot of them. Okay, he told himself, Octave had to be close by. Xerxes chained his bike to the rack, sent a quick email to Stephanie to let the crew know he was by the funhouse and to high-tail it over here.

Xerxes spotted a line of people waiting to enter. Didn't make sense, he thought, to enter that way. Octave and these other guys, these Rat Bastards, must be somewhere close. Xerxes wandered around the back and spotted a door...maybe for employees? He pulled on the handle and found it was unlocked. He slipped inside. Okay, this was what a funhouse was supposed to be, dark and eerie, because it certainly was that. He gulped, steeled his nerves and pressed on. The floor was angled up, making it hard to walk. Some fun. In no time, he found himself in a room full of mirrors not knowing which way to turn but got caught up looking at himself, couldn't help it really, there really wasn't anything else to do and his image loomed at him, distorted into weird shapes, pulling his face in different directions and it was kind of funny...so he laughed nervously. Couldn't figure out what direction to turn, every route was blocked, he bumped up into glass and another crazy distortion, like the mirrors were closing in on him. Xerxes shook it off, this strange feeling, just the distortion getting to him. He took another step and suddenly the floor disappeared, he couldn't keep his balance and he fell forward scrabbling at the surface with his hands. Despite his flailing, he slid and slid and slid and dropped down into a hole, bounced on to a slide, one that rivaled Sea World except this one wasn't full of water but seemed just as long and curvy and he slid just as fast.

XI

Xerxes flew off the slide and hit the floor with a thump. Pairs of hands pulled him roughly to his feet, pinned his arms behind his back, not too carefully, and before he could say anything a blindfold covered his eyes. Then he was marched off into oblivion. He was prodded from behind, shoved actually, and he walked for what seemed to be a long time. He was turned in different directions and lost track of where he'd started, couldn't remember how many steps he'd taken, he was so disoriented. Xerxes hoped that the wireless remote could reach the outside world and he hoped that Stephanie was still monitoring the signal. His hopes weren't terribly high on that score, however.

Finally, they stopped and he was prodded sharply. Xerxes stumbled forward and fell to the ground. He felt his face for the blindfold and tried to pull it off.

"Don't," a guttural voice warned him, and Xerxes' hands froze before he could even touch the material.

"Where am I? Who's behind all of this? What's going on here?"

"Shut your face or I'll shut it for you," the guttural voice said in heavily accented English. Xerxes clammed up. A lengthy silence followed, Xerxes strained to hear anything, but all was silent.

The voice rang out again. "This is a warning to the both of you…we can find you anywhere, anytime. Remember that." Footsteps sounded all around him, moving in the opposite direction, a mob stepping quickly, the sound dimmed as the pairs of feet echoed farther and farther until they faded completely and there was silence. Xerxes ripped off the blindfold and snapped on his helmet light; he swung it around the room, which was dirty, dank and definitely smelly.

"Man, stinks in here." Then he caught sight of a shoe, which upon further investigation was attached to a leg, and even more, attached to Octave. Xerxes lit up the scene. Octave had his mouth taped, eyes blindfolded and his hands and legs bound.

Xerxes ripped off the tape; Octave winced but began to breathe more freely, drawing in air heavily. The blindfold came off and from the pouch at his waist, Xerxes retrieved his Swiss Army knife, it always came in handy, and cut Octave's arms and legs free.

Octave shaded his eyes. "Eeeks? I cannot thank you enough. This is amazing. You have come in the nicks of time, yes?"

Xerxes put his hands on his hips and stepped back fixing Octave with a cynical look. "Come on," he said.

Octave had been shading his eyes against the glare and

then slowly dropped them to his sides as he sat up. "Okay, you are right to be a little angry with me..."

"A litte. This is not a little..."

Octave sighed. "So...it was not about a bicycle race...as I see you have probably guessed by now. About two months ago, I went to a club and I met this girl there. We became very, how should I say...friendly. I take her to her home that evening. So, the story has a bad ending. I think she feels for me what I feel for her but she is the girlfriend of the leader of this gang, these *rats d'égouts* but I didn't know this. Anyway, we are not seeing each other anymore because it is too dangerous for us. I swear to you, that is the whole story, through and through. There is nothing further. I am innocent and have done nothing wrong. That is the whole truth."

Okay, okay. So, Xerxes read *Romeo and Juliet* in school and knew something about unrequited love and found himself sympathizing with the guy. "You know, a body could be stashed down here for a long time and nobody would find it."

"Yes, I know," Octave said sadly. "I am lucky this time."

Then Xerxes thought about what the Rat Bastards might think if they knew he'd got them on video and audiotape. True, there wasn't much in the way of light but still, something must have come out. As Xerxes was thinking through this and his newfound friend huddled miserably in the dirt, voices echoed faintly. He indicated to Octave to be quiet, "Sssh!" and snapped off the helmet light and waited. What if they came back?

The voices remained a low murmur and Xerxes caught the sweep of a flashlight beam, and whoever was behind it stepped into the room, the beam of light arcing back and forth in a search pattern until Xerxes and Octave were caught in full beam. Xerxes grinned and waved while Octave remained perfectly still.

Behind the light, it didn't appear to be the Rat Bastards and he didn't hear any familiar voices from the crew, so who the heck was it?

"I am Capitaine Fabrice Poulin of the Surêté, young gentlemen. You both are very lucky. We have been keeping these gang members under surveillance for a long time and I can assure you they are a very bad and a very dangerous group. We observed the young Monsieur being manhandled by the gang and we followed as closely as possible without giving our presence away, you understand? But with the crowd of the Foire and the traffic being so congested, it was very difficult to keep up when the gang was on bicycle and could jump the sidewalks and cut across garden parks. They are very clever this way, no? Still, we were able to trace you to this place and this, er, dungeon."

"*Les flics!*" Xerxes cried with his limited knowledge of French. "I've been dying to say that ever since I got here. What's cracking?" Fortunately, he couldn't fully see Capitaine Poulin's sour expression.

"This is my colleague, Sergeant Pierre Fortin," the Capitaine said formally. Sergeant Poulin gave a small bow.

"Come, it is time to leave this place." Sergeant Poulin helped Octave up and the policemen led them out of the funhouse basement.

They emerged out of the darkness into the light of day and the strolling and contented crowds. Xerxes shielded his eyes until they readjusted to the brightness. He spotted the crew nearby, searching the area. He called out to them and at the same time got a good first look at the French policemen. He guessed they were undercover because they wore golf shirts and jeans and wraparound sunglasses, unless this was common for casual wear in Paris, but Xerxes didn't think so.

"Thank God!" Stephanie cried and galloped over, which wasn't easy in a pair of Manolos but somehow she managed. "Are you guys all right?" Yolanda and Rufus, still shouldering the videocam, followed and then Julien sauntered up behind.

"We're cool," Xerxes said. "Right?" and he turned to Octave.

"Yes, it is fine, thank you very much. Okay."

"And these are the police," Xerxes said. "Capitaine Poulin and Sergeant Fortin…Stephanie, our producer, Yolanda, our production assistant, Rufus, our director and cameraman and Julien, our guide here in Paris."

Poulin waved at Rufus. "Please, no filming… at least, for the moment. Er, please to meet you ladies and gentlemen…you are aware that an incident has taken place. It could have been very dangerous but today we were lucky and certainly Monsieur Pompidou had the luck, how do you say? Big time? Now, we are thinking of a little plan and need of course, the cooperation from all of you...?" And here, Poulin searched out each of the faces. He was a man of medium height and graying hair; he seemed trim and in good shape. "Well...?"

"What is this plan?" Stephanie asked. "Is it dangerous?"

"No," Poulin said. "Not really...but then, it could be. Nothing is for certain, is it?" The crew looked a bit confused. "You see, Monsieur Pompidou is our best link to this gang that has been chasing him all over the city and we wish to exploit this, take advantage, you see? Monsieur Pompidou is the bait... we shall lure this gang out of its lair and then...pounce on them. What do you think?" There was a deafening silence. Poulin looked at Fortin, who shrugged noncommittally. "Well, there are a few details we need to work out yet."

"Do you guys have any leads? Like, do you know who these gang guys are?" Xerxes asked.

"Well, er, no, we do not as of yet. They keep their faces behind the masks and they are difficult to identify. We do believe, however, that some of them are of Vietnamese origin. This young lady that Monsieur Pompidou met some weeks ago, she is Vietnamese."

All eyes turned to Octave, who blushed. "Yes, this is true." He fell silent. "So, you want me to be a target?"

"Just so," Poulin confirmed.

"And what if the gang is successful and the Sûreté is not?"

Poulin's expression brightened. "Ah, no, no, no, ...I assure you that we will be closely looking out for you and that nothing will go wrong and you will be safe at all times. We are very experienced in these matters." Xerxes could tell by Octave's expression he wasn't convinced of this. "And now," the Capitaine continued, "let me formally welcome all of you to Paris." There were murmurs of stunned thank-yous. "What is it you are filming here?"

Stephanie explained the concept of the show.

"Ah, I see, that is very clever... and you have all of the necessary permits?"

Stephanie looked exasperated. "Yes, Captain, of course we do. We've gone through all of the proper channels." And of course she never mentioned the secret race down the steps of the Eiffel Tower for which there was no permit precisely but she hoped she'd reach an understanding with the officials at that time.

Poulin appeared satisfied with her explanation and then handed out his card to everyone. "If anything should happen, please contact me right away, day or night. Either myself or Sergeant Fortin will assist you at once. Now, please, may I have your cell phone number?" Stephanie rooted out her phone and read the number to him and the policeman took Octave's cell phone number as well.

"Remember, please, that wherever you go during the next days, we will be with you and watching. May I have a copy of your itinerary, if you please?" Stephanie handed one over. "Excellent."

"Capitaine," Octave said.

"*Oui?*"

"I will help you. These are very bad people and must be stopped."

The policeman stepped forward and shook his hand. "You are doing the right thing, Monsieur," Poulin said, with a confidence and zeal that Octave didn't share. "You are a true patriot of France."

"Oh, this is so cool," Xerxes said. "Man, this is going to make this episode a humdinger."

Stephanie's mind strayed to all the unknowns, all the things she couldn't plan; this now became too unstructured for her. "I don't know," she said.

"What about safety?" Yolanda said. "Octave and X could get hurt." This caught Xerxes' attention. She'd never expressed any concern for him before. "Then I'd be out of a job and that would be a bummer."

"I just want to get great shots," Rufus said simply.

Julien had wandered out of earshot.

Capitaine Poulin cleared his throat. "Let me assure you that our surveillance will be all hours of the day and the night, what you call twenty-four/seven, no? We offer you the best effort, you see?"

Octave nodded and shook the Capitaine's hand. Xerxes slapped palms with Sergeant Fortin as the two policemen took their leave and then faded into the crowd.

"Listen guys, why don't we grab something to eat here and take some shots since we're here and this is a big event, right?"

"Sounds good," Xerxes said. "I'm up for a little grub, how about you Octave?"

Octave smiled weakly. "Yes, of course. Whatever my friend Eeeks wishes to do, it is fine with me. I always have the appetite and you can get some different things here. It is very multicultural."

Stephanie called Julien over and told him they were planning to grab something to eat then wander over to the Foire and take some footage while they were here—they would need the van ready to go in about an hour or so. Julien nodded assent and smiled quietly.

As they moved through the crowd, Octave seemed a bit shaky.

"You all right?" Xerxes asked him.

"Yes. I'm thinking too much. You know how it is, when something is happening you don't have time to think but afterward, then the reality of it all hits you. It is a big force, eh?"

Xerxes slapped him on the back. He really didn't think of him as a Pompous Ass anymore. "You'll get over it. You're a trained athlete, right? Your competitive instincts are keen. Your resolve is like molten steel, no one can take that away from you. So why should you let these rat guys do that to you? They're not worthy. Right?"

"Right, you are right, of course. You have an interesting viewpoint, Eeeks."

"I do my best," Xerxes replied.

After a few crêpes and a café au lait, Octave seemed better; he'd recovered his poise and most of his confidence. Xerxes decided to look out for him just the same. After all, he figured, it wasn't every day that a person became the target of a criminal enterprise and a police decoy all rolled into one. He couldn't wait to email Lionel and Maya about this. Of course, nothing would be said to Darius and Hilka; they wouldn't understand and would probably just worry. Or have the embassy come and get him and lock him away for his own safety. Xerxes was liking this; he found energy in this newfound freedom...and being out of school wasn't too shabby either. He just had to shut Principal Hammerschlager out of his mind that was all. And that was a no-brainer.

On the way back to the hotel, Stephanie had a thought. "Listen, Octave, I've got an idea. Maybe you should stay with us. We can get you a room. It would be more convenient and you would be closer by. What do you say?"

"I think it is a good idea, actually," Octave said. "My parents are away for a few weeks and I am on my own, so it would be more accessible to be here. And I wouldn't have to get up so early."

"Great. After Julien drops us at the hotel, he'll take you home and you can pick up what you need there. While you're doing that, I'll get you a room. Deal?"

"Yes, deal," Octave said and he and Stephanie shook on it.

At the hotel, Stephanie went up to her room to call Mira and Max and apprise them of these latest developments. Octave went off with Julien to pack some things he'd need over the next few days. Xerxes couldn't wait to email Lionel and Maya and tell them what was up. All this stuff was way too cool and a bit edgy too because of the danger element all of a sudden, not that he took it too seriously. Even still, Xerxes was glad he'd kept up his kickboxing regimen. You never knew when it would come in handy. Xerxes also noticed that Yolanda was giving him looks, but he decided to forget about her. She was just poison.

Xerxes practically leapt onto the elevator and punched the penthouse button. Carefully, he carded the door and entered quietly, taking a moment to look around. Nothing had been disturbed. He breathed a long sigh of relief, dropped his knapsack on the floor and went to his computer, ready to fire it up. Again, squelching the image of Maya and Rick Oswald, he decided to write to her first. He'd been a bit disappointed because, so far, she hadn't emailed him back. He figured she was busy but still … it hurt a bit.

The crew rendezvoused in the lobby at eight, which seemed to be the magic number. Julien picked them up and drove them to the Café Moderne, one of Octave's favorite places at 40 rue Notre-Dame-des-Victoires. Julien had let them off about a block from the restaurant and then went to park the van.

The crew walked to the entrance of the restaurant. Stephanie and Yolanda were in front chatting. Rufus, Octave and Xerxes walked behind them discussing the day's events. Octave noticed it first and nudged Xerxes, who looked around him. A phalanx of young Asian-looking men appeared, melted out of nowhere and formed a wide, mobile square around them.

"What the . . . ?" Rufus said. Stephanie and Yolanda kept walking.

The Asian men didn't speak, make any gestures or look at them but moved along with the crew keeping perfect pace. Xerxes found it a bit spooky.

"This is very weird, is it not?" Octave whispered.

Rufus had the handicam out and went to work. Xerxes shrugged. Just as they reached the entrance of the restaurant, the Asian men broke off and headed away in different directions. None looked back and not a word was spoken.

"Trainee dog walkers," Rufus said. "That's why they kept such perfect formation."

"You think this is it?" Octave asked.

"I have no idea," Rufus admitted. "But it sounded good."

They followed Stephanie and Yolanda into the restaurant. They hadn't noticed a thing.

Stephanie had worked out a deal with the maître d'hôtel to have the meal comped because the show was giving the restaurant free publicity by eating and filming in their establishment. It also didn't hurt that the show was seen in thirty countries around the world and across North America.

Halfway through the first course, Xerxes sensed that Octave was fading a little and that the thrill of being on television had faded too. He saw the pursed lips, the hesitation when he lifted his fork and the forced smile on his face.

Octave was concerned about his safety, which Xerxes could well understand. He kept glancing around, discreetly he hoped, to see if he could spot any police at the tables adjacent to them and wondered who among them they might be.

Xerxes clapped Octave hard on the back, so hard that the surprised Frenchman almost coughed up some French onion soup. "How ya' doin'? You okay, Octave? Hanging in?"

Octave gave him a long-suffering look. "Yes, my friend, Eeeks, I am okay. But I wouldn't mind swallowing my food before you bang me on the back, okay?"

"Sorry," Xerxes said, thinking his fellow cyclist was a bit testy. "Didn't mean to hit you so hard."

"It's okay. I'm just a bit, how would you say…stressed…yes?"

"I get it and it's a natural feeling, for sure. This is all a big, bad nerve strain."

"Nerve strain?"

"Right."

"Then that is what it is, nerve strain…soul train….North American expressions are very different. They don't make a lot of sense, not very logical…"

Xerxes smiled. "You got that right, buddy."

The meal broke up and they piled into the van. Julien drove calmly through the darkened streets. There wasn't much chit chat. Each was left to his or her own thoughts. It had been a full day and they were feeling the effects of it.

Julien dropped them off at the hotel entrance then pulled away from the curb with a wave. The crew members each headed up to their rooms. Even Yolanda decided to stay in that night. Xerxes noticed she seemed a bit distracted, even worried.

Xerxes was emailing away when there was a knock. He checked the peephole and saw that it was, guess who? Yolanda. He opened the door as casually as he could, leaning up against it dangerously close to falling over.

"Can I come in for a minute?" Then seeing his expression added, "Please."

Xerxes checked his pulse and as soon as it dropped below 100, he said, "Yeah, sure." And stepped clear of the door.

Yolanda swept in and dropped into one of the wingbacks in the sitting area. She swept her hair off her forehead but said nothing.

"To what do I . . . ? Uh, you want a pop or something?" She shook her head. "So," he sat opposite her. "What's going on?" Her fingernails were bitten down to the cuticles.

"I can guess what you think of me," she said.

"You can?" She nodded. "So, let me get this straight. You're thinking that I'm thinking you're not very nice. You're rude and inconsiderate and selfish? Something like that? Is that what you're thinking?"

Yolanda reddened right up to her hairline but nodded. "Maybe."

Xerxes jumped up, restless and full of erratic energy. "Or could it be that I see someone who is a bit insecure, someone who wants to get ahead and break into this crazy business and is afraid it will all go wrong and she'll have missed her great opportunity. Is that a possibility?"

Yolanda stared at him, her mouth agape. Finally, she shut it, snapping her jaws. "It's a possibility."

"So, what can I do for you?"

"I'm scared, I guess. Just like you said. I think some weird things are happening and I never signed on for this, you know? I was looking for a way into the industry and was lucky enough that Mira took a chance and gave me a job, a fairly lowly one, but I don't mind starting at the bottom and learning as I go."

"Good. That's a good thing, right?"

"I just have this feeling something is going to happen."

"What do you mean?"

Yolanda wrinkled up her nose in thought and Xerxes' heart melted. Bye-bye Maya and Rick. "I don't know, but everyone in my family is psychic. I just have a bad feeling about things and when I get these feelings, they very often turn out to be true."

"Sounds a bit spooky."

"It can be," Yolanda said. "I don't know what's going to happen or when, but something is and I'm worried about it."

"Have you told Stephanie?"

Yolanda shook her head and blonde, wavy hair cascaded across her face. "She's too busy being Miss Bossy Boots to pay attention."

"Well, I think she does have a lot on her mind. There's always a lot to do, things to check out, you know."

"Sure I know and I should be doing a lot more of it but she's just a control freak, and Rufus is just in love with his cameras, so that left you, wonder boy, to talk to and that's what I'm doing. But don't think it means anything, okay? I just need to get this out of me because it helps and you were available, all right?" she asked, her tone hardening.

Xerxes stopped pacing to listen and then held up his hands. "I hear you. Message received loud and clear." And he cupped his hands over his mouth. "Helloooo..."

Yolanda recoiled and then got up. "Well, thanks for listening anyway, for all the good that it did."

"Hey, anytime. That's what friends are for."

Yolanda gave him a dirty look. "You've got to be kidding."

"Okay, maybe it was a bit lame."

"A bit?"

"Hey, I'm only seventeen. I'm working on it, okay. I think you should lighten up a little."

Yolanda pursed her lips. "I knew it was a mistake coming here. Everybody's a crackpot."

Xerxes grinned. "You've got that right."

Yolanda headed to the door, made a face at him and then stuck out her tongue. In a second, she was gone, leaving Xerxes standing on his own, scratching his head. Couldn't figure her out and probably shouldn't even try.

Xerxes continued his emailing. A moment later, there was another loud knock. What's this? Yolanda come back to apologize? But no, it was Octave.

"Hello, Eeeks, am I bothering you? You are busy?"

"Heck no. Just sending some emails, come on in." Octave swept past him. "What's up?"

Octave shrugged. "I have the fatigue but I cannot find the sleep, you know? I feel, how do you say, when there is energy and it is all over the place?"

"Jumpy? Restless?"

Octave snapped his fingers. "*Oui*. Just so."

"So…?"

"There is only one thing to do."

"What's that?"

"I need to go for a ride."

"Ride? As in bike ride?"

"Yes. It is absolutely necessary."

"Well…"

"And I want some company, so what do you say?"

"I don't know, Octave. What about the police? Maybe it is taking an unnecessary risk?"

"Yes, but the Capitaine said they would be watching us twenty-four/seven, yes? Then there should be nothing to worry about. We should be safe?"

"I suppose so… it's just that those rat guys snatched you before and well…"

"Ah, but we will be vigilant this time, okay? On the look-out for them. That is why we need to go as two, to keep each other company and watch out for strangers. Come on, I am feeling the need, Eeeks, and won't be able to get to sleep and then tomorrow, the show will suffer because I will be making the yawns and will have the buggy eyes and so on…"

"All right, if you're determined. It's better that you don't go alone, anyway."

"Excellent. I knew I could count on you."

"I guess I'm pretty predictable."

Octave smiled. "I think you are, yes."

Octave left and Xerxes pulled on his cycling gear—jersey, shorts and shoes. He grabbed the helmet and made sure the camcorder was loaded and ready to go. And as a last-minute thought, he strapped the wireless keyboard to his wrist. A guy just never knew when the urge to email might suddenly strike him.

It was after midnight and the streets were quieter than Xerxes had ever seen them; he was thinking that between midnight and six in the morning was the downtime for traffic. The air was cool but not too cool and just perfect for riding.

Octave and Xerxes headed toward the Champs Elysées because it was wide open and led directly to the Arc de Triomphe, which Xerxes hadn't really taken in yet. They started pedaling up the Avenue du New York, cut over to Avenue Montaigne and hung a sweeping left on to the Elysian Fields.

As they rode side by side, Octave felt the need to talk. It was pleasant and the air had a sweet smell, distinct from the lingering odor of car exhaust, of course.

"I am an only child," Octave began.

"So am I."

"Ah…I must have recognized this in you, perhaps, Eeeks. And you like the cycling as well. Perhaps it is not a coincidence that you are here…"

"Who knows?" Xerxes replied.

"Yes, indeed…my father…he was…is a cycling fanatic, you see and his one and only ambition in life was to qualify for the Tour de France. Unfortunately, for him the circumstances didn't help. When he was twenty-two years old, he was in a very serious cycling accident and his leg was broken in three or four different places. The leg never healed properly. We must remember that this was years ago and surgical techniques were not what they are now and the rehabilitation also was not as good. My father was never able to compete in a road race ever again."

"That's too bad."

"Yes, well for him, it was tragic. His dream was over. He felt like his life was over. He became very depressed and let everything go. Eventually, this pain and loss within him subsided a little. He married my mother and was happy enough but still, he knew there was this void, this hole in his life. When I was born, all of this changed for him. He transferred his desire to race in the Tour de France to me, ever since I was very young, he has coached me, pushed me to go further and to do better.

In the beginning, I want to please him but then I discovered that I too, had this desire. So, I took up the challenge and ever since I was very small, I ride every day, no matter the weather. Usually three to four hours without fail during the week and even longer on the weekends. So, this challenge has now become a quest, you understand?"

"Like the Knights of the Roundtable?" Octave shot him a look as they coasted through a long, flat section of the street. "I read about it in school."

"Well," Octave said. "I wouldn't say it was a holy quest but I think it is close, as close as I can make it, anyway."

"Okay."

"But," he shrugged. "I am a teenager and what teenager doesn't like to have a good time, to go out, you know? So, that is why I went to that club, Le Cab, and I met Regine there. She is very beautiful and also very nice, but that is when the troubles began with *les rats d'égouts* and they started to come after me ever since. So I have been ducking them all over Paris."

As they accelerated along the Champs Elysées, a sleek, black BMW pulled up beside them. Xerxes glanced over but the car had tinted windows and he couldn't see in. He started getting nervous. The car was keeping even with them, neither moving ahead nor dropping behind, just like a pace car at the track. Menace oozed out of it through every motion, the hum of the tires, the dark, evil coloring, the vibration of the aerodynamic body.

Octave looked over his shoulder at Xerxes and shrugged. "Where are *les flics* now?" Xerxes called and as he said this, another black BMW pulled up behind them, keeping its distance, but the effect of being boxed in by the two sinister cars was unnerving.

Octave picked up the pace, then hissed. "When I hit it, just follow me, all right? Are you up for it?" Xerxes gulped, his throat dry, but he nodded his assent.

Octave looked behind him again and gave a little grin, like he was saying, "I'm tired of hanging around, it's time for action." Then he veered sharply to the left and pulled up to the driver's side of the forward BMW. Xerxes had no choice but to follow.

Octave put his head down and really began to pump, his feet exploded in the pedals. Holy smokes. Xerxes glanced at the speedometer and saw they were up to 50 kilometers an hour. Behind him, he heard tires squealing. Octave slowed, Xerxes was practically standing on his rear wheel…then Octave cut a sharp left turn onto rue Lincoln and headed away from their pursuers.

The BMWs were caught off-guard and hit the brakes, overshot the turn, reversed quickly and burned rubber after them.

Octave and Xerxes cut up to Bauchart, then cut left again on to rue Venet and peeled away, running parallel to the Champs Elysées. The BMWs chased them but hadn't followed their route, the cutting back and forth had been spontaneous and sharp.

Octave swerved hard on rue Galilee and left again on Champs Elysées, then hung a quick right, angling perilously close to the tarmac, took a short hard left on rue Lord Byron making a dizzying zigzag as Xerxes struggled to follow without wiping out, sweat running down his face and streaming onto his jersey, hands slick on the handlebars.

Then Octave hit the brakes furiously, fishtailing for 20 meters at least. Xerxes almost flipped his bike trying to match him. They leapt off their bikes and the two cyclists ducked behind a hedgerow, crouched down on their haunches and waited, panting rapidly.

After a moment, Octave and Xerxes poked through the shrubbery. They saw one BMW come from the top end of the street and the other drove down from the opposite direction. The cars skidded angrily until the front ends practically kissed. Each driver threw open his door and stepped out onto the tarmac.

"Geez," Xerxes hissed. "It's Capitaine Poulin and Sergeant Fortin. They don't look happy."

"Sshh," Octave warned.

Truthfully, the policemen scowled and exchanged irritated words at having lost the two cyclists. They watched as the two conferred, shaking their heads at each other, spitting invective, then got back in the cars and drove slowly off.

"I never knew cops drove Beemers," Xerxes said.

"Yes, it is strange," Octave said, thinking of the Citroëns he was accustomed to seeing.

After waiting a few moments, the road seemed clear and the two fugitives emerged from their hiding place. "Good thing that's a healthy bush," Xerxes said. "Or we'd have been found in no time."

They mounted their bikes and cycled leisurely along. "I think I will sleep well now," Octave said.

Out of the muted hues of the night, a phalanx of cyclists, dressed all in red, surrounded them. They kept pace with Octave and Xerxes. There was nothing threatening in their attitude or behavior, but still it was disconcerting. No overt gestures were made. No one said anything. Octave and Xerxes sped up, so did the red riders. They slowed down. Ditto the red riders. It was like these guys were attuned to them and matched each and every one of their motions, and it all was conducted naturally, effortlessly. They seemed to know beforehand which direction Octave and Xerxes would take and fluidly, seamlessly, turned with them, as if by mutual consent or some hidden signal. Then, about two blocks from the hotel, the red riders dispersed, like pheasants bursting out of the rough, in sharp trajectories and angles. Not one looked back. How odd. It was a strange day followed by an even stranger night and capped off by this mysterious visitation.

Xerxes again was more puzzled than alarmed and Octave was merely baffled. One more incident in a series of bizarre happenings.

The midnight cyclists headed up to their rooms in the hotel. Xerxes carded the door, dropped his clothes in a heap and toppled into bed. He was instantly asleep.

At breakfast the next morning everyone looked bleary-eyed, everyone except Octave and Xerxes, who'd slept remarkably well even though they arrived back at the hotel after one in the morning and it was just seven now. The crew held on tightly to their café au laits, as if the hot drinks were a lifeline, while Stephanie got down to business. Everyone was a bit jumpy from the incidents of yesterday.

"Here are the call sheets," she said, handing round pieces of paper. She handed one to Julien, who was slumped in his chair, eyes half-open, but who appeared to be listening. He grunted when his name was called or when spoken to, all signs of life including blinking and sipping a café au lait.

"Okay, so first up today is a montage sequence, then the Louvre," Stephanie said. "We're going to start shooting in the forecourt. X is going to do his standup with Octave and we'll get a pan of the whole complex? What do you think, Rufe...?" Her cell phone bleeped. She grabbed it from her purse. "Hello?" She listened for a moment and then handed it to Octave, who was startled. He, in turn, listened to the caller, pulled an angry face and replied to something in rapid and guttural French. Then he handed the phone to Xerxes, who took it, clearly puzzled. What was this, a new version of broken telephone?

"Hello?" he said reluctantly.

"This is Capitaine Poulin..."

"Oh yes, hello..."

"I have spoken to Monsieur Pompidou but I am wondering

just what you and your friend were thinking last night. It was a very foolish thing to do, cycling on your own late at night, after things had been explained very clearly, or so I thought."

"Ah, sorry about that…"

"And perhaps you might be able to explain why you were foolish enough to try to evade us, what is the point of this, Monsieur?" The policeman was irritable.

Xerxes now knew a rhetorical question when he heard one and didn't think there was any point in coming up with an answer, which would be pretty lame anyway. He figured the policeman was trying to save face—his dignity was at stake. "It won't happen again, I promise you."

"Be certain it does not. How can we protect you otherwise, if you go scurrying away like insects? That was very, very silly, Monsieur."

"Sorry," he said glumly and then snapped the phone shut and handed it back to Stephanie, while Octave gave him a sheepish look. She looked at the two of them curiously, not knowing what had gone on. Sensing the mood and general torpor, Stephanie opted for action.

"Come on, drink up everybody. Let's get to work." She hustled everybody out of the café and into the van to head for the first location of the day.

The weather was clear and dry but not too hot—a perfect day for shooting and the same for tourists. Rufus got his shots done for the montage, although it took longer than planned and ate up the entire morning, but just getting outside and having everybody busy and working improved the mood.

The crew broke for lunch at a restaurant that specialized in *tartes flambés*. This is a specialty from the Alsace region of France. The dish represents a sense of collaboration between Alsace and Paris because it was a butcher and a baker from each area who worked together to invent the dish, a French version of pizza, and which was assembled and cooked by the patrons of the restaurant.

As Octave and Xerxes made their own *tartes flambés*, Rufus shot the sequence, which made for a nice break from all of the fast-paced cycling shots. By the time the *tartes* were placed in the oven and the aroma flooded the restaurant, everybody's mouth was watering.

"What do you think?" Octave asked, his mouth full of food.

"Pretty darn good," Xerxes said, cutting into the freshly baked dough, seeing the steam rise, smelling the melted cheese, the grilled onions and mushrooms. "I see a chain of *tartes flambés* franchises back home."

"Ah, we shall be the partners in business, eh?" Octave laughed.

"You got it, Bro'."

After packing in enough *tartes flambés* for a football squad, the crew headed over to the expansive courtyard in front of the Louvre for the next setup.

Rufus began with a close-up of an ARAGO Medallion set into the wall of a building next to the Comedie Française across from the Louvre. He pulled back out into a wide shot and showed Xerxes and Octave cycling through the towering pillars of l'arc du Carrousel at the west end of the Louvre; they crossed over the glass top of the inverted pyramid, the clear and cool underground mall, cycling leisurely toward the towering glass pyramid itself, designed by the famous architect I.M. Pei.

"So," Octave said, with a sweeping gesture. "This is the Louvre. What do you think?"

"Impressive," Xerxes said. "Definitely impressive. The glass pyramid is awesome."

"Yes, but it caused a bit of conflict too. Not everybody liked it at first. There are many traditionalists in France."

"Too modern you mean?"

"Exactly. But I personally, think it is very graceful and very beautiful. Because it is glass, the rest of the Louvre melts into it, if you can understand what I'm saying…"

"You mean, because you can see through the pyramid, it's almost as if it becomes a part of the other buildings?"

"*Oui.* Yes, precisely. And as we know the Louvre is one of the largest museums in the world and holds about three hundred thousand pieces of art, much more than can be put on display at any time…"

"That's a lot of varnish."

"Varnish?" Octave had a moment and then his face lit up. "Ah, you make a joke…?

But Xerxes' attention had been distracted. He noticed a black-clad cyclist bearing down on them out of the sun at a sharp angle and a high rate of speed. Xerxes and Octave looked on, curiously rooted to the spot, not sure what they were seeing as the cyclist whizzed by, brushing Xerxes' bike. Something flashed in the dazzling light as the cyclist's hand swept by in a sinister cutting motion. Octave recoiled.

"I think that was a knife," Xerxes said looking after the mysterious cyclist only to spot another one coming from the opposite direction headed their way. Xerxes and Octave exchanged looks. "We've got more company."

Before Rufus could look up from the camera, Octave jumped on his bike. "Eeeks, we've got to get out of here." And he took off. Xerxes followed him as the black-clad cyclist swooped by and swiped, catching the fabric of Xerxes' cycling jersey and ripping a wide gash through it.

"Yikes!"

"This way," Octave yelled and he headed straight for the main entrance of the Louvre, with Xerxes closing in behind. Xerxes glanced back and saw six of the dark riders in pursuit, moving in formation like a menacing wedge.

"Who are these guys? Don't they ever give up?"

Octave got to the stairs and jumped off his bike, hauled it over his shoulder and dashed up two steps at a time. Xerxes didn't think. He did what Octave did. Just as they reached the main doors, one opened. An attendant held the door for a heavy-set man exiting the building. Octave and Xerxes burst through, pushing past him awkwardly and squeezing themselves and their bikes by him, leaving the man and the attendant speechless, mouths open, gasping in outrage.

Octave set his bike down and jumped on, seeing there was just enough space to wheel around the turnstile. On automatic pilot. Xerxes did the same while behind them the black-clad riders piled through the door. Howls of protest were heard from an elderly woman vainly trying to get out while the attendant called for security on his walkie talkie, but the dark riders were moving so quickly, they were past and mounting their bikes.

Octave and Xerxes tore down the main hallway, weaving in and out of groups of astonished visitors and tourists who had come to quietly view the great works of art in the famous museum. Xerxes flashed on the paintings, the gilt-edged frames, the elaborate tile work, the height of the ceiling and the width of the doorways—all a blur as he sped along. The dark riders formed a Vee, knocking anything and any-one out of their way—a chase team who tore after their prey—scattering people in their wake. One tour group and its guide were decimated.

Xerxes wondered if Octave knew what he was doing or where he was going as they rounded corners, putting a foot down to steady their bikes and control their turns as Octave yelled, "*Attention! Attention!*" by way of warning. Screams and yells echoed in their ears. Xerxes went into a half slide and hit the far wall, his rear wheel catching the legs of a mahogany side table and a set of vases on display. He watched in horror as the vases rattled, then rocked, and he prayed they wouldn't topple and break, but he had no time to stay and watch. He'd lost precious seconds and pushed off, pedaling furiously.

"Eeeks," Octave called and pointed. Xerxes looked up ahead, then behind. The dark riders were gaining on them. Up ahead a set of elevator doors were beginning to close. "Let's go." And put his head down.

Octave shot through the doors and wheeled his bike around sideways, gesturing frantically to Xerxes to hurry up. Xerxes rammed through. Octave caught his front wheel just as the doors closed on his rear tire. Together they yanked it through and the doors closed just as the dark riders flew up. Xerxes caught a glimpse of the glare of their helmets through the closing crack, heard their palms slapping at the walls, felt their anger and frustration just as the elevator lifted off.

"*Mon Dieu*," Octave heaved. "That was close."

"Where to? Lingerie? Toys? Escape route?"

Octave punched Three. "I have the idea."

The elevator shuddered to a stop.

They rolled out one after the other at a fairly leisurely pace, trying to remain innocuous but drawing curious looks nonetheless. "Tour de France," Xerxes said to one American couple, who began talking excitedly between themselves.

Octave led Xerxes down a long corridor, through a set of glass doors and then suddenly the world flooded with light. They were inside the pyramid at the top of a set of steep, steel stairs.

Outside, the crew didn't know what was going on. Stephanie, Rufus and Yolanda tried to get through the main doors but they were barred by security officers, who weren't letting anyone in or out.

As Octave began descending the stairs and Xerxes followed him, thinking just like being at home, there were gasps and cries from those around them. People on the stairs scrambled to get out of the way. "*Attention! Attention!*" Octave called, waving one arm. He even caught a woman's hat before it hit the ground. "This is yours, Madame," he said. Xerxes thought that was very smooth.

They hit the ground and Octave headed for the exit doors before another group of security guards yelling at them from above could make their way down the now crowded staircase, which was clotted up with people watching the odd sight of the two cyclists now sprinting for the exit. Octave and Xerxes burst through into the open air and sped toward the crew who were heading back to the van.

"Get the van in gear," Xerxes yelled. "Guys! Let's go!"

Stephanie looked up and waved and then beckoned for them. She turned and, ushering the others along, ran toward Julien, who stood leaning up against the van with his arms folded. Hearing Stephanie's cries, he straightened up suddenly, went around the driver's door, and got in. A second later, the engine was running and Octave and Xerxes reached it just as the crew arrived on foot. Rufus was lugging his equipment.

"What'd I miss?" he cried. "Did you get it on the helmet-cam?"

"I sure hope so," Xerxes said. "It was on, that's for sure."

"Get in," Stephanie said. "Chit chat later."

Octave and Xerxes lifted their bikes into the back of the van and closed the doors. There was a commotion by the main entrance and they turned to look. A cluster of security guards had their backs to them. Then they fell over backward like a group of pins, cartwheeling down the stairs. From above, the dark riders smashed through the doors, jockeying down the steps over the fallen figures not caring who or what they squashed.

"We'd better go, I think," Octave said.

"Good idea."

XII

The doors slammed and Julien took off.

"This is getting weirder and weirder," Yolanda said.

"But exciting," Rufus replied, fiddling with the lens cap of the camcorder. Yolanda gave him a dirty look.

"Same guys, huh?" Xerxes asked Octave.

"I believe so," Octave replied.

"The slashing knives were a giveaway," Xerxes said.

"Yes," and Octave laughed nervously. "Fortunately, they missed."

"Not by much," Xerxes said and showed the back of his jersey where it had been sliced through.

"*Mon Dieu*," Octave exclaimed. "That was very close."

"It's drafty back there," Xerxes said, trying to sound nonchalant even though he didn't feel that way at all. "So, where were the police when this was going down?" Octave shrugged. "Think we'll get another nasty phone call from Capitaine Poulin? He seems good at that sort of thing." Julien turned his head as Xerxes spoke but didn't contribute to the conversation, just quietly listened. For the moment, Xerxes and Octave had forgotten about the red riders from the previous evening. Another complicating factor.

Stephanie studied her call sheet and then conferred with Rufus. "Guys, I think we're going to call it a day. It's almost four now; you guys can relax back at the hotel. Rufus will go out with Julien to catch more montage shots for the show. Any objections?" There wasn't a peep. "Didn't think so." She sighed. "Honestly, I don't know what kind of show we're going to end up with."

They trooped back to the hotel where Xerxes and Octave headed to their rooms to crash before dinner. Stephanie asked Xerxes for the helmet-cam tapes so she could review them.

Xerxes was thinking about the black riders and how they knew where they were going to be and when. Then it hit him. Of course. All of that info was posted on the *Get Outta Town!* website, so kids could follow along as the show was being shot. Wouldn't they be surprised by all of the recent goings-on? Xerxes phoned down to Stephanie's room.

"Hello?"

"Stephanie . . . "

"X . . . ? What's up?"

"Listen, I was thinking . . . I know, that's rare for me . . . "

"I wasn't going to say that."

"Okay . . . just so you know . . . I'm not an empty vessel . . . "

"You mean like a ship? Or a Styrofoam cup?"

"Right. Either. Listen, anyway, I think these guys are

tracking us through the website. I mean, the whole schedule is posted there, right? They know our every move because we've been giving it to them."

"Right," Stephanie replied. "I'll have it taken down for the next few days, okay? After that, it shouldn't matter because we're outta here."

"Sounds like a plan," Xerxes said and hung up.

Xerxes fired up his computer. He was falling behind in his emailing.

"Hey Maya and Lionel, how you guys doing? Things have been pretty cool around here. I've cycled all over Paris, like maybe fifty times (just exaggerating a little bit, but sure feels like it) but it is a very pretty city and the weather has been amazing. Sunny and warm but not too hot, every day. Streets here are packed. Tourists up the yin-yang. A lot of fat people in plaid shorts and white socks. Go figure. And it's not even the real tourist season yet. Lots of beautiful buildings here. Tons of old stuff to see. Maya, you'd really like it. Amazing architecture. The Louvre was a blast...we got to ride our bikes down the halls...but more about that later. And love the food... croissants, crêpes and café au lait. You can't beat it. Cool stuff happening outdoors here. Went to this massive fair the other day and it had everything, scary rides, a creepy funhouse, games by the mile and neat stalls where you bargain with guys to buy stuff and try to beat down the price. A ton of fun. Well, anyway, it's getting late and I gotta get ready for dinner. Will message later. Give Brutal a kiss for me (just kidding). X"

Like all teenagers, Xerxes had a great capacity for sleep. He and Octave were up late the night before and booted out of bed pretty early that morning, so Xerxes decided to grab a few winks. Just as he was falling asleep, there was a tap at the door.

Xerxes looked through the peephole. Octave. Hope he didn't want to go for another ride. Xerxes had Zenned out on all that for the time being.

Octave came in looking very worried. "Eeeks, I went to Yolanda's room and she was not there."

Xerxes shrugged. "Maybe she went somewhere else in the hotel, you know, like the spa or pool or checking out the shops?"

"I looked everywhere and still she was not there…"

Although he was starting to feel nervous, Xerxes said, "There's no reason to panic. I'm sure there's a perfectly reasonable explanation…" He stopped and thought. "Hey, why're you going to her room in the first place?"

"She has given me the invitation," Octave said.

This admission didn't help Xerxes' mood any, which darkened considerably after hearing that. "Let's look again, just to be sure."

The two searched all over the hotel, they checked the spa, asked an attendant to look in the changing area, then poked their heads into the sauna, the beauty salon, cruised the shops, even walked through the bar although they weren't old enough to drink alcohol legally. They knocked on Rufus' door but he must have still been out shooting with Julien. They went to Stephanie's room to see if Yolanda was there.

Before they could even knock, Stephanie threw open the door; she had an odd expression on her face.

"You better come in," she said. When they entered, Stephanie handed Xerxes her cell phone. Puzzled, he put it up to his ear.

"We have the girl," a high-pitched voice said. "Do not go to the police. If you do, we will know and she will be hurt. The police are useless and incompetent. If you notify them, the girl will disappear forever."

Xerxes thought that forever seemed like a very long time, like googolplex, one of the few things he remembered from Math class. "What do you want?" he rasped.

"I will explain…"

Xerxes signaled for paper and pen, which Stephanie provided as the caller spoke; he scribbled the instructions.

"I want to speak to Yolanda." He heard some muffled talk, then what sounded like scuffling and muted voices.

"X! Help me…" That was all she said before the phone was yanked away. Xerxes had seen tons of old TV shows with these kinds of hokey plots but he never thought he'd be living one. Now what would Adam West or Homer Simpson or Family Guy or even Steve Urkel do? Good question, but he had no particular answer. He handed the phone back to Stephanie and merely slumped down on her bed.

"What did they say?" Stephanie asked. Xerxes thought about the question and how to answer truthfully without telling the entire truth as he saw it. Sort of in-between lying and not lying, for her own good, of course. He began to describe the kidnapper's demands. He noticed that Octave seemed to grow paler and paler to the point where he thought the Frenchman might pass out on the spot. He thought about asking him if he was okay and what was wrong, beyond the actual circumstances, of course, which were very upsetting. Xerxes decided he'd have a word in private afterward.

"We need to find the others and call the police," Stephanie said.

"No police," Xerxes replied. "They were very clear about that. Yolanda would be hurt badly if they found out."

"Listen, X, I am responsible for everybody here and if something happened…"

"Which is why we can't call the police, Stephanie. Not yet. You're going to have to go along…"

"Let the police handle this."

Xerxes smashed his fist down on the coffee table and a small dish full of hard candies wrapped in foil leapt into the air. "No, we can't." No one spoke for a long moment. "We have to play the game," he continued quietly. "To see how it turns out and keep Yolanda safe."

"This isn't a video game," Stephanie said. "This is reality and we're dealing with actual lives and the police are best equipped to handle this."

"Stephanie, these people know every move the police are making. I know this isn't a videogame and no one wants

Yolanda to be safe more than me, so we need to cooperate or she will be hurt, that much is for sure."

Stephanie bit her lip and then spoke very carefully. "From all of the police shows I've seen and detective novels I've read, it is possible that Yolanda may be harmed anyway or dealt with before we even get to wherever it is we need to go."

"Now who's playing in La-La Land?" Xerxes asked. "You're just going to have to trust me on this." He turned to Octave. "What is the Circle of Death?"

Octave turned totally white, gasped for air and then fainted dead away.

Stephanie and Xerxes exchanged frightened looks, none of this inspired much confidence; however, Stephanie, ever-efficient and businesslike, knelt by Octave's side and pinched his cheeks, then gave him a slap and then another, so crisp they sounded like a wide, soft belly smacking the water.

Octave opened his eyes, winced, massaged his cheeks and then sat up, blinking and shaking his head. "What happened?"

"You fainted," Xerxes replied.

Stephanie stepped away from him now that her job was done and folded her arms. "Now tell us about this Circle of Death."

Octave shook his head again, then once more. "No, I can't tell you," he croaked. "I must speak with Eeeks, alone."

Looking exasperated, Stephanie muttered under her breath, then stomped out of the room, slamming the door. Xerxes flinched. Octave then spoke in low tones and explained the Circle of Death to Xerxes who, as he listened intently, didn't feel particularly well—in fact, he felt positively ill.

Octave shrugged. "Of course, I will help in any way that I can. I will take your place..."

"No," Xerxes said. "The guy was pretty insistent it be me and only me, or there was no deal. He called me 'TV Star,' and then sneered. It was nice. Like a snake hissing."

Julien and Rufus returned to the hotel. Stephanie called an emergency meeting in her room. She explained the circumstances and gave instructions. They were all shaken up by the situation. Julien had wanted to smoke but decided to wait until later when he could get outside. He always felt this way when he was agitated and at the moment, he was extremely agitated.

It was agreed that they'd all stay in that evening and order room service. Xerxes returned to his room. Nothing much interested him. He didn't want to talk to anybody and there was nothing remotely interesting on TV. He laughed bitterly. Here they were in Paris and he was trapped in his room like a prisoner.

Xerxes decided to write a goodbye letter, kind of like a last will and testament, except he really didn't have much to leave anyone. He'd send it to his server with instructions to Email All after twenty-four hours if he didn't send in a disable command.

"This is the Last Will and Testament of Xerxes Frankel. I know you will all find this extremely weird and I feel the same way just writing it. If you receive this message, then something pretty bad has happened to me and I am no longer with you. I don't want you to be upset (well you can be a little) because I will have participated in something noble—the saving of a life. I can't explain the circumstances but trust that others will fill you all in. I just want to say that I love you, Mom and Dad. You have been great parents to me all along. Mom, I love the fact that you listen to me without judging, that your affection is unconditional. Dad, you've got to chill out and enjoy what you have and believe me, that's a lot. Mom is a pretty hot chick and you'd better appreciate that fact. But I like how you've been a role model and tried to show me how to be more responsible. That's what dads are for.

Lionel, buddy, you're the coolest courier in town. Keep working at the double-bass, there's a jazz band in your future. You can have my PlayStation and MP3 and my Roger Maris bat and my mountain bike. If you're reading this, buddy, I won't be needing them. You can have my baseball card collection too if you promise not to sell it for at least ten years. I'll miss your goofy smile and dumb jokes and the way you spit food when you eat.

Maya, what can I say? I thought we'd have some part of destiny together, but we've been on parallel bike paths lately. I'm not good about expressing myself, always have to hide behind jokes but when a guy is faced with a serious situation, then it doesn't seem to matter anymore if you're embarrassed about something. I was hoping we could spend a lot of time together in the coming years but who knows if that would have been the case? You're sweet and beautiful and smart and a great friend, the best any guy could have. I've picked up a little something for you here in Paris and hope to get it to you one way or the other. Just stay away from Rick Oswald and all the other doofus guys like him, all right?

Guys, I don't know what is going to happen...but let's just say, so far...it's been a blast.

Love, Xerxes"

Xerxes fell into a restless sleep, tossing and turning, twisting in the blankets, hot, then cold, sweating, then freezing, like he was coming down with the flu. He dreamed about Yolanda, saw her in a stark room, bound and gagged, dark figures menacing her. He saw her tears, heard the fear in her voice, saw the terror on her face and the helplessness in the set of her limbs, the bowing of her head, blonde curls falling across her face. He knew she was scared witless and feeling terribly alone. In his dream, as in the waking world, he vowed to secure her freedom no matter the cost.

The kidnapper had told him they had to be in the hotel lobby by seven a.m. Xerxes surveyed the faces and saw they were as haggard and hollow-eyed as his. Once assembled, the kidnapper said they would receive further instructions. Stepping outside his door, Xerxes noticed an envelope on the carpeted hallway floor. He retrieved it and upon opening saw a Polaroid taken of Yolanda. Her body position was a kilter, with a stark, gray wall in the background, her limbs trussed with rope, a gag scissoring her mouth, her eyes shockingly wide screaming fear and helplessness. Clearly, these guys weren't fooling around. Feeling low and grim, Xerxes replaced the photo. He'd show it to Octave but no one else; no point in alarming the crew needlessly.

Xerxes knew they had sent the photo to unnerve him, to squeeze out every shred of confidence he may have felt but then he didn't know how he'd feel until he got to the spot and see what had to be done. He pocketed the envelope and took the elevator down to the lobby to join the others.

The mood was somber, even depressed, and the normally animated Stephanie, with the take-charge attitude, was deflated. Rufus merely nodded and Julien sipped a café au lait silently.

Stephanie's phone rang. She answered, listened for a moment and then handed the phone to Xerxes, who held it to his ear and then snapped it shut.

"We're to head out of the city," Xerxes said. "Then they'll call us on the way with further instructions. Julien, do you have a good map with you?"

"*Bien sûr,*" Julien replied. "Of course."

Xerxes got his cycling gear together and the crew piled into the van. Xerxes looked around for Octave. He had disappeared, but then he reappeared a moment later with his cycling gear in tow.

"What are you doing?" Xerxes asked.

"Trust me," Octave said.

"You won't be doing anything?"

"Let's see what happens when we get there," Octave said. "Nothing wrong with having another bike along, I don't think, Eeeks."

"Okay."

They lifted their bikes inside and closed the doors to the van. Xerxes sat up in the passenger seat while Julien drove. He headed out of the city as per the instructions but once they got on the motorway, the traffic was stop-and-go and according to the traffic report, there was a massive pile-up bringing it all to a standstill, making it to St-Denis on the outskirts of the city.

Stephanie's phone rang again. Xerxes had it cradled in his lap. He answered and then handed the phone to Julien, who spoke in rapid French, explaining the situation. The conversation went back and forth quickly and sharply, words exploding out of Julien's lips. Then he snapped the phone shut angrily and handed it back to Xerxes.

"They are not happy," he said. "But what are we to do in this mess, take a helicopter?" Xerxes smiled wryly but felt no joy. His thoughts turned to Yolanda and the photo where she looked so frightened and vulnerable. He'd quickly shown it to Octave as they were loading up the bikes. He glanced back and Octave gave him a thumbs up.

"I know where we are to go," Julien said. "But I do not know how long it will take to get there because of this traffic challenge."

After an hour of stop-and-go, the van pulled off to an exit where the ramp traffic was actually moving along at a reasonable rate of speed and the crew breathed a collective sigh of relief. They were actually getting somewhere. It was not a short trip. Some two hours later, Julien pulled off the highway and turned down a side road just before the entrance to a small town called Étoile—Star. Julien followed the road to the very end, turned down a dirt track and bumped along for almost half an hour and then pulled off to the side. "We have arrived," he said.

The crew tumbled out of the van. Muscles were stretched, yawns stifled, as Xerxes shivered involuntarily even though the day was mild. But the sun was masked by a cloudy morass. He retrieved his bicycle from the back of the van. Stephanie had the rest of his gear, the helmet and cycling shoes. Octave stopped him. He took Xerxes' bike from him and laid it in the back of the van.

"What are you doing?"

"You never asked me how I know about the Circle of Death," Octave replied quietly.

Xerxes had to strain to hear him. "Okay." He looked around at the others, who seemed distracted and weren't watching them. "How do you know?"

"You remember I told you that my father had a terrible cycling accident and broke his leg very badly?"

"Yes."

"He was young and foolish and had accepted a dare from a friend. That dare was to ride the Circle of

Death…and now you know the result. He was never able to ride again."

"But he survived."

"Yes," Octave admitted. "He survived, Eeeks." Octave spun the rear wheel of Xerxes' bike. "Pick up the bike and carry it over your shoulder, all right? Do not wheel it down the path."

Xerxes searched Octave's smooth, handsome face, seeking an answer. "Okay," he said and shrugged. He picked up the bike and put it over his shoulders. The others had turned to watch curiously but remained silent as they followed Julien down the path, over the rise toward the Circle of Death.

The path continued for some 300 meters where it mushroomed into a clearing. The first thing Xerxes saw was Yolanda, sitting on a tree stump with her hands tied behind her and her mouth gagged. But she looked all right, unharmed, at least physically. She was surrounded by black-clad riders—uniform, as if cut from a mold, same height and width and holding the same rigid posture, militaristic and menacing.

Xerxes stopped and the others stopped behind him. Julien was a few paces out front. Before them was a natural barrier; they were perched on a cliff face but a round section of the cliff was missing as if it had been cut out and the missing chunk looked to be 30 or 40 meters in diameter. The edges consisted of rock, some dark species of granite, and a ledge ran around the perimeter of the great, gaping hole before them.

Along the sides, the ledge was narrow, perhaps 30 centimeters, maybe less; on the opposite sides, top and bottom, the ledge thickened to about 2 meters in depth. One of the riders held a canister with a nozzle and was spraying a dark substance onto the ledge surface.

Octave moved up beside Xerxes. "What's that he's spraying?" Xerxes asked.

"It is oil. To make the ledge slippery." Xerxes' stomach clenched at this good news. "Of course, you have an advantage," Octave said.

"Oh yeah? What's that?"

"I have sprayed a light adhesive onto your tires to give you more of a grip so it is less likely that you will slip … but it will slow you down a little bit perhaps. It is up to you, Eeeks, what to do. You can use my bike without the adhesive and you will go faster."

"Great choice," Xerxes replied. "How far down is it?"

"About 15 meters. My father fell the whole way but he bounced off the sides first and landed on the grass below. That year, the spring rains had come early and the grass was thick. A bush slowed his fall and he did not die, so in this way, he was very lucky. It took a long time for the rescue. Back then, it was a big operation. Since that time, it has been forbidden to ride the Circle of Death. But my father spoke of it once or twice and I was able to do my own research. I don't know how *les rats d'égouts* found out about this place."

"I'm going to stick with the sticky bike," Xerxes said.

As Xerxes mulled over all of the enchanting possibilities, one of the black-clad riders stepped forward with a bike and motioned to him. Xerxes put his bike down on the ledge and walked it over. He could feel his feet sliding and at that moment he was grateful to Octave for thinking ahead and helping him out.

The dark rider spoke in a loud voice. He was making an announcement in French. Octave translated. Essentially, he was barking the ground rules for the competition. Here's how it worked: each rider had two two-minute heats where they rode around the ledge. The rider who completed the most laps won the heat. Of course, there was always the possibility of slipping and falling over the edge where serious injury or even, death, could occur. If Xerxes won the combined two heats, then Yolanda would be set free. The loser of the two heats had to then ride the ledge blindfolded and if the loser was Xerxes and he didn't drop over the ledge, again Yolanda would be set free. In fact, if he went over the edge, she would be set free in any case. If he went over, Xerxes would be in serious shape and in this isolated area, it would be unlikely he'd get help quickly, so this would also achieve the goals of the dark riders, who essentially wanted to teach Xerxes and his friends a hard, life lesson. This was way worse than final exams, Xerxes thought.

Octave had a very worried expression on his face as he recited the words to the gathered crowd. He hesitated a few times and his voice broke once or twice, thinking to himself, that *it should be me. It is my destiny to right the* wrong that happened to my father. Eeeks is just a novice, he doesn't have the experience and this is an impossible task for him, simply impossible, and *les rats d'égouts* know that, *bien sûr*.

The dark rider pointed at Xerxes ominously and asked if he was ready. Xerxes clamped his jaw, jammed on his helmet, adjusted the chinstrap and nodded. I'll have to feel my way the first few laps, he told himself.

The dark rider mounted his bike as one of the gang held it in position for him. The official scorekeeper, another ganger, held out a stopwatch, counted down and then the rider set off. Xerxes watched closely and it was obvious this guy had practiced. He'd done this before.

Octave stood beside Xerxes and whispered instructions. "Don't lean in too much on that curve, the ledge slopes slightly and you'll lose the balance, watch the mossy patch opposite. Try to keep upright; this isn't like the sprint, yes? Your body position needs to stay even, pump the pedals on the straighter parts and coast through the turns but at the arc of the turn, pump again. Don't jerk the handlebars, the front wheel will get crossed up…" And on and on until Xerxes' head was spinning.

"Okay, enough," he said.

The dark rider finished the first heat. He'd ridden well and completed thirteen full circuits in the first two minutes. Octave approached the timekeeper.

"I will be watching," he said. "There will be no hanky-panky, yes? No playing with the time, *comprenez?*" And he shook his forefinger at him. The dark-helmeted gang member remained impassive and didn't respond.

Octave helped Xerxes onto the bike. "Whatever you do, Eeeks, don't look over the ledge, yes? Just focus on the front wheel and no more. Make believe that the ledge is 20 meters wide, visualize it in your mind and you'll be okay. *D'accord?*" Xerxes nodded his agreement even if he didn't feel it, and his mouth and throat were so dry the Sahara could have been a reservoir, and his gut stretched tighter than a drum.

The timekeeper raised his hand. Xerxes gripped the handlebars as Octave rocked the bike as the count came down, three...two...one...he was off, wobbling at first but he quickly brought the bike under control. Somewhere in the background he heard yelling but he focused like a laser beam on the ledge and tuned everything else out.

Xerxes rode tentatively through the first curve as he felt the back wheel slide, but he jerked it back on track. Relax and focus...visualize like Octave said, expand the ledge, see it as 2 meters, then 3, then as wide as a highway...he took deep breaths and counted...and before him lay an expanse...six lanes of hardtop shimmering in the sun, heat rising off the tarred surface...

Through the second lap, Xerxes felt more confident and pushed the speed, taking the corners more tightly, pedaling up on the short straightaways, feeling the tires hug the curves.

By the third lap, Xerxes was in a comfortable zone, he'd lost the jitters and felt his way along the path, knew now where the pits lay, where the surface was smooth, feeling the grip of the tires and once again, he thanked Octave silently for the adhesive spray. Genius, he thought, pure genius.

Xerxes pushed himself through the fourth lap, feeling his legs loosen up as he relaxed into the motion. Something pinged off his helmet, and then again and again and again. Careful not to lose focus or concentration, he glanced quickly up, then left and then to the right. The figures were all a blur but he realized the Rat Bastards were throwing things at him…stones…sticks…all kinds of debris…whatever they could pick up and whip at him. Fortunately, the surrounding area was sparsely covered so there wasn't that much to find. No one had said anything about not throwing stuff and his crew was outnumbered. I am invincible, he told himself. No paltry bits of dirt or rock are going to slow me down or throw me off track, and to ram home the point, he accelerated, pushed the speed and turned slightly to smile at the crowd as he streamed by them.

The timekeeper barked and the heat was over. Xerxes had made eleven laps within the official period, which he felt wasn't bad for a first go-round, and he knew he could make up the two laps if he needed to.

Octave was slapping him on the back and shaking his hand. "Eeeks, that was awesome, yes? You rode like a pro. I think we are giving them runs for the money, yes?"

"Run for the money," Xerxes panted. "Pound it." And he held his fist up and they touched knuckles.

"That was amazing," Stephanie said but still looked worried. "You did incredibly well…"

"Great shots," Rufus said quietly, pulling back his wind-breaker to reveal the handicam. "Got it all. This is going to be one amazing episode."

"If we get out of here in one piece," Stephanie said. "Listen," she said, turning back to Xerxes. "I know this sounds lame but don't take any unnecessary chances, okay? I mean, if you have to bail, do it."

Xerxes nodded, realizing this thing was far from over. He'd done okay for the first part but there was more to come.

Yolanda had kept her eyes closed the entire time not daring to look but when she heard the hubbub she opened them and from the expression, what little he could see of her face, Xerxes thought she seemed relieved to see that he was still in one piece.

The timekeeper barked. Round two was about to get underway. The black-clad rider rode with confidence and it looked as if he would exceed the number of laps he'd completed in the first heat. The bike looked as if it were glued to that track, like it was on some sort of super accelerator, and it whizzed around…but then…on lap six, the rider over-compensated on the far corner, the back tire slid dangerously close to the edge…he jerked it back and the front twisted to the left…the bike fishtailed back and forth crazily while the dark rider adjusted his body position, wrangling the bike under control…he put his foot down to stop the momentum and the bike slid over the edge, coming to a dead stop…he paused for a split second, then sprang back into motion, trying to make up for the time he'd lost.

The Rat Bastard finished heat two with twelve laps and a combined total of twenty-five laps.

Xerxes got back on his bike and then blew air in and out, flooding his brain with oxygen. "Keep doing what you have done, Eeeks," Octave said. "Just go faster and stronger and do not worry…if these *rats d'égouts* throw anything, we will take care of it…focus on the riding alone, okay?"

Xerxes smiled at the defiance—the brazenness of it appealed to him…it buoyed him up and he felt calmer and more confident…not as hard as Drag Racers, he thought…one of his favorite videogames…if he could beat that game, then this was nothing, right?

The timekeeper's hand went up and Octave chimed in on the countdown. Xerxes put his feet into the stirrups, found his balance, as Octave held the bike from the rear and began rocking it back and forth…then he pushed off and was away, no wobble this time but solid and pushing through the curves and short flats with poise and certainty. Xerxes began to feel like he'd been doing this all his life and he knew he could do it, knew he could do better than his first heat. The question was...how much better? And would it be good enough to win?

Xerxes pushed everything else out of his mind. He didn't think about Yolanda or the consequences if he finished behind his rival...just gritted his teeth and kept his wits about him and watched the ledge intently, letting his instincts take over, and he felt the balance of the bike and the grip of the tires. Make it an extension of yourself...feel the ledge...the grip on the rock...

Xerxes sensed how close to the ledge he could go and kept his balance steady, no rocking or wobbling. Again, the faces blurred and melded into a single expressive stream as he whizzed by. He was going so fast he only caught fragments of images, the set of a mouth, the lifting of eyebrows, the wonder in a pair of eyes, worry lines etched into a forehead...a scowl here...a sneer there.

And then...the time was up...fourteen laps, three more than before and, as he braked in front of Octave skidding up to him, he wondered, what would their keepers do now? The heats were tied, twenty-five laps each. Would they exercise fair play and let them go, no questions asked?

Octave jumped up and down. He and Xerxes slapped hands as Stephanie and Rufus crowded around to congratulate him. After a long moment of euphoria, the group calmed down and Xerxes looked across the divide.

"What will they do now?"

Octave shook his head. "I don't know, Eeeks...I..." and he trailed off without finishing.

Curiosity reigned as the *rats d'égouts* put their helmeted heads together to figure out the next steps. The Rat Bastards were agitated; snatches of loud, angry phrases carried to them, arms and bodies twitched and jerked as the discussion carried on.

Finally, the Rat Bastards broke the huddle and the leader, the one who had ridden against Xerxes, jerked his hand toward them. Xerxes and Octave approached while Stephanie and Rufus hung back; however, Rufus was careful to keep the tiny handicam concealed but rolling the entire time.

The Rat Bastards spread out in a line in front of the Circle of Death assuming aggressive and defiant postures. The leader growled his instructions as Octave listened intently and when he'd finished, he turned to Xerxes.

"There is to be one last race…a, how do you say it…a chicken race? The two of you are to start at the top of the hill some 100 meters back and race forward to the Circle of Death. The first rider to stop will be the loser. If you, Eeeks, stop first…"

"Bail, you mean?"

"Right, the bail…he said that Yolanda would die. If he is the one to, er, bail…then Yolanda will be liberated."

"*Voilà*," the Rat Bastard leader spat and poked Xerxes viciously in the chest. Xerxes grabbed his forefinger and bent it away from him, forcing the Rat Bastard to grimace in pain. Before his gang could jump in, Xerxes let him go. The Rat Bastard leader straightened up slowly, his attention focused only on Xerxes.

"I think you have made him a bit angry," Octave whispered. They walked away from the gang toward the bikes.

"Good. Maybe he'll have second thoughts." Octave shrugged, as if saying, this could be possible.

"What's going on?" Stephanie demanded.

"A chicken run," Xerxes said. "From that hill back there to the edge of the Circle of Death."

"Oh no," Stephanie said. "No way...you cannot do this...under no circumstances."

"So we let Yolanda die?"

"They're not going to kill her."

"How do you know?" Xerxes asked, exasperated and angry.

Stephanie leaned in. "Because we'll be witnesses and they'd have to kill us too."

"You've been reading way too many detective novels," Xerxes said. "Witnesses to what? We can't identify any of them. If I don't do this, Yolanda has no chance and you've got nothing to say about it." Xerxes walked away.

Stephanie, not to be outdone, stamped her feet and gritted her teeth. "Oh...you..." She fumed. She stomped off in the opposite direction.

Octave took Xerxes by the arm and walked him to the van. "This time, I think, you use my bike, okay?"

Xerxes looked at him, saw the concern on his face and then nodded. "Okay."

They lifted the bike out of the van and set it on the ground. The Rat Bastard leader approached with four of his crew; his mouth formed a wide sneer under the visor and then he spat something out in rapid French.

Xerxes looked at Octave whose eyes were blazing but he shook his head, refusing to translate. Xerxes shrugged and looked into himself.

Xerxes went to his core…started with the breathing, just like he was taught in the dojo when he was younger. There was the life force, the pure energy he'd need to see him through this encounter, this episode, and he narrowed his worldview and focused on himself. Electricity flowed through his limbs—the sound of his breath and the beating of his heart, each action came like a frame of film, slow and fractured, flickering before him…he watched it unfold…

The timekeeper raised his hand, Xerxes saw his mouth open and heard slow, elongated sound emerge…counting down…numbers stretching into eternity… three… two… one…Xerxes felt his bike rocking back and forth, lulling and cradling him as he drew breath in and the bike was free…hurtling down the hill toward the Circle of Death…energy flowed into his body and he knew what he had to do, knew unequivocally that there was only one choice. He'd known it all along, but it wasn't until that moment that he fully realized it was the only way…the only guarantee of a complete victory. Drag Racer…nothin' compared to this. Way too cool.

Octave screamed encouragement as he watched Xerxes and the Rat Bastard leader take off, tires spinning, legs pumping, torsos rigid, helmets bent over the handlebars but then he thought... *un moment*... something was wrong... terribly wrong, and his yells of encouragement turned into screams, into cries of help and warning...then Octave exploded into action sprinting toward the Circle of Death.

Stephanie couldn't watch; she turned her face away and shut her eyes and ears out from the noise and the spectacle. If it was something she couldn't control, she didn't want to know about it. And she didn't want to think about the consequences if something should go terribly wrong.

Rufus was riveted to the spot. He knelt down and while the hubbub and excitement burbled around him, he kept his camera focused on the action and My God, he exclaimed silently, it was amazing. He prayed that Xerxes' helmet-cam didn't crap out on them. Like all cameramen, he kept himself emotionally distanced from the unfolding action. By viewing it through a lens, he was barricaded from the direct experience; it couldn't touch him.

No one else seemed to have noticed in all of the craziness, but Julien had disappeared somewhere.

Yolanda was frightened, more frightened than she'd ever been in her life. She couldn't believe what was happening, that she was in this bizarre situation and that Xerxes, of all people, would risk his life for her. She wanted to cry out, to warn him to get away, to stop this madness, but her screams only echoed in her own ears. All she could do was grunt and moan through the tape stretched viciously across her mouth.

She watched, horrified, as Xerxes pumped toward the Circle of Death. He and the dark rider were even, neck and neck, their legs jackhammering at the pedals, moving furiously as they leapt toward the cauldron, the unforgiving, black hole that would swallow them up…finally…she couldn't stand it, she couldn't just sit there and do nothing…she'd never forgive herself if she did. All eyes were riveted on the two riders…

Yolanda stood up, then lowered her body and rammed the Rat Bastard nearest her. He toppled over, off-balance and taken totally by surprise…and then it was all a chain reaction as the area exploded. Yolanda saw what she thought was an army of red ants on bicycles swarming in, blanketing the Rat Bastards and suddenly she was adrift in a sea of writhing bodies as Reds fought the Blacks and one by one forced the Rat Bastards to the ground and handcuffed them. It was like some kung fu fantasy, red and black battling each other, arms chopping, legs kicking out. Behind her, she saw Julien, who smiled, then swiveled and pointed, shouting to those closest to him. Yolanda turned and emitted a muffled gasp.

Xerxes kept his tunnel vision…oblivious to the actions around him. Within his organic radar, he computed the distance to the ledge and increased his velocity; he became the hurricane, the windmill unleashing unbridled power, pent-up and panting, engaging him to soar.

A hand ripped the tape from across her mouth just as Yolanda screamed, "Nnnnoooo!"

The Rat Bastard leader jerked to the right, putting his bike into a skid, hitting the ground, falling to his side while he clawed desperately at the meager grass and scrub, praying for a grip, something, anything, to grab on to. He opened his throat and emitted a deep, gut-wrenching groan as the bike shot out into the distance and banged off the rock walls, careening and twisting like a tortured animal, and then smashed itself on the jagged outcrop below. A boot stomped on the Rat Bastard's wrist, holding him while he dangled. Callused hands reached down, grabbing his shoulders and jersey, hauling him up roughly to the surface where he was forced face down into the ground, arms behind him. Handcuffs were snapped smartly around his wrists as he writhed and bellowed his rage and humiliation.

Then all ceased and the air was calm. Yolanda couldn't move, couldn't do anything as everyone turned and watched. Even Stephanie forced herself to look. Octave clenched his fists and prayed.

Xerxes bike rocketed off the ledge, soaring as he tucked himself in, riding a fiery chariot across the sky; it caught the glow of the sun, light radiated from his helmet, dazzling, awe-inspiring, downright scary and the eyes and heads of the assembly turned and followed his path, measured every millimeter of progress as the bike arced, reached its zenith over the center of the Circle of Death, and gradually began its descent. The question remained...did he have enough momentum? These watching faces were ancient, excavated from ruins, discovered in famous museums—a medieval frieze, a snapshot of the longest moment in time when every heart, every breath stopped.

Xerxes' front tire touched the far ledge; he jerked forward over the handlebars. The tire found its grip then spun toward nowhere, sending smoke and dust straight up in a desperate plume and then it slipped and the faces in the frieze formed a collective "OH" of horror and fear...the front of the bike slid down the rock face, handlebars pointed downward as the back of the bike and its rear wheel went vertical, somersaulting forward. Xerxes released his grip, tucked his head into his chest and flew forward...the bike plummeted like an anvil but Xerxes was gone, flying ahead, flipping over and over onto the grassy surface until he came to rest on the far side of the Circle of Death lying flattened, his breath knocked totally out of him...weakly...he raised his fist skyward and croaked out a triumphant squeak. That was better than Drag Racing 2 and Road Warrior combined, he said to himself as he rolled to his side and shakily, one foot at a time, climbed to his feet, where he wavered in the slight breeze.

Stephanie and Rufus raced toward him. Octave leapt into the air screaming his delight. Yolanda cried, sobbing into her hands.

The Red Riders stripped off their helmets and lo and behold, their leader was none other than Capitaine Poulin, who said, "You have led us on the merry dance, Monsieur. My apologies for our tardiness." Xerxes looked around in disbelief. The rest of the Red Riders were the compact Vietnamese men that had boxed them in before entering the restaurant, except for Sergeant Fortin, and they were the riders who'd appeared when he and Octave had gone out cycling.

"Wow," Xerxes said. "I'm impressed." The others remained speechless.

Julien came over and shook Poulin's hand, who in turn faced the crew. "Please let me introduce you to my superior officer, Chief Inspector Julien Renard."

"What?" Stephanie and Rufus cried as sirens shrilled through the afternoon dampness and several vans and police cars appeared flashing their lights.

"Good to meet you, Chief Inspector. Just in the nick of time," Xerxes said, pumping Julien's hand.

"I too, was a little bit worried, my friend. But I think it worked out in the end."

Octave shook Julien's hand as well. "I will never underestimate the Sûreté again," he said.

Julien shrugged. "We are accustomed to this . . . and it is a good way to surprise the enemy, I think."

Yolanda was untied finally, and she marched up to Xerxes. He flinched, not knowing what to expect. She stared at him for a long, tense moment . . . then threw her arms around him in a crushing hug; then she stepped back and slapped him hard on the face. Xerxes spun around, his cheek stinging. "You big idiot," she said. "You could have been killed." And then she hugged him again.

Xerxes was confused but figured it was worth it. He looked down. "Hey, what are you crying for? Everything's okay…just don't slap me again. Man, that stings."

Yolanda laughed through her tears. "You don't get it, do you?"

"Get what?"

"I've been so mean to you…"

Xerxes thought of her attitude and cutting remarks. "Oh that, hey a few words here and there…you know…"

Yolanda groaned and stepped back. "Why do you have to be so nice?"

"Huh? Sorry…I…uh, I…"

"You don't get it," she said shrilly. Xerxes looked at Octave who gave him a look that said go easy, she's really demented. Then Yolanda pushed him hard in the chest. "It was me, you idiot…me…me…me…who did all those things to you…trashed your bike…shot at you with BBs in the park…put the mousetraps by your door…splashed painted on your mom's car…trashed your hotel room…hello?"

"Bbbuttt why?"

Stephanie strolled up with a dark look on her face. "Tell him," she said.

Yolanda looked at Stephanie, then at Xerxes and nodded. "I was angry and bitter and jealous. You see, X, my brother had auditioned for Mira and Max and they liked him. He was supposed to have this job, not you. Then you came along and . . . well, he lost out, so . . . I tried everything I could to scare you off . . . but then this big, ugly, creepy guy kept showing up and I decided to back off a little bit . . ."

Xerxes laughed. "That was Brutal . . ."

"A friend of yours?"

Xerxes bent over. "No," he said. "No, that's the thing. He's my worst enemy . . ."

"I don't get it," Yolanda said.

Xerxes straightened up. "Me neither. The guy's weird . . ."

Yolanda shuddered. "And creepy."

Xerxes turned to Stephanie. "You knew about this?"

"Not the pranks, X. Just the fact that Yolanda was steamed about her brother. But I told her to be a professional about it and put it all behind her. She promised me, she would . . ."

As they talked, the Rat Bastards were hauled up and loaded into the vans and police cars. Julien came over to them.

"We have been tracking this gang for a very long time," he said. "We were aware of the young Monsieur's problems with them and kept him under surveillance. We also knew about your television series, *Get Outta Town!* and were prepared when you all flew into Paris. We know, too, about your secret mission . . . your secret ride down the Eiffel Tower . . . there is not too much we don't know."

Stephanie and Rufus exchanged blank looks. Xerxes was impressed and he pointed at Julien who gave him the "I got you" signal and they exchanged grins. "But we're still going to be able to do it, right? The ride. I mean, we've got to … it's the perfect end to the show, what do you say, Julien, I mean, Chief Inspector? It'd be good for tourism."

Julien pawed the ground with his right shoe for a moment. "I suppose, we might turn a blind eye, just this once…"

Xerxes let out a whoop and gave Octave a high five and a series of finger slaps and hooks, ending with a brotherly hug.

"I did not think you were going to make it over the Circle of Death," Octave said.

"It was pretty close," Xerxes admitted, "closer than I would have liked, for sure. I figured I had enough speed going but it was a bit risky."

Octave laughed at Xerxes' understatement. "Yes, you could say that," he replied.

The crew piled into the van. Julien assigned a police driver and they headed back to the hotel for a much-needed break. Back in his room, Xerxes stripped out of his cycling gear and took a long, hot shower. His back was sore from the hard landing he took but otherwise he was okay, and then he stretched out on the bed for a quick nap. He had an hour before they were to meet up for dinner. Julien arranged for the police driver to stay with them for the next few days.

Xerxes was dropping off to sleep when the phone rang. Groggily, he reached for the receiver.

"Ah, young Monsieur, Julien Renard here..."

"Mmm, Chief Inspector..."

"My apologies for disturbing you but I am calling every-one. A serious matter has occurred. In the confusion of the day, with all of the excitement, one of the gang members has escaped. I wish to give you a fair warning, young Monsieur, to be careful and look over your shoulder, yes? We are remaining vigilant and you will remain under our surveillance in case this criminal does something danger-ous or foolish... like an act of revenge, perhaps..."

"Ah, I see. That's wonderful news. Thank you for letting me know, Chief Inspector. We will be very careful."

"Good. Good. As I said, we will be watching, discreetly, of course. Goodbye for the moment."

"Goodbye."

Xerxes hung up the phone and tried to fall back asleep but found he couldn't. He got dressed and took the eleva-tor down to Octave's room and knocked on the door. Octave answered, talking on a cell phone, and beckoned Xerxes in.

XIII

Octave spoke for a moment longer and then snapped the phone shut. "I have been talking to my parents. They will be home in a week's time. They were asking how things were going with the filming and I told them that everything was fine. There were no problems. It had all gone very smoothly," he said, flashing an impish grin. It's a good thing parents don't know everything that goes on. Usually the last to know, in fact. Xerxes thought about Darius and Hilka and how much he'd be telling them and concluded, not much.

"Renard called you?" Xerxes asked.

"*Oui.* It is worrisome, don't you think?"

Xerxes sloughed it off. "The guy's got nothing. His entire crew is behind bars facing serious charges. He's probably in Switzerland by now."

"You are confident of this?"

"Absolutely," he replied with a total lack of the confidence he'd put out there for Octave's sake. "Totally. Let's go eat."

Downstairs in the lobby, Stephanie had a surprise. Max and Mira had flown in to be with them for the final day of shooting. The next day was a holiday and there was to be a massive fireworks display and a concert at the Eiffel Tower, which Rufus hoped to include as the perfect wrap-up to the show.

As a treat, Max and Mira were taking the whole crew to L'Atelier de Joel Robuchon, one of the most popular and exclusive restaurants in Paris, situated at 5 rue de Montalembert.

"I have heard of this place and the chef, he is quite famous," Octave said. "But never have I eaten there. My parents told me about it and said it was not to be missed."

"Sounds like good eats," Xerxes said. "I could eat an entire soufflé. Let's hit the road." Stephanie and Yolanda had on their good duds—a dress for each of them, which wasn't a stretch for Stephanie, and Xerxes wondered if she'd loaned Yolanda something. Still, they both looked great. Sheepishly, he looked over his khakis, clean though, and scuffed trainers and Polo shirt. No jacket and tie, and he wondered if they'd let him in. "Ladies, you are both looking lovely this evening."

"Such a flatterer," Mira said and cackled.

"Thank you," Stephanie said.

"Thanks," Yolanda said curtly, still not used to the fact that it was okay to be nice to him now. "I think I liked it better when I hated you."

"Heh-heh," Xerxes said.

Max trailed behind Mira as they piled into the van.

The restaurant was designed like a series of bars, with open cooking areas where the patrons sat at counters and watched the food being made. Each dish was served directly from the stove, oven or griddle, depending on what was ordered, and cooked individually to order.

The crew ate well. Xerxes didn't hold back. He sampled spaghetti *à notre façon*, turbot and potato purée, clams stuffed with garlic, crisp mackerel tart and a mango and banana dessert crêpe that was to die for. At the end of it, Xerxes thought he was going to die.

"Man, that was heaven but I am feeling like a bursting balloon."

"Don't explode," Octave said laughing.

"No guarantees," Xerxes replied.

Xerxes and Octave even scored a glass of wine each, even though technically they were underage. Octave drank wine regularly at home with his parents during meals, as many teens do in France and other European countries.

It was a night to blow off steam, to release all the tensions and stress and not worry about perpetrators of revenge. Yolanda, to show she was human and warming up to him, actually squeezed Xerxes' bicep once with what was almost something approaching affection. As they left the restaurant, she even took his arm and kissed him on the cheek by the elevator...so it was all rather divine. The crew couldn't stay out too late; they had an early call in the morning and were back in the hotel by eleven o'clock.

Xerxes got back to his room and crashed, too tired to send a few emails or keep his blogs up to date.

He awoke the next morning at 6:30 a.m. and jumped into the shower— a good thing because most, if not all, the hot water disappeared at a little past nine when most of the guests awoke. He got dressed and was downstairs on time for 7:15 a.m.

Everyone was there, including their new driver, a fellow called Pierre who was young with long, wispy hair and a bright smile.

"Morning everyone," Mira cackled. "So this is it. The wrap day. The end of our first shoot together. I think we've got a great show in the can. So, let's end it how it began... with a bang."

"She doesn't mean that literally," Max said calmly, as he handed out juices, cafés au lait and croissants he'd picked up. Despite the gargantuan meal of the evening before, Xerxes and Octave dug in.

Mira poked Xerxes in the belly. "Where did that all go?" He grinned, crumbs flaking his lips. "Ah, to be young again." And she chortled away. Xerxes held the grin until he thought his face would crack.

The presence of Max and Mira meant that another van was required. The two acted more like parents, shooing and cooing, fussing and clacking, than hard-nosed producers. It was decided that Max would drive the second van and follow Pierre.

The police had retrieved Octave's bike from the floor of the Circle of Death but it was pretty badly damaged. The front wheel had collapsed and the rear-wheel rim had sustained multiple dents. Train wreck, Xerxes thought. Both tire tubes had exploded but the frame was intact as were the gears, so it was salvageable.

Max had found a bike shop that loaned them slick, new mountain bikes in exchange for a credit on the show. A deal was done and Xerxes and Octave each had new bikes, not to mention, the bikes had to be special—they had to fold down and fit into a large knapsack and smuggled into the Eiffel Tower in preparation for the ride down.

The small convoy proceeded up Boulevard Garibaldi, streaming into traffic, horns blaring continually, cars glued to the bumper in front, in short, a normal traffic day in Paris. Max had lived in LA and was used to gridlock. He stayed calm, keeping close to Pierre in front. After Place Cambronnie, Boulevard Garibaldi turned into Boulevard de Grenelle. Then at Quai Branley, they took a quick right turn just at the banks of the Seine near the Port de Suffren and the Tower itself. The rather short trip took almost forty-five minutes.

"Hurry up and wait," Rufus muttered, always anxious to get going as the shots accumulated in his mind; he needed to get them out and make them real.

Stephanie had snagged the special parking permits allowing them to park near the base of the Tower so they didn't have to lug their gear too far. The vans stopped and everyone got out and began unloading.

Xerxes and Octave practiced folding up the bikes without too much luck because neither had done it before and the bikes weren't the usual ones they rode. To the casual observer, they looked like frustrated tourists trying to fold down large road maps snapping in the wind.

Mira cackled. Stephanie and Yolanda pointed and sniggered while Rufus got it all on tape. All of the antics made the two even more frustrated.

Finally, Xerxes gave his bike a kick and it jerked into place. "Hey, it worked. Maybe I'll try banging on the TV when it goes on the blink."

Octave watched him sourly. "What is this...on the blink." And he blinked his eyes repeatedly.

"Ah no," Xerxes said. "You know, Bro', when the boob tube gives up the ghost, goes all fuzzy, you know? So you give it a good chop and slap it back into line."

"This works?"

"Hardly ever...but sometimes..." Then he looked directly at the camera. "Don't try that or this at home, folks. You need a special license." Then he stared disgustedly at the bike, now positioned at strange angles, lying on the grass.

"Fellas," Max said. "Let me give you a hand. Used to work in a bike shop when I was in college." Calmly, he showed the two hotheads how to fold the bikes down, then open them up, making certain all the parts locked into place. The last thing a rider wanted was the front end of the bike collapsing while shooting down a steep, bumpy and potentially treacherous decline. "Got it? Now you give it a try on your own."

Xerxes and Octave sighed deeply, but followed Max's instructions slowly and carefully. Each went through the frustrating maneuver twice before Max nodded his assent. Rufus gave the thumbs up as Xerxes raised his hands in triumph.

"Even better than beating the Circle of Death," he said.

"Pound it," Octave replied and the two touched knuckles. Rufus was laughing so hard he could barely keep the camera steady.

Xerxes and Octave hefted their knapsacks onto their backs and the crew trooped toward the Tower entrance. Xerxes stopped and stared.

"Now, that is something else," he said, looking straight up.

Stephanie flashed the passes to gain admittance and the crew went through the turnstiles while Mira and Max and Stephanie spoke with the security officials.

Rufus, Yolanda, Xerxes and Octave took the elevator up and got out at the second level. Rufus got busy with his setup and mounted portable lights on the camera so he could follow the action as he needed up and down the stairs. Xerxes had his helmet-cam set up and Rufus had rigged one for Octave as well, so they would capture both perspectives. Stephanie manned a second camera at the bottom of the stairs. Rufus was confident they'd get good video coverage and could stop and start as it suited them.

It was still early, just before opening time, so the corridors were empty for the moment but tourists and other members of the public would soon be let in.

Thirty minutes passed while Xerxes and Octave waited patiently at the top of the stairs and Rufus comple light and sound checks. Stephanie had co-opted some walkie talkies from the security office so they could coordinate the action at the top and track it coming down. Rufus and Stephanie figured it would take about five minutes for the actual ride and perhaps even less depending on how quickly Octave and Xerxes were able to move down the steps and if they'd need to stop and do another setup further down.

Xerxes and Octave assembled the bikes. Rufus checked to make sure everything was snapped into place. "Looks solid," he said. "Don't want you fellahs to take a tumble if you don't have to …"

"I second that notion," Xerxes said.

"Me also," said Octave. "If I fall, it will be because I do not ride well and then I can blame myself but this …" and he gestured at the bike, "a mechanical failure would be a disaster, no?"

"Yes," Rufus said. "We don't want any of those and we don't want anyone to get hurt." Voices began to echo up the stairwell. "Looks like the Tower is in business, boys."

Octave was first up and swung a leg over his bike while Xerxes steadied him. Yolanda had a stopwatch going that she synchronized with Stephanie at the bottom of the Tower so they could get an accurate read on how much the race down would take.

?"

e the squawky voice back.

"

"Okay…in five…four…three…" She gestured to Octave, showing him the numbers on her fingers. "Two…one…go…"

Like a skier at the top of a mountain, Octave tensed at the countdown, then pushed off and sailed out into space. "AAAhhhhhhhhh…!" He took off so fast that he nearly rammed Rufus, who staggered back grasping for balance and slipping on the steps. Octave reached out and steadied the camera while squeezing the rear-brake caliper to slow his progress. Rufus banged into some tourists coming up the stairs and that stopped his momentum.

"Sorry, so sorry," Rufus said, then turned around and looked at who he'd smacked into. The fellow was tall as a building and almost as wide. "Really, really, sorry," he said. The big man glowered at him and merely shook his head. He let Rufus go and kept on climbing, his diminutive wife beside him frantically scrambling to keep up as he took the stairs three at a time.

Octave swept past and Rufus swung around and caught a shot from behind and then charged up the steps to where Xerxes waited tensely.

"Some guy as big as a barn gave me a real dirty look," Xerxes said.

"Uh, yuh, we met," Rufus said. "Ready to roll?" He glanced at Yolanda, who held her hand up and began the countdown while looking at the stopwatch.

"Three…two…one…Go!" Yolanda called.

Xerxes bounced off down the stairs, bumping and shaking. It brought back memories of the Boulevard of Broken

Dreams and, man, that seemed like such a long time ago. And he knew the Eiffel Tower wouldn't be as challenging as that narrow and treacherous ride.

The lighting in the corridor was harsh and threw him off. He found the physical adjustment awkward. The steps unfolded in a slow spiraling curve that required control, but it wasn't anything he hadn't done before and after the Circle of Death, well, this was a mere piffle really. He was a bit higher up in the beginning but it all appeared to be quite tame, so, just to demonstrate he was on the ball, he fired off a quick blog for the website: "Eiffel Tower, heading down, bumpy but fun, great for the kidneys."

Xerxes was making good time. There was a lot of vibration but no more than a turbulent plane ride or a roller-coaster. It felt like he was getting into a rhythm.

He dodged in and out of clumps of tourists puffing up the steps, eliciting cries of surprise, protest, some laughter and a little bit of anger and outrage. Somehow, he ended up holding an older woman's Pekingese that had jumped into his arms, yapping and licking his face. "Sheesh, down boy or girl or whatever you are..." Xerxes pulled hard on the brakes, grabbing at the side railing to slow himself down and then screeched to a halt. Carefully, he let the dog down and turned to resume the ride. It whimpered and then scampered after its mistress. A black-clad figure rose in front of him with a balaclava pulled down over its face.

Xerxes wobbled and when he saw a knife with the largest and sharpest-looking blade slicing the air in front of his nose, he arched back as if he were riding a bucking bronco; the front wheel reared up.

"Yikes!"

The hand with the knife struck the wheel and tangled in the spokes. Xerxes threw his weight forward, forcing the knife hand down, twisting it at an angle. His assailant let out a cry of surprise and pain, letting go of the blade and yanking frantically to free his hand. The assailant's body followed the pull on his wrist, forcing him face down on the steps, and Xerxes rolled right over him, kicking the attacker's hand free of the spokes as he passed, eliciting more cries of pain and anguish. Xerxes was pumped now— adrenalin surged through him and he didn't care, he hit the afterburners and tore down the steps, ignoring anyone he hit or scattered before him.

"Out of the way," he roared.

Xerxes was going so fast that he caught up with Octave, who, sensing chaos and commotion behind him, turned and saw Xerxes bombing down the stairs, looking like a kamikaze pilot on the loose.

"*Mon Dieu!*" Xerxes' bike jerked so much he thought the vibration alone would break him and the bike into a million pieces. Then Octave saw the black-clad maniac and a vicious knife gleaming under the fluorescent lights in his outstretched hand.

Octave didn't need any prompting; he took it all in within a split-second and kicked his bike into high gear and he and

Xerxes, now just inches apart, careened down the steps as their crazed assailant took the stairs downward at leaps, barely keeping his balance, swiping and jabbing as he went, hiss and spittle spraying from his lips.

Stephanie was perplexed. She heard Rufus' garbled, high-pitched patter, not understanding a word of his gibberish. These darn walkie talkies sucked. Puzzled, she looked up and spotted Octave scorching toward her with Xerxes hard on his heels and some lunatic lunging and spitting behind them.

Stephanie backed up, then turned and ran toward the main entrance, screaming. Hold it, Steph. Stop. You're a professional. Get the shot. Get the shot, she told herself. So, she turned and knelt and focused the camera.

Octave whizzed by her, infinitesimally followed by Xerxes and a microsecond later, the groaning and grunting maniac, who ignored her as they zoomed by. She swiveled to get the shot.

First Octave, then Xerxes, and finally, the maniac, burst through the exit doors. They bumped down the steps ... the rogue Rat Bastard bunched at the knees. In one fluid motion he uncoiled into a powerful full-frontal leap into space, latching himself onto Xerxes' back, his powerful hands gripping Xerxes' shoulders, feet dragging on the ground as Xerxes pedaled furiously, hoping to throw him off, but the maniac's grip ratcheted around him.

As Xerxes pedaled faster and faster, the Rat Bastard dug his nails deeper but then slipped on the smooth material of

Xerxes' jersey and was dragging his ankles on the pavement. Xerxes pedaled and pedaled through molasses slowed by the extra weight of his assailant.

Octave split off and swung around in a wide arc, rode up parallel to them and kicked at the man's hands. By now, the assailant had the knife between his teeth; he released his left hand slowly, seized the blade and swiped wildly at Octave who lashed out with his right foot striking the rogue Rat Bastard in the abdomen, doubling him up. A thin line of blood opened up along Octave's thigh. He looked down, not realizing he'd been cut, but felt something wet running down his leg. Then a searing pain burned him. He cried out and dropped back suddenly; the bike swam woozily along the tarmac.

Xerxes craned around and saw what happened. He realized the knife would be plunging into his neck at any moment. He squeezed the brakes and pulled his weight over, sending the bike into a wild skid, pulling left, then right, forcing himself and the rogue Rat Bastard off-balance. The swings of the knife went wild, missing their lethal mark. Xerxes ducked left, ducked right, did everything he could to avoid the sinister blade.

Xerxes forced the bike to its side, hitting the ground and pinning the rogue Rat Bastard's left hand beneath the frame. In a nanosecond, Xerxes was up, had his feet out of the stirrups and sprinted toward the parking lot and the vans. He took a quick peek behind him and the rogue Rat Bastard was up on his feet, his left hand rigid, wrist cocked, arm whipping behind and then unfurled in a surging action; a whizzing sound sang out, the rogue Rat Bastard tensed, another whiz like bees buzzing and the second dart found its mark. The rogue Rat Bastard convulsed going up on his toes, teetering, teetering, his eyes rolled in his head, then he slid face forward, throwing the knife into the tarmac as horrified parents covered their children, husbands shielded their wives and some Samaritans guarded their pets, all quivering in terror. The rogue Rat Bastard lay peacefully snoring in a crumpled heap oblivious to all.

Xerxes turned and watched. Before he could register what was happening, police cars screamed up, lights flashing, tires screeching. Capitaine Poulin and Sergeant Fortin jumped out of the back of a car, guns drawn, and cautiously approached the dark-clad figure lying prone on the ground sleeping like a baby.

Capitaine Poulin knelt over the body, holstered his pistol and gestured impatiently to the paramedics. "*Viennez içi. Vite. Vite.*" The rogue Rat Bastard moaned, unconsciously reaching for the knife, but Sergeant Fortin sent it skittering away from him where it was picked up and bagged as evidence by a police officer. Two paramedics lifted a gurney out of the back of an ambulance. The rogue Rat Bastard was lifted and strapped in. Poulin gestured for two of his men to go with the paramedics. The ambulance then backed away and took off with two of the squad cars following on to the hospital, siren wailing.

Another paramedic was cleaning Octave's wound. He grimaced when the antiseptic was applied but when he saw Xerxes observing him, quickly gave the thumbs up.

"How you doin', Bro'?"

"Eeeks, it is going to be okay."

"You're sure?"

Octave spoke to the paramedic. "The wound is not deep," the paramedic said. "It will require the antiseptic and perhaps a shot of the tetanus…to be safe." Then he nodded, closed up his bag and walked back to the idling ambulance.

"You see?" Octave said.

"Well, you're lucky."

"Why is that?" Thinking that lucky was the last thing he would call himself.

"Your cycling career will continue, unlike your dad's."

Octave thought for a moment, then his eyes opened up and he nodded thoughtfully. "Yes, you are right about that. The Circle of Death did not get me."

"Or me, Bro', or me." Xerxes paused. "This has been one heckuva trip."

"Pound it." Octave held up his fist and he and Xerxes touched knuckles grinning at each other like a couple of helpless fools.

Yolanda and Stephanie dashed up. "Are you okay?" Yolanda asked.

"It is nothing," Octave replied stoically.

"It doesn't look like nothing," Stephanie replied. "You don't have to be macho around us, you know."

"Macho?"

"You know what I mean."

Xerxes stood behind her and pretended to flex his muscles and puff out his chest. "Er, yes, yes, I do…I think…" Then he stifled a snort.

Octave got to his feet and began to limp over to the van. Yolanda took his bike for him and the *Get Outta Town!* crew walked into the early-afternoon sun.

That evening the Eiffel Tower was lit up, majestic and magnificent against the skyline. Fireworks shot into the sky as tens of thousands of people camped out at its base. Music blasted out of suspended speakers. Andrea Bocelli's "Romanza" filled the air as the sky blinked and winked and dazzled with phosphorescent light. The music was not to Xerxes' taste but he had to admit, it created a mood of inspiration. Rufus was in heaven, recording it all. He had Xerxes and Octave in the frame with the Tower in the background, flares and rockets shooting out behind them, music swelling up around them. This was Xerxes' final stand up in Paris.

"I had an amazing time here," he said facing the camera. "Paris is one of the most exciting cities in the world and if you open your mind and let the city and its people welcome you, you will have an experience you will never forget." He turned to Octave. "Octave, my friend, you have been an amazing host, a terrific competitor and an all-round great guy. I'm glad to have met you and I'm happy that we had the chance to cycle around this magnificent city together."

"Eeeks, I had a blast. It was great meeting up with you too. You have inspired me to continue on with my goal of competing in the Tour de France."

Xerxes, back at the camera: "Paris is definitely a place to visit for action and adventure, but remember…don't try this at home. I'll see you next time on *Get Outta Town!* Pound it." He turned to Octave and they touched knuckles together.

"Cut!" Rufus called. "That's a wrap, everybody." Cheers and clapping from the crew. Mira came around and kissed everybody, even some of the bystanders, who watched with good-natured amusement. Chief Inspector Julien Renaud was there, along with Capitaine Poulin and Sergeant Fortin, who shook hands with everyone.

"We may need to call you back," Julien said to Xerxes. "In case of a trial."

"Happy to come back," Xerxes said. "I can crash with Octave, right?"

"*Absolument*," Octave said. "Of course."

"We'll let you know. And on behalf of the Sûreté, I wish to thank you in the formal sense for all your aid during your stay, and that of your companions."

"Our pleasure," Xerxes said, cutting in before anyone could answer. They shook hands all round and then the police took their leave.

Xerxes caught Yolanda giving him a thoughtful look but his mind saw in the night sky, smack in the centre of a

Roman candle, Maya and Rick Oswald in a steep embrace. He smiled back at her distractedly but Yolanda stuck out her tongue at him. Well, he thought, situation normal. He figured he'd have a few stories to tell his homies for sure. It had been an intense and exciting experience. And although he was anxious to get home…at the same time, Xerxes Frankel began to itch a little bit for the next adventure… just around the corner.

Next Episode: Mr. X and the Cog Train from Heaven

PARIS:
PLACES TO GO

RESTAURANTS:

Il Gallo Nero
This restaurant is located on a corner with big, full-length windows that allow you to look out and see everyone traveling by – and, passers-by can look in to see what you are eating. Il Gallo Nero is a friendly place with tasty espresso ice cream.
Address: 36, rue Raymond Losserand, 14th

Le Paradis Thai
Sure, it might look tacky from the outside with its pink neon sign and a mock Thai temple entrance guarded by elephant statues, but when you walk in, live fish swim beneath your feet under a glass floor.
Address: 132, rue de Tolbiac, 13th

Chez Hanna
This restaurant is cheap(ish) and cheerful – it serves great falafel while playing cheesy 80s music. It's somewhere fun to stop for decent food with good-sized portions. As an added bonus, it's pink with twinkly lights!
Address: 34, rue de Rosiers, 3rd

Le Bistral
Le Bistral's floor has old, inlaid wine crates, and the walls are decorated with fun pictures. Book in advance to be sure you get a table at this busy restaurant – a sure sign that the food is tasty! Try the *tarte tatin* made of endives and goat cheese for a starter, and lamb with Parmesan sauce, aubergines, tomatoes and endives for a main course.
Address: 80, rue Lemercier, 17th

Fumoir

The food here is special: you get a little bowl of mussel soup when you sit down just to whet the appetite. Next, try the tuna poached with fennel, dill and pastis, and then try the blueberry pie. The Fumoir is just opposite the Louvre, which makes it very handy for sufferers of fine art fatigue.
Address: rue de L'Amiral Coligny

Chez Izoi

This restaurant is small, super-romantic and fun. Not a *great* restaurant, but oh so Parisian!
Address: 1, rue de l'ecole polytechnique
Tel: 01 43 25 95 77

Le Gamin de Paris

Franco-Moroccan, and famous for the honey duck.
Address: 49, rue Vieille du temple

Refuge des Fondues

This dinner spot is not to be missed. Go with a group of friends or go just as a couple, but be sure to make reservations. Order the cheese fondue and you'll have a delicious time.
Address: 17, rue Trois Frères
Tel: 01 42 55 22 65

Willy's Wine Bar

Said to be the best wine bar in Paris.
Address: 13, rue Petits Champs

Au Vieux Paris d'Arcole

An all-time favorite located near Notre Dame. If you're hungry, try the escargot (snails). Go down the stairs to visit the wine cave.
Address: 24, rue Chanoinesse

Le Pain Quotidien

The place to go if you're craving brunch!
Address: 2, rue Petits Carreaux or 18, place Marché St Honoré

Le loir dans la théeire

Another "no-miss" for brunch or lunch.
Address: 3, rue des Rosiers

For a hip night out on the town, visit these trendy places:

Buddy Bar (near the American embassy, Métro Concorde, also a good dinner), Bar Fly (Champs Élysées), Opus Café.
Website: www.frenchguys.com

Outdoor Amusement Parks:

Disneyland
Disneyland is Paris' biggest attraction. It is located 20 miles from the center of Paris and connected by public transport. The magical world of Walt Disney will please children of all ages. It offers entertainment, sports and leisure facilities and other attractions such as day and night parades, shows, a variety of shops and restaurants.
How to get there: RER line A: TGV station straight at the park; Car: motorway A4 Metz-Nancy to exit 14
Open: 9am to 8pm
Price: from 1 to 3 days: adults from 27 euros to 73 euros, children from 23 euros to 62 euros
Websites: www.disneylandparis.com; www.parisbreak.co.uk/leisure/kids.asp

France Miniature
France Miniature is an outdoor park easily accessible from Paris. It displays the different faces of France in miniature scale, using over 200 models. New models are added every year. All of France's major sites, castles and monuments can be toured very "quickly," all in one special park. It is particularly aimed at children and designed to be educational and fun. The aquatic sound and light show were added in 1999.
Address: 25, Route du Mesnil, 78990 Elancourt
How to get there: La Verriere train station, then bus to the park
Open: 10am to 7pm
Price: Adults from 12 euros, children (from 4 to 16) 8.50 euros
Websites: www.franceminiature.com; www.parisbreak.co.uk/leisure/kids.asp

Astérix
Besides Disneyland, Paris' other popular theme park is Parc Astérix. It is located about 35 kilometers north of Paris and is easily accessible from Charles de Gaulle airport. The park is based on the Astérix comic books, and you can meet the heroes of the comic (Astérix, Obélix and friends) in the park. The park is home to plenty of rides, including water rides, hair-raising rides and the new Oxygenarium ride in inflatable boats. There is also a dolphin show. It has

many other attractions for children and adults. There are restaurants and take-away outlets.

Address: Boite Postalel, 60128-Plailly
How to get there: Bus Shuttle from RER Roissy-Charles-de-Gaulle
Car: off the A1 autoroute
Open: From April to October: 10 am to 6 pm
Price: adults 28 euros, children (from 3 to 11) 20 euros
Tel: 03 44 62 34 04
Websites: www.asterix.tm.fr; www.parisbreak.co.uk/leisure/kids.asp

Cité des Sciences et de l'industrie

Located in the north of Paris, Cité des Sciences is an ultra-modern science muse-um and has its own internal television. Its bridges, suspended walkways and transparent escalators and elevators make you feel as though you are visiting a futuristic city. The museum offers a variety of activities and workshops for kids with three floors of interactive exhibits. Its high-tech sections are very popular.
Address: Parc de la Villette, 30 Avenue Corentin-Cariou, Paris 19e
How to get there: Metro line 5 or 7: Porte de la Villette, Porte de Pantin
Bus: PC
Open: Tuesday to Sunday: 10am to 6pm. Closed Monday.
Price: adults: 7.50 euros; reduced: 5.50 euros; under 7s: free
Tel: 01 40 05 70 00
Websites: www.cite-sciences.fr; www.parisbreak.co.uk/leisure/kids.asp

Cafés:

Website: www.paris.org/Cafes

Aux Villes du Nord

Address: rue de Dunkerque, 10th
Métro: Gare du nord
Price: 1.14 euros
Service: The service is fast and friendly.
Quality of the coffee: A blend of sweet Arabic coffees.

Brasserie Lipp

Brasserie Lipp is a preserve of the *Belle Epoque* world of 1900. Léonard Lipp opened his brasserie in the 1870's after fleeing Alsace during the Franco-Prussian War. As such, its menu is typical of that region and includes beer, sausage, sauerkraut, etc. The brasserie has also been a meeting place for televi-sion personalities, ministers (it is halfway between the French Senate and National Assembly), and actors, among others.
Address: 151, blvd St-Germain, 6th
Métro: St-Germain-des-Prés
Open: 8am to 12:45am daily; closed in August

Buffet de la Gare de Paris-Austerlitz

The café's small terrace can be nice on sunny days, and you can be sure to be well off the tourist track if you come here. Don't expect anything more from this café than you would from any other train station anywhere else in the world. Then again, perhaps this slice of daily life is what you are looking for.

Address: rue de Dunkerque, 10th
Métro: Austerlitz
RER: Austerlitz
Price: 1.22 euros

Le Dauphin

Le Dauphin is an unassuming turn-of-the-century brasserie and café one block north of the Louvre, just outside André Malraux Square. The brasserie has been family-owned and operated since 1945 and offers a variety of traditional entrees, a modest selection of regional wines, and memorable desserts such as the hot prune pie with Armagnac. Espresso and other coffees are standard for this type of café. The rear dining room provides a dark, slightly decaying, refuge to linger over dinner or coffee and is a stark contrast to the traffic-congested square just outside.

Address: 167, rue St. Honoré, 1st
Métro: Palais Royal; Musée du Louvre

Café de Flore

Like its celebrated rival Les Deux Magots, Café de Flore can claim to have been the heart of the Existentialist Movement during the early part of this century with Sartre, Simone de Beauvoir, Camus and others regularly meeting here.

Address: 172, blvd St Germain, 6th
Métro: St-Germain-des-Prés
Open: 7am to 1:30pm daily

Café de la Paix

The Café de la Paix is one of Paris' most famous spots. Designed by Garnier, the same man who created the Opéra Garnier, the decor recalls a past era. The Opéra area was once the hub of café society in Paris, and while the "hub" is no longer, the elegance of that time remains. You won't find the coffee inexpensive here, but it may still be a bargain given the surroundings.

Address: 12, blvd des Capucines, 9th
Métro: Opéra
Near: Opéra Garnier

Café Le Paris

Le Paris probably has the least expensive coffee on all of the Champs Élysées. Rather than a tourist place, Le Paris has a clientele of regulars. These are people who work on the Champs, people from CCF, which is just a few meters up

the street, as well as other businesses. The waiters and proprietor are friendly and know their customers. Overall, it is a small oasis from the tourists outside.
Address: 93, ave des Champs Élysées, 8th
Métro: George V
Price: 1.68 euros

Le Café Marly

The place to be and be seen, Le Café Marly is in the Richelieu wing of the Louvre Palace. Its terrace is on the Cour Napoléon; the Pyramid is no more than 50 yards away. Inside the café, glass walls are all that separate the salon from sculpture and works of art in the Louvre itself.
Address: Cour Napoléon; 93, rue de Rivoli, 1st
Métro: Palais-Royal Musée du Louvre
Tel: 49 26 06 60

Le Campo

Situated just across from the engineering school for computer science EPITA, Le Campo is a friendly, small café. Many students congregate here, so the ambiance is student-like and Parisian, yet calm and not too noisy. The interior of the café, the placement of the tables, and the decor allows one to enjoy a quick break. The service is simple, rapid and efficient – exactly as it should be!
Address: Boulevard de l'Hopital, 13th
Métro: Campo-Formio, Ligne 5
Tel: 43 31 28 80

Le Canon des Gobelins

Well situated at the intersection formed by Boulevard Saint Marcel and Avenue des Gobelins – very near Place d'Italie and in the center of the main streets for the *quartiers* Montparnasse (Boulevard Port-Royal) and Gare d'Austerlitz (Jardin des Plantes) – this is a magnificent brasserie with a very Parisian decor. The coffee (espresso) is served accompanied by a piece of black chocolate.
Note: This is not the usual chocolate wrapped up in plastic and aluminum, but a *true* chocolate: certainly not a *Leonidas* but a *parline* desirable for accompanying the coffee. The coffee is a pure Arabica. Le Canon des Gobelins also has excellent decaffeinated coffee for those who prefer it.
Address: Avenue des Gobelins and Boulevard Saint Marcel, 13th
Métro: Gobelins (Bus number 91; stop: St. Marcel)
Price: 1.83 euros (a bit expensive, but the coffee is quality)
Service: Excellent

Les Deux Magots

Named after the two wooden statues (the two *magots*), which still dominate the room, Les Deux Magots is one the most famous cafés in Paris. Jean-Paul

Sartre and Ernest Hemingway were both patrons in an earlier era. Its rival, Café de Flore, is just next door.
Address: 170, blvd St Germain, 6th
Métro: St-Germain-des-Prés
Open: 8am to 2pm daily; closed the second week of January.

Le Rendez-Vous des Belges

The waiters are very friendly and enjoy talking with customers. This coffee shop is small and in a long room, but the ambiance is typical for Paris, notably with lots of taxi drivers drinking beer at the counter, talking over their stories of the day.
Address: rue de Dunkerque, 10th
Métro: Gare du nord
Price: 1.22 euros
Service: Fast, very friendly and well done.
Quality of the Coffee: Special blend of 100% pure Arabic: delicious!

Shopping:

Marché Saint Pierre

Address: 2, rue Charles Nodier, 75018 Paris
Métro: Anvers
Tel: 01 46 06 92 25
Website: www.marche-saint-pierre.fr

Fifty-Fifty

Fifty-Fifty is a classy eighth arrondissement institution where vintage Givenchy blazers compete with the latest runway creations from Marc Jacobs all at reasonable prices, considering their not-so-humble origins. Foraging in Fifty-Fifty is like raiding a friend's closet and paying a mere pittance to transfer these designer duds to your own.
Address: 4, rue Corvetto, 75008 Paris
Tel: 01 45 61 05 65
Website: www.paris-expat.com/guide/4-04_chic.html

Dépôt-Vente de Buci-Bourbon

While paying less for more is always attractive, the goods can be dated and financially out of reach for your average consumer. On the other hand, as with any grandmother's attic, an occasional probe can yield unexpected treasure.
Address: 6, rue de Bourbon-le-Château, 75006 Paris
Tel: 01 46 34 45 05
Website: www.paris-expat.com/guide/4-04_chic.html

Les Puces de St-Ouen
Fashion/Clothing, Markets
Address: 48, rue Jules Vallès, (Marche des Antiquaires), Saint-Ouen, 93400
France
Tel: +33 1 40 12 70 36
E-mail: info@les-puces.com
Websites: www.les-puces.com; http://travel.yahoo.com/p-travelguide-2775876-puces_de_st_ouen_les_paris-i;_ylt=Ak9EfiT4XvchH7.NU3QDosusFWoL

Marche D'Aligre
Address: Place d'Aligre, 75012 Paris
Website: http://travel.yahoo.com/p-travelguide-2775875-marche_d_aligre_paris-i;_ylt=Apibbyq0_4..4btJSq0RBi.sFWoL

Marche aux Oiseaux
Address: Place Louis Lepine, 75001 Paris

Rues Des Francs-Bourgeois
Fashion/Clothing, Department Stores & Shopping Centers
Address: Place des Vosges, 75003 Paris
Tel: +33 1 49 52 53 10
Website: http://travel.yahoo.com/p-travelguide-2775865-rue_des_francs_bourgeois_paris-i;_ylt=AkcZGdrU8czqQZQEhFVPktasFWoL

Tati
Fashion/Clothing, Department Stores & Shopping Centers
Address: 5, rue Belhomme, 75018 Paris
Tel: +33 1 55 29 50 00
E-mail: contact@tati.fr
Website: www.tati.fr

La Samaritaine
Fashion/Clothing, Specialty, Bookshops, Department Stores & Shopping
Centers
Address: 19, rue de la Monnaie, 75001 Paris
Tel: +33 1 40 41 20 20
Website: www.lasamaritaine.com

Louis Vuitton
Fashion/Clothing
Address: 38, avenue des Champs-Élysées, 75008 Paris
Tel: +33 01 810 810 010
Website: www.vuitton.com

Chanel
Fashion/Clothing
Address: 31, rue Cambon, 75001 Paris
Tel: +33 1 42 86 28 00
Website: www.chanel.com

BHV – Bazaar De L'Hotel de Ville
Fashion/Clothing, Bookshops, Department Stores & Shopping Centers
Address: 52, Rue de Rivoli, 75001 Paris
Tel: +33 1 42 74 90 00
Website: www.bhv.fr

Music Stores:

Website: http://travel.discovery.com/destinations/fodors/paris/
shopping_20388_1.html

Afric'Music
Afric'Music is a hub for the city's African population. Tiny as it may be, the store blasts with music from the Congo, Zaire, Senegal, Haiti, the West Indies, and elsewhere. If you're curious about something, the owner will play it for you right off the bat.
Address: 3, rue des Plantes, 14th
Métro: Alésia
Location: Montparnasse
Tel: 01 45 42 43 52

Born Bad
Born Bad is the place to go for rare underground finds – stop by the branch Born Bad Exotica, on rue Saint-Sabin, if you'd like to listen to a soundtrack of every James Bond movie ever made or check out a host of old records with dancing Hawaiian hula girls on the cover. In other words, you'll find all that is kitsch and underground and otherwise elusive.
Address: 17, rue Keller, 11th
Métro: Bastille
Location: Bastille/Nation
Other location: 11, rue St-Sabin, 11th
Tel: 01 49 23 98 05

FNAC
FNAC is a high-profile French chain selling music, books, and photo, TV, and audio equipment at good prices – by French standards.
Address: 136, rue de Rennes, 6th
Métro: Les Halles

Other locations: 74, ave des Champs-Élysées, 8th
Tel: 01 53 53 64 64
Métro: Franklin-D.-Roosevelt
Tel: 01 49 54 30 00
Métro: St-Placide
Location: Beaubourg/Les Halles
Address: Forum des Halles, 1st
Tel: 01 40 41 40 00

Paris Accordéon
At Paris Accordéon you can check out an impressive collection of antique
accordions, choose a CD of classic, accordion-driven bal musette music, and
perhaps catch an impromptu performance by the owner.
Métro: Denfert-Rochereau.
Address: 80, rue Daguerre, 14th
Location: Montparnasse
Tel: 01 43 22 13 48

Virgin Megastore
Virgin Megastore has acres of albums; the Champs Élysées store has a large
book section too.
Métro: Franklin-D.-Roosevelt
Other location: In Carrousel du Louvre, 99 rue de Rivoli, 1st
Tel: 01 49 3 52 90
Métro: Palais-Royal
Location: Champs-Élysées
Address: 52, ave des Champs-Élysées, 8th
Tel: 01 49 53 50 00

Shopping for Food:

http://travel.discovery.com/destinations/fodors/paris/shopping_20356_1.html

À la Mère de Famille
À la Mère de Famille is an enchanting shop well versed in French regional
specialties and old-fashioned bonbons, sugar candy and more.
Métro: Cadet.
Address: 35, rue du Faubourg-Montmartre, 9th
Location: Opera/Grands Boulevards
Tel: 01 47 70 83 69

Boulevard Raspail

On Boulevard Raspail, between rue du Cherche-Midi and rue de Rennes, is the city's major marché biologique, or organic market, bursting with produce, fish, and eco-friendly products. It's open Tuesday and Friday.

Métro: Rennes.

Location: St-Germain-des-Prés, 6th

Debauve & Gallais

Debauve & Gallais was founded in 1800. The two former chemists who ran it became the royal chocolate purveyors and were famed for their "health chocolates," made with almond milk. Test the benefits yourself with ganaches, truffles, or pistoles, flavored dark-chocolate disks.

Address: 30 rue des Sts-Pères, 7th

Métro: St-Germain-des-Prés.

Location: St-Germain-des-Prés

Tel: 01 45 48 54 67

Fauchon

Fauchon remains the most iconic of all Parisian food stores. It's now expanding globally, but the flagship is still right behind the Madeleine church. Established in 1886, it sells renowned pâté, honey, jelly, tea and private-label champagne. Expats come for hard-to-find foreign foods (US pancake mix, British lemon curd); those with a sweet tooth make a beeline for the macaroons (airy, ganache-filled cookies) in the patisserie. There's also a café for a quick bite. Prices can be eye-popping – marzipan fruits for 95 euros a pound – but who can say no to a Fauchon cadeau?

Address: 26. place de la Madeleine, 8th

Métro: Madeleine

Location: Opera/Grands Boulevards

Tel: 01 47 42 60 11

Hédiard

Hédiard, established in 1854, was famous in the 19th century for its high-quality imported spices. These – along with rare teas and beautifully packaged house brands of jam, mustard, and cookies – continue to be a draw.

Métro: Madeleine.

Address: 21, place de la Madeleine, 8th

Location: Opera/Grands Boulevards

Tel: 01 43 12 88 88

Major Tourist Attractions:

The Louvre
F-75058 Paris Cedex 01
Information desk: Open every day except Tuesdays, from 9am to 6:45pm
(9:45pm on Wednesdays and Fridays)
Tel.: +33 1 40 20 53 17
Operator: +33 1 40 20 50 50
Fax: +33 1 40 20 54 52
E-mail: info@louvre.fr

Eiffel Tower
Address: Champ de Mars, 75007 Paris
For general information call: 33 (0) 1 44 11 23 23
Website: www.tour-eiffel.fr

Arc de Triomphe
This huge arch (164 feet high, 148 feet long and 72 feet wide) stands at the
end of the Avenue des Champs Élysées and in the center of the Place de
l'Étoile, formed by the intersection of 12 radiating streets. Although it is much
larger, the arch derives from Roman examples.
Website: www.bluffton.edu/~sullivanm/arctriomphe/arc.html

Bateaux Mouches
This unique experience takes in such sights as the Louvre, Notre Dame, Orsay
Museum, the Eiffel Tower, and the Statue of Liberty, while floating down the
River Seine. You can also take time to dine. There are luxury lounges and indi-
vidual tables, all set behind panoramic viewing glass. Paris is presented with
style, grace and charm. Derived from original passenger boat services and
driven by a passion for Paris, *bateaux mouches* have flourished upon a tradition
of independence and innovation. Each boat is named after one of the tradi-
tional vessels that once served Paris.
Address: Compagnie des Bateaux-Mouches
Pont de l'Alma, rive droite, 75008 Paris
Tel: 01 42 25 96 10
E-mail: info@bateaux-mouches.fr
Website: www.bateaux-mouches.fr

Sacre Coeur
The interior of the church contains one of the world's largest mosaics, and
depicts Christ with outstretched arms. The nearby bell tower contains the
"Savoyarde."
Address: Parvis du Sacré Coeur, 75018 Paris

Anvers, Abbesses, Château-Rouge, Lamarck-Caulaincourt
Open: Basilica: 6:45am to 11pm, Dome and crypt: 9am to 6pm. Late night
opening: Basilica: 11pm
Price: basilica: free access; dome, crypt: 2.29 euros; reduced dome and crypt:
1.22 euros.
Website: www.paris.org/Monuments/Sacre.Coeur

Notre Dame

A gothic masterpiece, Notre Dame was conceived by Maurice de Sully, and
was built between the twelfth and fourteenth centuries (1163-1345). Road dis-
tances in France are calculated on the basis of the "0 km" marked on the
square in front of the cathedral.
Address: Place du parvis de Notre Dame, 75004 Paris
Website: www.paris.org/Monuments/NDame/info.html

Pont Neuf

This is the oldest bridge in Paris; work started on it in 1578 under Henry III,
and it was finished in 1606 under Henry IV. Its design, however, is extremely
modern, when compared to the designs of bridges before it. All of the other
bridges in the city, in fact, had been lined with high houses hiding the view of
the river. From here, however, if you look from the perspective of the Seine, the
bridge, with its two spans right at the centre, becomes an enormous balcony
spread over the breadth of the river. Parisians immediately understood the
beauty and the importance of the bridge, and it became a meeting point and a
place for a promenade.
Address: 75001 Paris
Websites: www.welcometoparis.it/Louvre/louvre5.uk.html;
http://travel.yahoo.com/p-travelguide-2775910-pont_neuf_paris-i

Versailles

The Château de Versailles stands 15 miles (24km) southwest of Paris and is
one of France's noted attractions. Most of the palace was built between 1664
and 1715 by Louis XIV (known as the Sun King), who turned his father's hunting lodge into the grandest palace ever built.
Open: Tues–Sun, except on certain French public holidays
26 Mar–31 Oct: 9am to 6:30pm
1 Nov–31Mar: 9am to 5:30pm
Price: palace: 7.50 euros (5.50 euros after 3:30pm) or 14 euros for extended
tours; Grand Trianon and Petit Trianon: 5 euros (3 euros after 3:30pm); gar-
dens: 3 euros. The park is free for pedestrians and cyclists, but cars must pay
an admission fee.
Tel: (01) 30 83 78 00
E-mail: direction.public@chateauversailles.fr
Website: www.chateauversailles.fr

Fontainebleau

In the 16th century, Henry II and Catherine de Medici commissioned architects Philibert Delorme and Jean Bullant to build a new palace within the Fontainebleau forest 40 miles (64km) south of Paris. Italian Mannerist artists Rosso Fiorentino and Primaticcio came to assist in the interior decoration, helping to found the School of Fontainebleau. The palace was a refuge for French monarchs from the days of the Renaissance; they valued it because of its distance from the slums of Paris and for the rich hunting grounds that surrounded it. Many important events have occurred here, perhaps none more memorable than when Napoleon stood on the grand steps in front of the palace and bade farewell to his shattered army before departing for Elba. Compared to the glories of Versailles, however, Fontainebleau can be a bit of an anticlimax; it is best to see it before Versailles.

Address: 4, rue Royale

Open: Daily except Tuesdays 9:30am to 6pm (until 5pm from October to May)

Price: 5.50 euros; 4 euros for 18–25s; free for under 18s

Tel: (0) 1 60 74 99 99

E-mail: info@fontainebleau-tourisme.com

Website: www.fontainebleau.fr

Les Invalides

Les Invalides comprises the largest single collection/complex of monuments in Paris, including: Musée de l'Armée, Musée des Plans-Reliefs, Musée de l'Ordre de la Libération, L'Eglise de St-Louis-des-Invalides. In 1670, Louis XIV (the Sun King) founded Les Invalides near what was then called the Grenelle Plain. As an old soldiers' home, it was funded by a five-year levy on the salaries of soldiers currently serving in the army at that time. The first stones were laid in 1671, for what was to become a complex providing quarters for 4,000. Construction followed plans drawn up by Libéral Bruant, and was completed in 1676. Robert de Cotte designed the Esplanade. Construction of the dome began in 1706. Designed by Jules Hardouin-Mansart and completed by de Cotte after Mansart died in 1708.

Address: Esplanade des Invalides, 75007 Paris

Website: www.paris.org/Musees/Invalides

Skateboarding Shops:

Street Machine
Address: 6, rue Bailleul, 75001 Paris
Métro: Louvre - Rivoli
Tel: 01 47 03 64 61 or 01 47 03 64 65
Fax: 01 47 03 64 61
E-mail: info@streetmachine.fr
Website: www.streetmachine.fr/front

Ekirok
Address: 45, blvd Sébastopol, 75001 Paris
Tel: 01 42 36 47 48
Address: 61 rue St Denis, 75001 Paris
Tel: 01 53 40 85 40
E-mail: info@ekirok.com
Website: www.ekirok-laboutique.com

Flipside
Address: 103, rue St Denis, 75001 Paris

Le shop
Address: 3, rue D'Argout, 75002 Paris
Tel: 01 40 28 95 94

Numéro 4 Skateshop
Address: 23, rue Louis le Grand, 75002 Paris
Métro: Opéra

Urban Surfers
Address: 65, rue St Jacques, 75005 Paris
Métro: Cluny-Sorbonne
RER: St Michel
Tel: 01 53 10 85 88

TOOG'S
Address: 39, rue de l'abbé Gregoire, 75006 Paris
Tel: 01 45 48 13 72

Chattanooga
Address: 53, avenue Bosquet, 75007 Paris
Tel: 01 45 51 76 65
Fax: 01 47 53 01 50

Doc shop
Address: 37, rue de Constantinople, 75008 Paris
Tel: 01 53 04 00 01
E-mail: info@docshop8.com
Website: www.docshop8.com

Nozbone Skate Shop
Address: 295, rue du faubourg St Antoine, 75011 Paris
Métro: Nation
Open: Monday from 2pm to 7pm, Tuesday to Sunday from 10:30am to 7:30pm.
Tel: 01 43 67 59 67
Fax: 01 43 67 74 29
E-mail: contact@nozbone.com
Website: www.nozbone.com

Snowbeach
Address: 30, boulevard Lenoir, 75011 Paris
Métro: Bréguet-Sabin or Bastille
Tel: 01 43 38 62 50
Fax: 01 43 38 62 44
E-mail: contact@snowbeach.com
Website: www.snowbeach.com

RideSpirit Boardshop
Address: 73, boulevard Vincent Auriol, 75013 Paris
Tel: 01 45 83 09 89
Fax: 01 45 83 09 86
Website: www.ridespirit.com

Urban-Ride
Address: 149-151, rue de Rome, 75017 Paris
Tel: 01 47 66 84 18
Website: www.urban-ride.com

Pro Shops, Île-de-France:

Hawaii Surf
Address: 9 ave D. Casanova, 94200 Ivry sur Seine
Tel: 01 46 72 07 10
Fax: 01 46 58 95 32
E-mail: skate@hawaiisurf.com
Website: www.hawaiisurf.com

All Mighty
Address: 114, ave du Général Leclerc, 92340 Bourg-La-Reine
RER: Bourg-La-Reine
Website: www.all-mighty.com

ISH-EYE
Address: 22, rue de Champigny, 94370 Sucy-en-Brie
Open: Tuesday to Sunday 10am to 1pm and 3pm to 7pm
Tel: 01 45 90 16 67
Fax: 01 45 90 36 61
E-mail: fisheye@tele2.fr

Impact Skateshop
Address: 5, rue Guy Baudoin, 77000 Melun

Other Skateshop
Address: 10, rue des Sablons, 77300 Fontainebleau
Tel: 01 64 23 40 55

Skate Avenue
Address: 8, rue Raymond du Temple, 94300 Vincennes
Tel: 01 41 93 11 35
Address: 53, ave du Bac, 94210 La Varenne St Hilaire
Tel: 01 48 89 80 17
Address: 4–6, rue de Noisy
Place du Colombier, 94360 Bry/Marne
Tel: 01 48 81 03 57

Tomato Skateshop
Address: 20, clos des Cascades, 93160 Noisy le Grand
Tel: 01 55 85 06 15
E-mail: noisy@tomatoskateshop.com
Website: www.tomatoskateshop.com

Tribute Skateshop
Address: 5, rue Marchand, 91000 Corbeil Essonnes
Tel: 01 64 96 76 38

QUAI OPS
Address: 16, route de Domfront, 61100 Flers
Tel: 02 33 65 46 35
E-mail: quaiops@aol.com

Is It Luck
Address: 124, rue Saint Denis, 77400 Lagny sur Marne
Tel: 01 64 02 04 52

Pacific Wear
Address: 9, rue André Bonnenfant, 78100 St Germain en Laye
Tel: 01 39 73 90 90

Skate Parks:

Prairie de Mauves
Address: 9, allée des Vinaigriers, 44300 Nantes
Tel: 02 51 13 26 80
E-mail: lehangar@fal44.org
Website: http://perso.wanadoo.fr/ylt/hangar/

Hostels:

Le Village Hostel
Address: 20, rue d'Orsel, 75018 Paris
Tel: 00 33 1 42 64 22 02
Fax: 00 33 1 42 64 22 04
Website: www.villagehostel.fr

3 Ducks Hostel
Address: 6, place Etienne Pernet, 75015 Paris
Tel: 00 33 (1) 48 42 04 05
Fax: 00 33 (1) 48 42 99 99 - M° Commerce
Website: www.3ducks.fr

Young and Happy
Address: 80 rue Mouffetard, 75005 Paris
Métro: Place Monge, Linge 7
Tel: 01 47 07 47 07
E-mail: smile@youngandhappy.fr
Website: www.youngandhappy.fr

La Maison
Address: 67, bis rue Dutot, 75015 Paris
Métro: Voluntaires, Linge 12
Tel: 0142 73 10 10
E-mail: cafe@mamaison.fr
Website: www.mamaison.fr

Aloha hostels
Address: 1, rue Borromée, 75015 Paris
Tel: 01 42 73 03 03
Fax: 01 42 73 14 14
E-mail: friends@aloha.fr
Website: www.aloha.fr

Caulaincourt Square Hotel Paris
Address: 2, square Caulaincourt, 75018 Paris
Tel: 00 33 (0) 1 46 06 46 06
Fax: 00 33 (0) 1 46 06 46 16
E-mail: bienvenue@caulaincourt.com
Website: www.caulaincourt.com

Le Regent Montmarte
Address: 37, blvd Rochechouart, 75009 Paris
Métro: Anvers
Tel: 00 33 1 48 78 24 00
Fax: 00 33 1 48 78 25 24
E-mail: bonjour@leregent.com
Website: www.leregent.com

Woodstock Hostel
48, rue Rodier, 75009 Paris
Tel: 01 48 78 01 63
E-mail: flowers@woodstock.fr
Website: www.woodstock.fr

Internet Cafés:

Accessnet
This lovely cybercafé is located in the middle of Paris near Georges Pompidou
Center and Chatelet les Halles, and has 12 computers.
Address: 76, rue Rambuteau, 75001 Paris
Open: 12pm to 10pm
Tel: 01 423 605 86
E-mail: accessnetcybercafe@email.com

c@fe CA&RI TELEMATION
Keyboards are available in Japanese, Korean, Russian, Arabic, Hebrew,
American British and French.
Address: 72–74, passage de Choiseul, 75002 Paris
Hours: Mon-Fri 10am to 8pm; Sat 2pm to 7pm; Sun closed
Tel: 33 1 47 03 36 12

E-mail: cafe@cari.com
Website: www.cari.com

Chabanet

This Internet café is located in the center of Paris near the "Opera Garnier," the National Library and the "Palais Royal." French, English and Japanese are spoken.
Address: 4, rue Chabanais, 75002 Paris
Hours: Mon-Fri 10:30 to 22:00, Sat-Sun 14:00 to 20:00/Holidays closed
Price: 2.50 euros/15min (6 euros/1h)
Tel: +33 (0) 1 42 96 64 02
E-mail: contact-us@paris-chabanet.com
Website: www.paris-chabanet.com

ClickSide

Address: 14, rue Domat, 75005 Paris
Tel: 33 1 56 81 03 00
E-mail: info@clickside.com

Cybercafe Latin

Twenty computers are available, as well as printers, scanners, video conference; AOL-"friendly."
Address: 35, bis rue de Fleurus, 75006 Paris
Open: 7 days a week, 9am to 10pm
Price: Between 2.5 and 4 euros/hour
Tel: +33 1422 220 118
E-mail: internet@cybercafelatin.net

Site Bergere

A friendly cyber café in the 9th arrondissement between les Galleries Lafayettes and Gare du nord.
Address: 13, rue de montholon, 75009 Paris
Tel: 01 42 46 24 667
E-mail: info@sitebergere.com
Website: www.sitebergere.com

Ars Longa

Ars Longa, both Cybergallery and Multimedia Cultural Space, is located right in the middle of the Belleville District near Oberkampf Street. It offers new books, secondhand books, coffee and passport photos, among other services.
Address: 94, rue Jean-Pierre Timbaud
Métro: Courronnes or Parmentiers
Tel: +33 (0) 1 43 55 47 71
Website: www.arslonga.org

VILLAGE WEB
Village Web is one of the first cybercafés in Paris. It is in the heart of the
Montmartre area and is open every day. Twenty computers are connected to
the Internet with high-speed connections. You can print, scan, fax, copy, and
use Office tools.
Address: 6, rue Ravignan, 75018 Paris
Price: 5 min for 0.5 euros
Open: Every day from 9am to 9pm
Tel: 33 1 42 64 77 70
E-mail: info@village-web.net
Website: www.village-web.net

Ciao
E-mail, Internet, scanning and desktop publishing are available.
Address: 5, rue Mignon, 75006 Paris
Tel: 01 53 10 30 50
E-mail: info@cybercube.fr
Website: www.cybercube.fr

Cafe Orbital
Thirty computers are available, with printers, scanners, video conferencing;
AOL-"friendly."
Address: 13, rue de Médicis, 75006 Paris
Métro: Odeon Travel
RER: Luxembourg
Open: 9am to 10pm
Tel: +33 (0)1 4325 7677
E-mail: info@orbital.fr

Jardin de l'Internet
Twenty computers are available, with printers, scanners, video conferencing,
etc. You can sit outside if you only want to drink coffee and enjoy the sun in
front of the Jardin du Luxembourg.
Address: 79, Boulevard Saint Michel, 75005 Paris
RER: Luxembourg
Open: Mon–Sat: 9am to 9pm; Sun: 10am to 10pm
Tel: +33 144 072 220
E-mail: cybercafe@jardin-internet.net
Website: www.jardin-internet.net

Cyberc@fe de Paris
The spacious Cyberc@fe de Paris is located in the very center of Paris just
above France's largest Métro station, Chatelet les Halles (exit Métro: 14 Rue
Ferronnie) and is full of Sony computers in English and French.

Address: 15, rue des Halles, 75001 Paris
Tel: 33 1 4221 1313
E-mail: info@cybercafedeparis.com
Website: www.cybercafedeparis.com

Luxembourg Micro

Very fast Internet access is provided; situated in the heart of Paris next to the
Jardin du Luxembourg. Twenty computers are available, with printers and
scanners; AOL-"friendly"; network: PC & Mac, ASDL
Address: 83, boulevard Saint Michel
Open: Mon–Sat: 9am to 10pm; Sun: 1pm to 8pm
Tel: 33 1 46 33 27 98
E-mail: cyber@luxembourg-micro.com
Website: www.luxembourg-micro.com

Absolute Cybercafe

Address: 11, rue des Halles, 75001 Paris
Location: next to the famous Cybercafe de Paris central
Métro: Chatelet les Halles
Open: 11am to 11pm every day
Tel: +33 1 4221 1111
E-mail: info@cybercafedeparis.com

Easy Everything

Coffee shop and Internet prices based on capacity of the store at the given time.
Website: www.easyeverything.com

Paris-Cy Internet Café

This café offers fast Internet access and access to office equipment, printers,
CD burners, disks, scanners and digital photocard readers, English and French
keyboards, and soft drinks.
Address: 8, rue de Jouy
Métro: between Saint-Paul and Pont-Marie.
Open: Mon-Sun: 10am to 10pm
Price: 2.50 euros /hr for cardholders
Tel: 1 42 71 37 37
E-mail: contact@paris-cy.com

Café Orbital

Established in 1995, this café is located in front of the Luxembourg Garden in
the Latin Quarter of Paris and has high-speed and wireless Internet access.
Open: Weekdays: 10am to 8pm; Weekends: 12am to 8pm
Price: 2 to7 euros/hr
Tel: +33 1 4325 7677
E-mail: info@cafeorbital.com

EPISODE 2

A sneak preview . . .

MR. X (And the Cog Train from Heaven)

 I

A cog train is a marvelous piece of mechanical wizardry, amply more than a piece of locomotive gimcrackery. The track has an additional rail with saw teeth buzzed into the steel and the train has a set of cog wheels that mesh neatly with these metal choppers. The result? Cog trains muscle themselves up incredibly steep inclines. They go where no other trains can go. The cog train in Lucerne, Switzerland, climbs the steepest incline in the world, powering straight up as it chugs along to the highest points of Mount Pilatus in the Swiss Alps. It is a breathtaking but harrowing trip. You've got to trust the technology that has been doing its job for over a hundred years.

Trust was very much on the mind of Xerxes Frankel, the 17-year-old star of the travel show *Get Outta Town!* He had flown to Lucerne to shoot a new episode, and was hooking up with Ludi Magister, a local teenager and snowboarding fanatic. Together, they were checking out the Lucerne sites and running the slopes. At least, that's what was supposed to happen.

How did he get himself into these situations?

Xerxes was on the cog train. Being on the cog train, meant "on" the cog train, as in, holding on for dear life, flattened to the roof as the wind howled and tore at his clothing, driving needles of snow into his face, eyes stinging, tears streaking his cheeks. He squinted over at Ludi, who lay huddled beside him. Ludi's broad face bore a hollow look of sheer terror. Comforting, Xerxes thought, very comforting.

"We are going to die," Ludi said.

Xerxes cupped his ear. "What?" he shouted over the screaming elements.

"We are going to die," Ludi repeated.

"No."

"We are going to die . . . we are going to die . . . we are going to die . . . we are going to die . . ." It became a hysterical mantra, humming into his brain, infusing his soul and spirit.

"Shut up," Xerxes shouted. "We are not going to die." Freeing one hand, he grabbed Ludi's sweater, bunching the turtleneck collar up around his neck. "Repeat after me," he hissed ferociously. "We . . . say it."

"We . . ."

"Are . . ."

"Are . . ."

"Not . . ."

"Not . . ."

"Going to . . ."

"Going to . . ."

"Die . . ." And he hit the "Dee" sound hard.

"Die . . ." Ludi closed his mouth, biting his lip. "How do you know, X? How can you be sure?"

"I'm just a natural optimist."

Ludi threw back his blond head and howled, hysterical with laughter. "You . . . are . . . an . . . optimist . . . ?"

Xerxes nodded and Ludi rebounded into another uncontrolled paroxysm of laughter, half-crying, half-wheezing. After a long moment, he subsided. "I feel better now. You can let go of my sweater."

Xerxes released the collar. "Good. Now let's focus on what we're going to do."

"Good idea," Ludi said. "I haven't a clue . . ." And he convulsed again.

Xerxes rolled his eyes. "Get serious, man."

Ludi stared at him. "How can I be serious?" he roared. "We are flattened to the roof of an out-of-control cog train driven by some maniac in the middle of a blizzard in June and we ARE probably going to die. We don't have a plan. We don't have any help, the weather is getting worse and you want me to be serious? You North Americans are a bizarre race . . ."

"Thank you. You know, I think you really are a glass-half-empty kind of a guy."

"In situations like this, the kind I've never before experienced? . . . then I agree with you. Who wouldn't be?"

The question stopped Xerxes for a second and he began to think about the events that led him here.

The train jerked, then jolted in its tracks sending a large, rambunctious vibration singing through one car after another, each kissing the next. Ludi slapped the palms of his gloved hands, beating the smooth metal surface made even slicker by the snow pelting down, instantly freezing against the frigid surface. Before Xerxes could react, Ludi began to slide backward as the cog train lurched upward at a frightening angle. He heard the metal groan as the wheels ground against the track. It was an eerie, sorrowful sound. Ludi's hand slaps became frantic, beating rapidly against the iron drum, while his body, spread-eagled and undulating, slid down the length of the train.

"X . . . X . . . help me . . . !"

Xerxes spun around so that he was facing the rear. He pulled himself forward. In a millisecond he was sliding and gaining speed, rocketing out of control. His body became a bullet, going faster and faster and faster until he caught up with Ludi, who stared at him. Their foreheads touched and they grabbed each other by the shoulders, feet and elbows digging in, frantically searching for a ridge or crevice to latch on to. Ludi's mouth was wide open, the shape of a forlorn "O" but no sound came out. His terror turned him mute.

"Hang on . . ." Xerxes yelled.

The rear of the train flashed up. Suddenly they were airborne, flying, a human saucer pirouetting out into space, flipping over and over and over, swallowed up in the swirling, frozen mists of nature . . .